BOSS
of Me

USA TODAY BESTSELLING AUTHOR

TIA LOUISE

This book is a work of fiction. Names, characters, places, and incidents are products of the author's imagination or are used fictitiously. Any resemblance to actual events or locales or persons, living or dead, is entirely coincidental.

Boss of Me
Copyright © TLM Productions LLC, 2019
Printed in the United States of America.

Cover design by Lori Jackson Design.
Photography by Wander Aguiar.

All rights reserved. No part of this publication can be reproduced, stored in a retrieval system, or transmitted in any form or by any means—electronic, photocopying, mechanical, or otherwise—without prior permission of the publisher and author.

They warned me not to take this job.
They said you were ruthless, impossible to please…
I said I was better than them.
I wouldn't fall for your charm, your arrogance, or how sexy you fill out that suit.
I wouldn't fall for your deep brown eyes or the way that muscle moves in your square jaw when you're pissed.

I said I could resist you.
I was wrong…

(BOSS OF ME is a STAND-ALONE workplace, military romance with a badass alpha boss and the feisty woman who steals and heals his heart. No cheating. No cliffhangers.)

"I'll never leave you behind, never forget."
　　　—George S. Fletcher II

Prologue
Patton

Seven years ago in a jungle south of the border...

THE CLOCK IS TICKING.

We have to move fast or this will go terribly wrong.

Sweat rolls down my sides, and I exhale slowly, calming my pulse.

The air around us is heavy and close, so thick it's almost visible and so hot it's almost impossible to breathe.

Tropical plants form a dense barrier of wide, shiny leaves around us, and we're hidden in the brush around a small, cinder-block hut.

Our target is a green dot on my screen blinking right in front of us.

He's here.

"Moving in, eleven o'clock." Taron's voice is low in my ear.

"Coming up from the southeast." Sawyer's distinct southern drawl is a quick response.

"No noise. No prisoners." I give the order, firm and clear.

I'm the leader of this three-man rescue mission, and we won't fail.

We surround the unpainted, cinder-block hovel. It's quiet in the shadows. The windows are black holes with no glass, empty squares that could be hiding anything—watchers with guns, lining us up in the crosshairs.

Or he could be alone.

No, it would never be that easy.

He could be dead.

My jaw tightens and I push back on the thought. *What good would he be to them dead?*

Taking a knee, I slowly lift my gun to my eye, setting my sites on the front door. We've been tracking radio signals, emails and IP addresses, until we isolated them here.

Two weeks have passed since Martin was jumped on a routine fuel run. From what we've been able to piece together, they took him down with PAVA spray, a paralyzing nerve gas. Then the videos started.

Two weeks of grainy images of our friend and fellow Marine tied to a chair with a bag over his head. They'd rip it off to reveal black eyes and bloodstained skin. Then the threats started—guns and money. It's what they all want. Until now, the moment of truth in the heart of a South American jungle.

We're tired, thirsty, and focused on retrieving our friend, kidnapped off-duty in a routine stop on our way to a peace-keeping mission in Caracas.

Sawyer checks in from his point, and we watch as Taron creeps across the face of the structure, approaching the weathered wooden door. His gun is at his chest as he carefully reaches out and knocks.

Three sharp raps, and we wait.

Nobody breathes.

No response.

He looks to me, and I give a nod. I'm front and center, ready to cover him.

Nobody gets past me.

Nobody takes my men.

We're brothers—no one forgotten, no one left behind.

My heart beats like a mallet against my ribs. As much as we've trained, this scene is entirely unpredictable. We hope to have the element of surprise. We hope his kidnappers believe we're still in Los Cabos, but they could be smarter than we give them credit for. With low growl, I shake my head. *Not likely*.

These drugged-up gangsters dared to kidnap a Marine. The only thing stopping us from torching this whole place is my belief we can extract him without causing unnecessary casualties.

Taron's jaw is set, the sleeves of his tan shirt showing from beneath the black Kevlar vest are stained with sweat, and his light-brown hair is wet. All our faces are scrubbed with camouflage, making the whites of our eyes seem to glow.

My breath stills. My cheek is pressed to my gun barrel, and the noise of cicadas rises like a chorus around us. It grows louder, a warning.

I shake off the thought. Taron is my focus.

The shadow of Sawyer emerges from the brush at the opposite end of the house. They're acting on my orders, but we're brothers. We've had each other's backs since Day One. This is more than a rescue. Martin is family.

Taron moves away from the concrete wall, and my finger is ready on the trigger. The only thing standing between us and what's about to happen is a wooden door…

He lifts his leg and gives the door a sharp kick, sending it flying against the wall with a blast that rattles the quiet jungle. His back is against the wall again, and he holds, waiting for a barrage of bullets.

None come.

Three heartbeats, three silent breaths—I give him a nod. He turns quickly, gun at eye level and steps through the space, swinging his weapon side to side. Sawyer is at his side, and I'm out of position moving forward to cover them.

"Marley!" Taron's gun lowers, and he rushes forward. I'm at the door to see him whip the bag off our friend's face, and it hits me like a sucker punch.

His head drops forward, bobbing like a top. I don't understand his mumbles. A thick stream of bloody spit drips from his swollen lips.

Rage mixes with adrenaline. He's been beaten almost to death, and cords of rope cut into his skin. Taron's quickly slicing his restraints as Sawyer and I case the hut. It appears deserted, which puts me on guard for IEDs. The unfurnished room has no interior light, casting long shadows in the corners. With a muted thud, Marley's knees hit the floor.

Taron bends to help lift him, and that's when I see her. Green eyes shining like cat in the darkness.

"No!" I shout as she rushes forward, screaming, just in time for Taron to whip around and see the raised machete in her hand.

Light flashes off the silver blade, the blast of Taron's pistol deafens us in the small space, and she drops like a stone, a bloody splatter like a megaphone fanning out on the floor in front of her small body. Long, caramel hair fans around her head, and she looks seventeen.

"God, no." He lets out a pained groan as the small gun falls to the floor.

For a moment, we're unable to move, unable to look away from the girl lying dead at our feet. My eyes heat, but I squeeze them shut briefly, clenching my teeth against the emotion. Marley mumbles incoherent words. He's barely conscious, beaten almost beyond recognition. I can't even tell if he recognizes us. The machete is at his feet, beside the dead girl.

She would have slashed them both if Taron hadn't done what he did.

Combat leaves no room for second-guessing. Hesitation is how you end up dead, cut in half by a teenager you'd otherwise overlook. A girl who never should have been here. Bastards using children to fight their battles.

"Get him out of here." My voice is a gruff order. When Taron doesn't move, I raise the volume. "I said GO!"

He struggles to lift Marley over his shoulder, and Sawyer steps forward to help him. I'm the last one to leave the hut, giving it a final sweep before I turn, in time to see Taron hit the ground and then cry out in pain.

"Mother—" He rolls to his side, blood soaking his lower back from where he landed on a broken sapling.

"Patton, stop!" Sawyer yells, and I see the trip wire.

How we missed it coming in is anybody's guess. Sawyer hoists Marley onto his shoulders. He's strong as an ox from working on his family's peach farm back home. I throw my rifle over my shoulder and lean down, grabbing Taron's arm.

"Can you walk?"

His face is scrunched in agony, but he manages to nod. "Get us out of here."

My jaw is tight, my brow set, and I force the determination we need to finish this rescue mission. Our ATV is down the hill, hidden in the brush, and we follow Sawyer, Taron leaning heavily on me.

His blood soaks through his clothes onto mine, dripping down to his pants. This injury might send him home, and Marley's worse. We're all worse on the inside. We saved our man, but we're all scarred by what we left behind.

It's too late to change it. We'll deal with the scars later.

When the fighting stops.

CHAPTER
One

Raquel

Present day

A HOT BREEZE WHIPS THROUGH THE STREETS OF DOWNTOWN Nashville, sweeping my light brown hair off my shoulders and throwing my black blazer open. I catch it, holding my bag and clutching my phone to my ear, hanging on my sister Renée's words like the voice of God.

"Make friends with Sandra. She's a good ally." Renée is encouraging, but my stomach is in knots. "Don't ask too many questions. If something doesn't make sense, wait and ask her later."

"I can't ask questions on my first day?" The orange hand appears at the crosswalk, and I take the opportunity to straighten my blouse. "What kind of mind reader do they think I am?"

"Trust me, Patton Fletcher doesn't have time to teach you how to do your job." She sounds like she might be quoting him.

"I've never even met Patton Fletcher."

"Who hired you? Taron? He's the only one who could get away with something like that."

"Ah, yeah." The walk sign appears, and I hustle across the four-lane street. "I interviewed with Taron Rhodes and Jerry Buckingham."

"Hmm..." Her skepticism fans my nerves.

"What?"

"You'll really have to be on your toes, then. If he didn't pick you, he'll be looking to get rid of you."

"Why?" Panic spreads into my chest.

"It's just how he is. He likes to be in control."

"So what do I do? You worked here." I push through the glass doors of Fletcher International, Inc., fresh out of Vanderbilt's Owen Grad School with a shiny new MBA.

Just like my sister, I graduated in the Top Ten in my class, and as such, I landed interviews with the top firms in the city. I wanted to go to Chicago or Dallas, but my advisor said Fletcher was a great starting point, a real feather in my cap if I could get a good recommendation. I assume this Patton Fletcher knows every CEO in the country... or his dad did.

When I searched Fletcher International, I found pages of articles on George Fletcher, not so much on his son.

"Don't let him push you around." Her voice turns thoughtful. "I couldn't tell if he did it on purpose or if it's just his personality..."

"How do I do that? He's the boss."

I wonder if she might tell me what happened to her here. My thoughts flicker back to when Renée started as an accounting intern at FII. She seemed to be doing great, one of *Nashville Magazine's* "Thirty under Thirty" rising stars in local business.

She passed the CPA exam on her first try... Then a year later, she dropped off the grid.

She stopped answering her phone, and when I called the office, a woman said she didn't work here anymore. I had to leave campus in the middle of exams, catch a city bus across town to her low-rent apartment in East Nashville, where it looked like she hadn't left her bed for days.

She wouldn't tell me what happened—she only said she wasn't doing it anymore. "It" meant anything having to do with her accounting degree.

That spring break, I ditched my plans to spend the week in South Walton to help her move back to Savannah, to our parents' tiny home near the watchful eye of Ms. Hazel Wakefield, their old neighbor.

Now she helps run Ms. Hazel's gift shop on Tybee Island and pays for rent by cleaning the old woman's house, running her errands, and cooking their meals. She doesn't have much choice since she walked away from her career with nothing but a crushing load of student loan debt.

"You want my advice on Patton Fletcher?" She huffs a laugh like it will take all day. "Don't mention his dad. It pisses him off."

My brow furrows. "Got it. Anything else?" I'm on the elevator rising too fast. Or she's talking too slowly.

"Never wear all black. He hates that."

"Shit." I glance down at my black slacks and matching black blazer. "I'll have to buy a scarf at lunch."

"Nope, he hates scarves even more."

"What's his problem?" My lips tighten, and my urge to fight starts to rise.

It's how I got my nickname, Rocky. My dad started it because even as a little girl, I never backed down from a bully.

"Remember when we were kids, and you liked to say 'You're not the boss of me'?"

"Yeah?"

"Don't *ever* say that to Patton Fletcher." I'm about to speak, when she adds conspiratorially. "But *never* stop saying it in your head. I think he secretly likes it."

"He sounds evil."

"Well..." Her voice goes higher. "Patton Fletcher is a devil. He's not *the* devil, but he's definitely one of them."

"I'm not afraid of the devil." I have no intention of letting some arrogant young CEO scare me away from my dreams—if that's what he did to Renée.

The elevator stops with a ding, and I wonder if that's the reason I said yes to this particular job offer, to prove the Morgan girls have grit, to prove we're tougher than we look.

"Whatever you do, don't fall for him." Her tone turns serious, and it almost makes me laugh.

"I have no intention of falling for him."

"I checked your star sign this morning. It's a good day for you to start something new."

I'm in the door, and not a moment too soon. When she starts on the holistic remedies and astral predictions, I'm done. "Thanks, sis. Gotta run. Love you!"

"Love you, too. Protect your chin."

"I will." It's our usual sign-off, a boxing reference.

I end the call as a slim young man in a pale blue, button-down and salmon-pink dockers behind the reception desk lowers his phone and gives me a bright smile.

"Welcome to Fletcher International, can I help you?"

"Hi, I'm Rock—ah, Raquel Morgan. I'm supposed to check in with Sandra—"

"Oh! You're the new hire. One moment, please." I wait while he punches a few buttons and speaks quickly into the receiver.

I only have a moment to glance around the immaculate, dark-wood, leather, and glass waiting area before he hops out of his chair, extending an arm toward the door leading to the back offices. "Right this way. Sandra's waiting for you."

"Thank you..."

"Dean." He smiles, turning back to answer the buzzing phone as Sandra appears in the hall.

I can't help noticing her lavender silk blouse and beige pencil skirt. I feel like the grim reaper compared to the two of them...

Which is ridiculous! I look very professional in my suit, and I'm wearing a cream silk blouse... I'll ditch my jacket once I'm in my office. Problem solved.

"Welcome aboard! It's so nice to have another girl at this sausage fest." Her hazel eyes shine behind heavy, tortoise-shell framed glasses, and I like her at once.

"Yeah." I glance down with an embarrassed grin. "I feel overdressed."

"They say you can never be overdressed, right?"

"I guess..." I'm not sure what to say. I stand out like a sore thumb, and I can't decide if it's a good thing or not.

Sandra leads me down a corridor with offices facing downtown on one side and cubicles in front of computers on the other. "This is your office in the middle."

Does that make me the monkey? I step into a good-sized room with a large window overlooking the river. A dark wood desk holds a newish-looking laptop with a sheet of paper beside it. A banker's box full of files is on the other side and another is on the floor.

I drop my bag in the maroon leather office chair. "This is great."

"Taron is in the corner office to your right." She points across her chest. "And Jerry is just on the other side. I think you met them both already?"

"Yes!" I smile. "They interviewed me."

She gives me a wink. "I think they were both concerned about who would occupy this space. Nobody wants a bad neighbor."

Everything about Sandra puts me at ease and makes me wonder why I was so nervous. I plan to text Renée the second she leaves and thank her for the heads-up when a dark figure glides in behind her.

"Sandra, I need you to open a file on the Madagascar account." A deep, rich voice joins us, and Sandra does a little jump and turns. Dark eyes under a lowered brow land on me.

"Patton Fletcher, meet our new hire, Raquel Morgan. She's taking over the international accounts for Taron."

My heart stutters in my chest, and all I can think is *Wow*.

"For Taron?" The muscle in his square jaw moves, and he looks to the right, toward Taron's office, as if he can see through the wall. For a moment, I wonder if he can... being the devil and all.

"So yes, Raquel Morgan..." Sandra repeats herself, leaving the introduction open as she gestures toward me. "Patton Fletcher."

"Right. Welcome." He seems angry.

I can't seem to find my voice. I've never been in the presence of someone so young yet so formidable in my life.

His dark hair is swept back from his face in glossy waves that just touch the back of his collar, and his shoulders are broad. His biceps strain against the sleeves of the blue blazer he's wearing, and when he extends a perfectly elegant hand to shake mine— long fingers, neat nails—the black tips of a tattoo peek out from beneath his white cuff. *Jesus, take the wheel.*

Our fingers touch, and heat floods my veins. "Thank you." My voice is practiced calm, but I feel weak. *Why didn't anyone tell me how insanely hot this devil is?*

"Then the Madagascar file will go to her." He holds a manila envelope toward Sandra, which she passes to me.

"She's your girl." His eyes narrow, but Sandra continues. "Raquel speaks five languages—"

"Reads," I quickly interrupt. "Sorry... I'm only a fluent speaker in one. Besides English, of course, but I can read the others fluently. For some reason, reading is easier than speaking."

Am I rambling?

Stop speaking, Rocky.

"I hope it's whatever they speak in Madagascar." Patton's tone is dismissive, and he pivots as if to go.

"French." My voice is a bit louder. "They speak French in Madagascar, and you're in luck."

He turns back, and I smile, doing my best to redeem my wobbly first impression. I'm a professional woman, not some swooning school girl.

His dark gaze sweeps up and down my body quickly, and my knees tingle. "Are you going to a funeral?"

The sarcasm in his tone irritates me. I hold my smile steady, and I remember what Renée told me, my mantra. "I'm working at one of the top firms in Nashville. From what I hear, it's a very professional place."

The corner of his mouth twitches, and I'm not sure if he's going to smile or frown. I'm briefly distracted by the fullness of his lips, but I kick that thought out of my brain. Patton Fletcher is testing me, just like my sister said he would. It's a fight or flight situation, and I'm not about to run.

"Try some color next time. We want our clients to feel positive about working with us, not depressed."

Rude! He starts to go, but I can't resist. "I think choosing my wardrobe is a job I can handle." I'm teasing, but only a little bit.

"I guess we'll find out." He glances over his shoulder, and I'm not sure—is he teasing, too?

"I have been dressing myself for a long time." My tone is thoughtful.

I could say as a self-respecting devil, *he* should be the one wearing all black...

But I don't.

"Have you been doing this job longer than me?"

I don't want to answer that.

"Right." He turns to Sandra. "Tell Taron to come to my office as soon as he arrives. We have a video conference with Hastings and Key at ten." I think that's it, and I realize I'm holding my breath. It catches again when he points at me. "Skype meeting with Madagascar tomorrow. Sandra will put everything you need on the G-drive. I expect you to be ready."

"I will be."

He's gone, and I glance at the thin envelope in my hands. *Shit*. What do I need to know by tomorrow?

When I look up again, Sandra is grinning, one eyebrow arched. "Sounds like you'd better get busy. Your passwords and everything you need are on the sheet by your computer. If you need anything else, let me know." She pushes off and leaves me alone in my office, but I hear her last words as she walks away. "This is going to be fun."

CHAPTER Two

Patton

WHAT THE FUCK? I push my door closed and stalk to my desk, flipping open my laptop and sending a quick text to Taron: ***Investor meeting in one hour. Don't be late.***

It's only the tip of what I want to say to him, but I'll wait until he's here.

Dropping into my leather chair, I lean back considering this new development. Taron hired a woman to handle our international accounts? I click through my emails to the one I ignored from him on Friday.

Quickly scanning her résumé, I confess, I'm impressed. Raquel Morgan graduated with honors from one of the top MBA schools in the country—and because of the deal my dad struck with Vanderbilt University a million years ago, we get first pick of the graduating class for interviews each year.

If we need someone.

I didn't know we did, but I let the guys do pretty much what they want. Now we have this very smart, very beautiful young female on our staff... Raquel Morgan. My jaw tightens. Does he seriously want to go down this road again?

Lifting the heavy pen from beside my computer, I tap the end against the desk pad. My eyes move around the room, from the pointer dog statue on the end of my mahogany desk to the heavy brass clock beside it, out to the leather wingback chairs across from me to the leather couch against the wall. Bookshelves are filled with hard-bound editions, some fiction, some reference volumes.

All our offices are this way. Everything in the firm coordinates—dark wood, rich leather, gleaming brass...

All men.

Sandra is the only woman for a reason, the primary one being Dad hired her before he left, and she managed to stick with us through the transition.

When Dad passed the reins of his baby, his commercial real estate firm, to me seven years ago like an Olympic torch, I took it and hit the ground running. I brought in Taron and Marley, and we transformed it to a tech-based company, got rid of all the paper, and started recruiting clients globally.

Fletcher International has become the Air B&B of the commercial real estate market. We match clients who need short-term office space with owners needing to fill them. Our model has been expanding in the smaller markets, until now we're ready to move into New York, Los Angeles, Chicago—we're poised to blow up. We just need a bit more up-front capital to secure the high-end properties we want in these markets.

Taron and Marley fit seamlessly here. They know international customs, and I trust them. We have each other's backs. Sawyer returned to his family's farm or he'd be here, too, just like always. We're brothers—nobody left behind. And nobody works for you like family does.

Only, lately it seems nobody takes advantage of you like family either. Marley is becoming more of a liability, showing up late and high or still drunk from the night before. Taron is slowly divesting himself of responsibilities, as if I wouldn't notice. Handing off international accounts is the latest in his string of downgrades.

I'd be angry, but he's damn good at locking down new clients. He's got a natural charm that draws people to us. Hell, he even charms me out of being pissed most of the time. So while I'm willing to accept his decision to hire a new person, what the hell was he thinking hiring *her*?

The bell on my clock dings, warning we're ten minutes from our meeting. I'm about to send Taron a pissed off text when my door opens, and he steps inside.

He grips the doorknob with a wince and clears his throat. "Sorry, moving slow this morning. Are we meeting in here?"

"Conference room. Don't sit." He nods and turns gingerly, and I know what's up.

"Trouble with your back?"

That fall in the jungle fucked up his spinal column. He spent a month on pain meds and ended up with two problems. Once he finally managed to get off the narcotics, he swore he'd never take another pain pill, which means he either drinks too much or tries to power through. Looks like today he's powering through with a slight hangover, but I won't hassle him about it.

It's been seven years, and I still feel responsible for what happened in that jungle.

"I can handle it if you need to sit this one out." I'm behind him, following his limping frame to the conference room.

He responds with a tight laugh. "Leave you alone with Stephen Hastings? We *do* want their money, right?"

"Remington will be there. He says they're interested. It's in the bag."

"They work in military defense and healthcare. We still have some selling to do to get them into commercial real estate."

Taron winces as he lowers himself into a cushioned leather seat around the long table. A huge computer screen is at one end and an iPad Pro in the center.

"It's a solid proposal, and we're a known entity, not some new kids out of Seattle." I'm not usually the diplomat, but I'm ready to expand, and these guys have the money we need to make it happen now, before someone beats us to the market.

They're also not asking for a massive cut—just fifteen percent of the profits and no control or oversight.

He gives me a tight grin. "They're here because of your dad."

The comment makes my skin bristle.

Dad was like Taron, diplomatic, the calm to my storm, but I brought this firm into the twenty-first century. I'm the man behind the curtain holding the whip.

The screen flickers to life and a split image of Remington Key on one side and Stephen Hastings on the other appears.

"Morning, Patton, Taron. Hot enough for you?" Remi is smiling and friendly, relaxed, not wearing a blazer.

"Just Nashville in the summer." Taron smiles, laying on the charm. "We're all feeling it, from what I hear."

Remi's located in South Carolina, while Stephen is in New York.

"Speaking of hot, have you seen the new Scan Eagle they're testing down in Key West?" Remi clicks on a laptop to his left, and a drone that looks like an aluminum paper airplane appears on the screen.

"I did." Taron leans forward, and they're like two kids sharing matchbox cars. "They're using them to stop drug smugglers from what I heard."

"They're using them for whatever they want." Remi laughs. "You should see one of these things take off—"

"Gentlemen." Stephen is not smiling, and his tweed coat is in place. "I'm sure we're all busy."

Taron leans back, and Remi shuts the laptop. So much for small talk. I don't mind—it's not my strong suit anyway.

Stephen takes over. "I've reviewed your proposal. I like what I'm seeing here."

I allow myself to relax slightly. I'm not smiling, but I'm encouraged by his opening.

Matching his tone, I slip in a brag. "We're poised to be the leader in this field. Fletcher International will be synonymous with short-term commercial rentals, like Xerox is to copiers."

"It sure looks like it. Way to get ahead of the game, guys." Remi rocks back in his chair, tossing a baseball-style stress ball. "I'm surprised nobody thought of this before."

"I started building this line when I took over as CEO." My jacket is in place, my forearms are on the table, and I'm watching Hastings, whose eyes are on the sheets in front of him. "Our global client base has grown exponentially. Now we're ready to expand our offerings, and we want to offer only the best."

Stephen's brow lowers. "You only have one client in the UAE."

Taron leans forward. "It's part of the reason we need to expand. Countries like Dubai and Abu Dhabi are looking for spaces in LA and New York. Once we have more properties on the books, they'll come pouring in. We find it, they come."

He ends on a positive note, but silence fills the room, broken only by the noise of papers being flipped back and forth.

"You've come pretty far pretty fast…" Stephen's sentence hangs, like a noose ready to tighten around my neck. "But you're not there yet."

The air seems to leave the room. My throat is tight, and anger is rising. "Excuse me?"

Hastings closes the folder and tosses it forward on his desk. "You need more big-ticket renters. Otherwise, we launch, and the US and European clients bypass us. They can do it themselves. Show me why they need this."

My lips press together. I'm not about to beg this guy.

Taron isn't ready to give up. "You're wrong." He stands too quickly, and I see him wince. He covers it. "We're already a concierge service. They don't want to bother with the real estate culture here, the security needs, the logistics. We have the experience and the contacts to make it seamless, and we offer only the best properties with top-notch security."

"I want to see bigger fish. Come back when you have them." Stephen's tone is final.

My eyes go to Remi, and he's all Poker face. I don't have time for this shit.

"I wanted to work with you guys." My tone is level, done. "I hope we still need investors when you come to your senses."

I reach forward ready to end the call, but Taron's right there with the olive branch. "Hang on, look guys, we get it. You want a sure thing. I've got some leads out there now. How about we reconvene in a week or so?"

Stephen's expression doesn't change, but Remi breaks into a smile. "Sounds like a plan. Shoot me a message when you're ready."

"You got it. Talk soon." Taron leans forward and hits the end call button. Then he exhales deeply.

I'm out of my chair, ready to go to the next name on our list. "Fuck them. Braden Investments messaged me last week ready to go."

Taron's palms are flat on the table, and he holds a beat. "Braden wants a bigger piece of the profits, more control of which markets roll out and when. You will hate that."

He knows me pretty well. "So what are you saying?"

"Give me a week. I'm talking to Pro Partner and AmCham, both in Abu Dhabi and both interested. Raquel can help you with Madagascar, and I'll focus on securing them. Then I'll touch back with Remi."

My fingers steeple in front of my lips, and I consider his

suggestion. "One week, and we'll give them one last chance." I stand, ready to return to my office. I'm at the door when I pause. "So why did you hire her of all people?"

He knows what I'm talking about—his wry grin confirms it. "She's good. We need her."

"We don't need anybody."

"We need Hastings and Key, and we need Raquel Morgan. She graduated at the top of her class."

"There wasn't a man who spoke five languages?"

"Haven't you heard of diversity?"

"An Arab man would've been perfect."

"Right." He exhales a laugh. "That would go over great with our Nashville clients. They're still our biggest book of business, you know."

"Remember when everybody spoke English?"

"And the sun never set on the British Empire? Yes, times have changed."

Scrubbing my hands against my forehead, I start for the door. "This is a small office. We work in close quarters. Women cause problems."

"What are you saying?"

"You should've hired a man."

The door opens on its own, and my throat tightens. She's standing in front of me, those gray-blue eyes fixed on me like some kind of witch.

She's the problem. It's not women, it's her.

"Hope I'm not interrupting anything."

I feel Taron's face turn toward us, but I can't look away. Her black jacket is gone, and her cream silk blouse is thin, almost transparent. I can see the faint outline of the lace cups of her bra against her olive skin, and my mouth goes dry.

Fuck, how long has it been since I've touched a woman? My fingers curl with wanting to touch her. *What the hell?*

Clearing my throat, I turn away. "What is it?"

"Sandra said you needed this translation before the end of the day." She holds out the thin manila folder I gave to her earlier.

"Is it on the server?" My tone is sharp.

"Of course. I thought you'd want to know it's ready now rather than having to find it later."

She's so fucking strong. It's her first day, and she acts like she owns the place.

I try to say thanks, but it comes out more like a growl. Stepping around her, I head for my office, but the lingering scent of ginger and coconut clings to me like quiet heat following me down the hall.

CHAPTER
Three

Raquel

BITING MY TOP LIP, I QUICKLY REVIEW WHAT JUST HAPPENED. I walked in on some meeting of the He-Man, Woman Hater's Club having finished my assignment early, and... Did Patton Fletcher just growl at me? I grin smugly.

People warned me about this job, about how impossible Patton Fletcher is to please. Well, take that, people. Round 1 goes to Rocky.

Taron is across the room watching me, and I quickly compose myself. "I guess I'll get back to unpacking my desk."

He slowly circles the table. "How's it going?" Taron's smile, his bright green eyes make him less threatening than Patton.

Still, he seems uncomfortable, like he doesn't want to be here. I wonder if that's why he hired me—it's abundantly clear he's the only reason I got this job.

"Going pretty well." I smile up at him. "Lucky break my first assignment was in French."

"Is that lucky?" He nods, and extends a hand toward the hall. "I would've been screwed."

We take the short walk back to my office, where the banker's boxes are right where he left them. The only thing I moved was my laptop, logging in and quickly starting on the new file as soon as Sandra loaded it on the server.

"I figured I'd move these into the drawers in the same order you have them here."

He nods. "Familiarize yourself with them, but you don't need to memorize. All the details are on the server. You can access it with your phone. Did Sandra get you set up?"

"Yep." I grin and nod. "I'm all set."

"I'm going to have to leave you with Patton on Madagascar. I'm working on a few new leads in the UAE." He steps back and shoves a lock of brown hair behind his ear. "I think you can handle it."

He goes to the door, and I give him a smile. "Thanks for giving me a chance."

"You earned it." He leaves, and I open the banker's box on the desk.

All of the folders are thin, with only a few very basic facts on single sheets inside. I assume because everything is on the G-drive. I've only sorted five when Jerry taps on my doorjamb. *What is this? Grand Central?*

"How's it going, New Girl?" Jerry Buckingham is completely different from Patton and Taron.

He talks a lot, which I can't imagine goes over well with the devil. His outfit is basic khakis and a button-down shirt, no tie and a blue blazer. Total frat boy, only he's too old to be a frat boy. His hands are meaty with short fingers, but I suppress my nose wrinkle.

"Pretty busy, actually." I smile and do my best to be nice but not encouraging.

I walk around my desk and lift the other banker's box from the floor, hoping to emphasize how busy I am, but when I straighten, I notice him obviously ogling my butt. Double ew.

He coughs and grins, sliding his palm down his lapel. "On

your first day? That can't be right. We usually give a few days' grace period before we work you to death."

"The boss didn't get that memo. Patton assigned me a new client when I walked in the door. Skype meeting tomorrow."

"Madagascar." He nods, leaning against the entrance. "That shouldn't be too hard for an international whiz like yourself." The way his eyes run down my blouse makes me want to put my blazer back on. "Hey, a group of us go out for drinks every Thursday after work. You should tag along."

I hesitate. "A group?"

"Yeah!" He brightens, encouraged. "Sandra, Dean, and me. We go to AJ's for happy hour."

Pressing my lips together, I consider the offer. Renée did tell me to make allies with Sandra. I just don't trust drinks with Jerry. "I don't think so." I smile and do my best to be distantly friendly.

He steps closer. "You're missing out. We'll be discussing all the gossip leading up to the company picnic on Saturday."

"Company picnic?" My throat goes tight. "Does that include me?"

"You're with the company now. It's out at Percy Priest. It's an annual thing to coincide with Labor Day—you have Monday off, by the way."

"Oh, yeah." I wonder if I should visit Renée, make sure she's doing okay, has enough money...

"So you going?"

"To the picnic?"

He laughs. "To AJ's. After work tomorrow."

"Oh, no." I shake my head, and smile, looking down. "I'll probably be up late tonight preparing for the meeting. By the end of the day, I'll be ready to crash."

"The offer's open if you change your mind." He steps to the door, but pauses to give me one last look, coupled with an eyebrow raise. "Think about it."

I'm sure he's trying to be nice, but it's coming across as creepy. "Sure. Thanks."

Once he's gone, I hustle over and shut my door. The rest of the afternoon, I spend sorting through the files. Even if Taron said I don't need to memorize them, I still want to spend a few minutes on each one, familiarizing myself with the basics.

I'm completely engrossed in my work when I hear a tapping on the glass. Looking up, I see Jerry standing outside holding his hands up. I look around and see the sun is setting. *Shit*, I worked straight through lunch. Another smile, a small wave, and he leaves. I stand and stretch, ready to call it a night.

A quick glance at the clock tells me it's after six, and it appears everyone is gone. Jerry, Taron, Mr. Randall who I have not met—all of their lights are off. A lone envelope is in the mail box outside my door, and when I pick it up, I see it's addressed to George Fletcher. My brow furrows, and I glance toward the opposite corner. I'm not surprised to see his light is still on.

Turning the business envelope over in my hands, I decide to check in before I go home. We do have a meeting together tomorrow with this new client, and who knows? This could be important. I toss my blazer over my arm, grab my bag, and pick up the small file for Madagascar, leaving my door open as I cross the corridor.

I tap on his door lightly and wait. No noises come from inside, so I knock a little louder.

"Yes?" His voice is stern, but I don't let it stop me.

"Sorry," I speak as I open the door and enter, looking at the envelope. "I seem to have gotten someone's mail by mistake."

When my eyes land on his, it's like a little earthquake that shakes me all the way to my core. His brow is furrowed like a storm brewing over his warm brown eyes, and an unlit cigarette dangles from his perfect fingers.

The inside of my lip slips between my teeth. I need to go on a date or something. I should not be responding to my new boss this way.

"Should I give this to you?" I hold out the missive, and his eyes go to it.

"There are at least four people between you and me. Give it to Sandra." *That voice.*

"Are you always so angry, Mr. Fletcher? Or is it just me?" I'm being playful, but I'm instantly locked in his gaze again.

For a moment, I can't breathe.

He stands, rising to his full six-foot-who knows what. All I know is I'm down below him, where I'm sure he thinks I belong. "Give it to me."

I step forward, holding it out to him, hating that my fingers tremble slightly. He snatches the letter, gives it a quick glance, then tosses it in the trash.

"But…" I move like I might catch it. "It might be important."

"I don't go by that name. My father retired six years ago. How important can it be?" He still isn't smiling. He's watching me like a predator, waiting to see what I'll do next. Waiting to pounce. Everything about him feels dangerous and thrilling… which is very unprofessional.

"Well, goodnight." I start to leave, and he takes a seat. At the door, I pause, thinking. "George?"

"No one calls me that." His tone drops lower, and for some reason, it makes me feel naughty.

"Someone does."

"No one who expects me to answer." His eyes are on the papers in front of him, and I don't want to stop looking at him.

I want to memorize everything about him. He's so perfect in that leather chair, his dark hair pushed back behind his ears, skimming his collar, long fingers rolling that cigarette back and forth. *Cigarettes? Seriously?* I mean, it looks sexy as hell in a daring, bad-boy way, but still…

"You're not really going to smoke that, are you?" My nose wrinkles, and again, those brown eyes snap up to mine. *So hot*.

"In case you missed it, I'm the boss. I do whatever I want. Now if you don't mind…"

I don't know why I'm taunting him. I really need this job, and I can't afford to get fired—not only because it would look bad on my résumé. I literally can't *afford* to get fired. I need the money for me and Renée.

My hand drops to the door handle, and I soften my tone. "I'm sorry. I'm ready for the meeting tomorrow. See you then."

He doesn't even look up.

CHAPTER Four

Patton

The door closes, and I lean back, trying to escape the lingering scent of her. It's a faintly persistent sweetness in the back of my throat. It's like everything about her, bright and tempting and refusing to be ignored... or bossed around.

I don't know what to make of it. One minute she acts shy, the next she's taunting, like some fucked up mix of a kitten and a minx.

Was she seriously criticizing me? I'll smoke if I want to.

I toss the unlit cigarette onto my desk and run my hands over my face. It's irritating that I'm attracted to her. I don't even know her. I need to stay focused on the big picture, our future plans, and launching this new commercial app.

Instead, my thoughts are dominated by flashing blue eyes, full lips parting to reveal straight white teeth, that sheer top...

The way she laughed and said my name...

It took all my willpower to keep my hands off her.

Fuck that, I *will* keep my hands off her.

Standing, I walk to the window and watch the nonstop stream of headlights flowing in and around the city. Our building is only a few blocks from Printer's Alley, which means even on a Wednesday, the streets are crowded with tourists partying and being loud.

I need a drink...

Which reminds me, *Where the fuck is Marley?*

I step back to snatch up my phone when it rings in my hand. The name grinds my jaw, but if I ignore him, he'll only call again until I answer. Then we'll both be pissed.

I exhale my annoyance and touch the green circle. "Hi, Dad, what's up?" *Why aren't you in a musty old club with your retiree pals smoking cigars and drinking scotch?*

"I heard the deal with Hastings and Key fell through."

Of course, he's calling about that. "It's on hold. Taron wants to follow up on some leads in the UAE, and Hastings wants to see if we land them."

He makes a noise of disapproval. "When I ran things, we didn't do business with the Arabs. Or the Chinese. Or the Russians."

It takes all my strength not to point out the obvious—he's no longer running things.

Instead, I *am* a diplomat. "Taron's smart. He wouldn't deal with questionable firms."

"If he knew about it. I'd keep Fletcher all-American. You can always trust Americans."

Another slow inhale, exhale. "It wouldn't be Fletcher International if we did that."

"You know, you don't have to do this launch. We're making plenty of money in the Nashville market."

"We do have to do it, and you'll be glad once it's done and the value of your shares goes through the roof."

He exhales like I'm a petulant teen, not the CEO of this

company. I wish he'd stick to playing golf and watching 24-hour news.

"Bill said Martin was on one of those gossip shows today. They've got pictures of him partying with Sissy Faith. On a Tuesday. Is he having issues again?"

"Sissy… the country singer?" I'd like to change my wish. Nothing is worse than my dad knowing more than I do about anything. "Tabloid gossip. Marley's working PR angles, picking up endorsements, you know."

He's quiet, and I hope I'm in the right ballpark with that lie.

"I'd hold off on partnering too quickly with young talent. You never know when they'll do something like twerk on national TV."

I don't even want to know where my aged father learned the word *twerk*. "Yeah, it was an idea, but I think you're right." Telling my father he's right is the best way to get him to roll over and go back to sleep.

"I trust you're keeping an eye on him, getting him help if he needs it."

"Of course." Another lie. Is Marley slipping? I need to find him.

"You boys did a good service to our country. Still, I can't have him mucking up our reputation—"

"He's not handling frontline business. I have him on social media and marketing."

"Social media." He grumbles, and I know I'm in for more bloviation. "Nothing beats good old-fashioned, face-to-face interaction."

"Right." I'm distracted by this new wrinkle in my day, and an awkward lull falls between us.

He clears his throat, lightening his tone. "It's after nine. You shouldn't work late every night, you'll burn out."

Like he didn't work late every night of my life. Where does

he think I learned it? At least I don't have a wife and kid waiting for me at home. The thought pricks at my mind. I look at the envelope in the trash and think about ginger and coconut...

I don't want that. My life is great as it is—except this Marley thing.

I'm ready to disconnect and track him down. "I was just finishing up when you called."

"Are you smoking in my office again? Nasty habit."

"Like anything could cut through thirty years of scotch and cigars."

"Cigars bring out the character in the wood. Cigarettes are just dirty."

"Was that all you needed?" I'm at the end of my patience now.

"If you're dead set on this expansion, lock down Hastings and Key. They're good people. Good Americans."

"Right."

"And get a handle on Martin. You don't need another situation with him."

Those words coming from my father's mouth make me furious.

"Night, Dad." I disconnect quickly, before the conversation goes completely south.

Even when I agree with him, the way he states his views makes me question myself. I don't have time for that tonight.

Holding the phone, I'm about to call Marley when a noise in the corridor makes me freeze in place. A bumping sound is followed by the sound of paper falling, more bumping, then a crash like a pen holder falling over on a desk.

I stride over and jerk open my door. "Who's there?"

Small lights around the Exit signs illuminate the empty space, and I squint into the darkness. A figure steps around a file cabinet.

"Patton! What the fuck are you doing here?" Marley holds out his arms, grinning like this is normal, as he walks to me.

"Work starts at 9 a.m., not 9 p.m. Where the fuck have you been?"

"Is it nine?" He laughs like it's all a big joke and pushes past me, going into my office, and dropping into one of my leather chairs. He's wearing the same blazer and slacks he had on when I left him yesterday evening. "You won't believe what happened."

My fists clench and unclench as I follow him inside. "Sounds like something I won't like."

"Have you heard of Sissy Faith?"

"Yes." My tone is sharp.

Celebrity or not, the girl is barely twenty-one, twelve years younger than us. I don't have time for his bullshit. He drops his leg and leans forward, reaching into his pocket and pulling out a blunt. He grabs the lighter off my desk and fires it up, taking a long pull.

"Her body is so tight." His voice is strained, and he grins lifting his chin to let the smoke out before passing the joint to me. "It's been a while since I've been with someone so… fresh."

"Jesus… You slept with her?" I scowl, taking the joint and holding it a second. At least it doesn't smell like that cheap, skunk shit. I wanted a drink, but this will suffice.

"Fuck, yeah." He chuckles at some memory. "After you went home last night, she showed up with some roadies or whatever. We hit the town and, *damn*."

His words make me think of Raquel, of touching her body, and the heat rises below my belt. I lean against my desk and take a long pull off the blunt before passing it back. I watch as he takes another hit, and my brain starts to relax. Dad's call pissed me off, but I'm feeling a little better now that Marley's in my office, not dead and not too far off track.

He offers the smoke to me again, but I decline. "I *am* planning to show up for work tomorrow."

"Suit yourself. She gave me the name of her supplier."

"Don't get caught with it." This guy thinks nothing of getting high, getting in a car, and speeding through The District.

"What did I miss today?" He pulls up his phone and starts tapping on the face.

"Not much."

"What's this? Welcome Raquel Morgan?" He turns the phone toward me and has the nerve to look interested.

"Taron hired her."

"Morgan... Is she related to—"

"Yes."

"Is she pretty?"

Yes, very. "It doesn't matter."

He leans back on the couch and looks at me a second before lifting the joint and taking another long pull. Then he looks out the window. Seconds pass. "Let's go to AJ's and see who's playing."

"I told you, I have to work tomorrow. We're meeting with Madagascar."

"Fuck that, you could do that in your sleep. We're only young once."

I study the deep lines around his eyes. I'm going to have to do something about him, and I'm pissed I didn't see it sooner. I'm pissed my dad is right. "We're not so young, and you need to sleep it off. I expect you to make an appearance here tomorrow."

"I guess now I have to." He stands, tapping out the J. "Have to check out this new Morgan chick in the office."

"Raquel works with me." It's possible the words come out a little too sharp. I don't care. "I want to see your marketing plan for the fourth quarter."

He doesn't bat an eye. "Already done. Instagram account @Fletchcom, hashtag luxrental, hashtag rentbnb, hashtag Fletcher. Now I just need to post a bunch of photos of our shit."

"And you think that'll work?"

"Works for Kylie Jenner."

"Am I supposed to know what that means?"

"It means we can get a drink at AJ's before we call it a night."

I'm not in the mood for people. "Taron's working on two new accounts. He can use the help. Did you drive here?"

"Uber."

Perfect. I lift my blazer off the back of my chair then scoop up my phone and keys. "I'll drive you home. I want you in his office first thing in the morning."

"You're the boss."

"Glad you remember."

He laughs like nothing is wrong, and after the day I've had, I decide to leave it there for now.

CHAPTER *Five*

Raquel

"I WAS A LITTLE FREAKED OUT. I DIDN'T EVEN HAVE MY computer password yet. But it was all in French, so I had it done in a few hours." Balancing my phone on my shoulder, I spoon take-out chicken Pad Thai into a bowl.

"Oh, yeah, they excel at starting you off hard and never letting up. You've got to find a way to impress Patton. That'll knock him off his high horse."

I take a bite and nod, even though she can't see me. "You were right. Patton Fletcher is something else."

"Don't fall for him." Renée's voice is distracted, and she says it more like a mantra.

It kind of worries me. "Did you?" I silently hold my breath waiting for her answer.

"Did I what?" The noise of banging fills the line, then her voice goes loud. "Fall for Patton Fletcher? Lord, no! I actually try to protect my emotional health."

My eyes close as I exhale slowly. *Thank God.* "He's kind of stern." *And hot as fuck.*

"Stern? That's a nice way of putting it. He's a pushy, insulting, arrogant, demanding—"

"He's the boss?" It's a gentle tease.

She huffs out a sarcastic *ha*. "Bosses don't have to act that way. He's a jerk."

Stabbing the slippery noodles with my fork, I think about the sexy man in question. "I didn't think he was a jerk. He more, sort of... hyper-focused." I take a big, spicy bite of chicken and crunchy carrots and broccoli. *Delicious*.

"Has he insulted your wardrobe yet?"

I make a little noise of defeat. "I'm not sure if it was an insult. He asked me if I was going to a funeral."

"Ha!" She fake-laughs. "Asshole. Like everyone was born with a trust fund, inherited their dad's successful business, and shops at Armani all the time."

"I'm more a Balenciaga gal myself." I'm really trying to diffuse the tension. I wasn't that mad about his comment, and once I ditched the blazer, he was downright friendly.

"How's it going with Hazel? Is she treating you like the help?"

"She's okay. Her cat count has officially risen to ten."

"Ten! How many cats is too many?"

"Well..." Her voice trails off. "They stay outside except the ones who've been declawed. It's such a cruel practice, declawing. It's like cutting off the tips of all your fingers, and as they get older, they develop arthritis making it painful to jump—"

"I'll never declaw a cat. Promise." It doesn't take much to get my sister on a soap box, and she has many causes. "How are you feeling? Are you happy there?"

"Of course! I wouldn't stay if I wasn't."

Chewing my lip, I think about her words. Since the loss of our parents, it's just Renée and me, and after her unexplained breakdown, I'm a little gun-shy. I finally have a job where I'm making good money, but I can't afford more medical bills. I certainly can't afford to go back to Savannah to take care of her. Not now.

"You'll tell me if you need anything, right? No disappearing again."

She doesn't answer right away, and I hear the sound of running water.

"Ray?"

"Look, Rocky, I'm fine, okay? You'd do well to follow my advice and take care of yourself."

I take another bite of dinner, letting the sudden tension diffuse. "I really liked Sandra. She was glad to hear you're doing well."

"Sandra's nice. Tell her I said hello." The warmth in her voice encourages me. While I chew, her tone becomes thoughtful. "Who else did you meet today?"

Stabbing another bite, I quickly review the day. "Dean is the receptionist. He's super nice, college aged, although I don't think he's enrolled anywhere."

"He must be new... Anybody else?"

"Nope." I take my last bite, talking around it. "I lost most of the day working on Madagascar. I didn't even get lunch."

"Hm." Another banging noise. "Well, I'd better go. I'm making soap."

"Hey, take care of yourself, okay? I love you."

"Protect your chin."

We disconnect, and I grab the remote, flipping to Netflix and letting Queer Eye play. The Fab Five are working with a man in a wheelchair, and his smile is so bright. I wonder if I could maintain my positive attitude in the face of physical adversity.

I've faced personal challenges. While Renée was going through her stuff, my social life all but disappeared. I couldn't afford to go out with the girls, and if I did have a free night or weekend, I either passed out from exhaustion or drove to Savannah to stay with her. I was barely twenty-one, but she needed me.

Now when she does the overprotective big sister routine, it feels so unnecessary. She's so worried about Patton Fletcher... *George*. My nose wrinkles.

It really is a crime how sexy he is. I've never had such an immediate, primitive response to a man. I've had boyfriends, of course, but this is different. This is like being offered a thick, juicy steak after being on a 40-day bread and water diet.

Setting my dinner on the end table, I lie on my side on the couch. I want to thread my fingers in his dark hair. It's so thick and glossy, I love that he wears it slightly longer. I want to trace my finger down the line in his forehead, erasing the anger there. Is it anger or is it tension?

Maybe if I ran my hands all over those broad shoulders... I could press my lips to the back of his neck, touch my tongue to his warm skin and taste the salt on his hard body.

I want to see what he's hiding under that suit, see his tattoos, feel the strength of his arms, slip my hand down his stomach and check the size of his package... My thighs squeeze together, and I consider fetching my vibrator.

I should probably stop fantasizing about my grumpy boss, but it doesn't count if he isn't interested in me, right?

Patton Fletcher, I exhale a sigh. He's either going to be the best or the worst thing that's ever happened to me...

Dashing into the office, I'm five minutes late. I can barely breathe, juggling my coffee and my bag with my cardigan over my arm. I don't have another suit, and it's too hot for winter coats. My only option was a pair of black cigarette pants, a chambray blouse, and my cream blazer.

"Nice French tuck." Dean does a little clap as I jog past his desk. He's in teal pants and a mustard crew-neck sweater. "Tan would be proud."

"I didn't know fashion would be a part of the job." I'm not joking. I'll have to hit up Target as soon as I get my paycheck and hope I can do enough rotations until then.

"I've found if you fly under the radar, you don't get hit."

I can't tell if he's intentionally making a military reference or not. I'm well aware all three of the partners here are decorated veterans. Some incident in the jungle I didn't have time to research.

"I'm not sure that theory will work for me." I already stick out, being the only female besides Sandra.

I almost jump a foot in the air when I round the corner to find Patton waiting in the corridor with a frown. "Glad you decided to join us."

My heart was flying from the fright, but now it's swooning from how hot he looks. I think he must be getting me back, because the white dress shirt he's wearing is thin enough that I can see his wife beater under it. I can also see more of the tattoo on his arm from the way his sleeves are rolled to his elbows. I see a band with *semper fi* on it in thick, chunky lettering.

He catches me looking and shoves his sleeves down, buttoning them at the wrists. He's so close, I can smell the crisp blend of soap and citrus hanging around him.

"In this meeting, you only translate. Nothing more." His deep voice sends heat filtering from my chest down into my stomach. "The deal is made. We're just finalizing it in person. It's essentially a Skype handshake."

Blinking up, I meet his dark eyes, and it's like a flash of electricity. His brow quirks, and he clears his throat, looking away.

For a moment, I'm confused. Did he just pull away from me? I'm sure I imagined it.

"I should stick to the script." *Like a good little girl.* I don't say it, but he cuts me a look.

For the span of a heartbeat, I feel something move between us. It's almost like he wants to say something, but he changes his mind. He turns and walks to the conference room, and without his blazer on, I get my first glimpse of his butt. *Holy shit*. Tight, square, perfect.

I'm melting into a hot puddle until he calls back loud enough for everyone to hear. "Ditch the cardigan. You're not eighty."

It's like a splash of cold water on my lust party. I jump back, looking down at my sweater and frowning. I'm not even wearing it, and when I am, I do not look eighty.

Turning, I see Sandra watching me with one eyebrow cocked. "You okay?"

"Sure... I'm great. I was just trying to figure out what to do with this." I start to hold out my sweater, but I don't want her to think I care if he hates it. "My notes... I guess I should stop by my office. I can drop this off while I'm in there. It's not really that chilly in here. You never know, though." *Jesus, stop talking, Rocky!*

I hate how I talk too much when I'm nervous. Or flustered. Or completely intimidated by the sexiest man I've ever seen.

A smile curls her lips, and she nods. "You'd better get going."

My face is burning hot as I hustle to catch up to Patton, who's already in the conference room and logging onto the website. I'm supposed to be impressing him, not fumbling around like an amateur.

"What took you so long?" He's back to gruff annoyance, which of course, makes me want to fire back.

"You've only been in here ten seconds."

He turns on his heel, and his brown eyes are hot when they hit mine. "Don't start with that smart mouth in front of these guys. They're used to women knowing their place."

"Is it a philosophy you agree with?" I blink at him innocently, *sarcastically*.

His lips press into a straight line, and he turns to the screen.

"It's possible they're onto something… when it comes to certain women."

My eyebrows shoot up. "Certain women?"

He cuts me off. "Follow my lead. We can't afford any fuck ups at this point."

"It's what I planned to do." I'm irritated with him now. "So their email said they'd like to conduct the meeting in French."

He pulls on a light brown blazer, pulling his cuffs down with a huff. "If they speak French, they speak English."

"I'm sure they speak English, but they want to speak French."

"Makes everything take twice as long as it should. An annoying power move."

He's grumbling, and I'm about to point out how being fluent in other languages makes us unique and more appealing to international companies when the enormous monitor flickers to life. A white room with a large window appears, and three men in gray suits sit side by side behind a long table facing us like we're in court.

No one is smiling.

"Good afternoon, gentlemen." Patton gestures to me. "Raquel Morgan here is our new Director of International Affairs. She'll be our translator."

He touches my shoulder, sparking a zing of electricity that I shoot down. I'm not entertaining those thoughts when I'm pissed at him.

The men on the screen don't respond. It's almost like they can't hear us.

A few seconds tick past, and Patton gives me another nudge. *Oh, shit!* I jump to life and quickly repeat what he said to them in French.

All of the men smile, and one nods. "Sali. K'aiza."

Patton glances at me, and my teeth clench. He knows I

almost missed it, but he's letting it go. I'm not. I remember Renée's advice: *Impress him.*

The man's greeting was not in French, but my work yesterday paid off. It's a common Malagasy greeting.

"They say, 'Hello, how's it going?'"

Patton's eyebrows flicker up, but after that crack about knowing my place, I'm ready to roll up my sleeves.

The conversation continues with Patton speaking in English and me translating it into French, and vice versa with the men. The rental is on one of the top floors in a high rise in Knoxville. They've seen photos, and Patton assures them the space has been newly renovated and is able to accommodate all the latest tech for a team of up to fifty.

They discuss the college town briefly and traffic patterns. It is pretty boring, and I'd probably have zoned out if I didn't have to translate all of it. It's doubly annoying because ten minutes in, it was clear these guys do indeed speak English, and Patton's right—the meeting would go a lot faster if we could drop this pretense.

We're finally at the end, ready to sign off on all the contracts when the door opens, and a guy I've never met swaggers into the room. He's tall with neat brown hair and wearing an expensive gray suit. His blue eyes strike me as world-weary, but he gives me a big grin in spite of it. I'm ready to like him, when I glance over and see the tension in Patton's face.

"What's going on in here?" The guy pulls out a chair across from us and drops into it.

"You know what." Patton's voice is even. I've only been here one day, but I can tell by that tone he's pissed. "We're meeting with Madagascar."

"Mada-gascar!" He says it in a mocking way, and my stomach clenches. I realize this guy is a loose cannon... He shouts at the screen, waving, "Are these our friends in Africa? Jumbo!"

My lips press together, and I'm not sure if I should translate or not. I think he might be high. The men on the screen seem confused, and Patton takes the lead.

"Taylor, Justin, Rickey, I'd like to introduce you to Martin Randall. He handles our marketing." His tone is all business. "Martin's had some late nights recently."

I translate this quickly, knowing these guys understand everything Patton said. Martin's eyes are on me, but it's not predatory like Jerry. He's studying me, watching me for clues.

"Was that French?" Martin's voice is still loud, and he turns from me to the screen. "I thought Madagascarians spoke Mulligatawney." He holds up a hand Native American style and quips, "Moto-Moto!"

Patton is on his feet at once and rounding the table as Martin falls back laughing. "Get it? I like to move it, move it..."

He's still going when Patton catches him by the arm, lifting him out of the chair. "Let's go."

"I heard they smoke a lot of pot in Madagascar... It's not legal in Tennessee. It's so confusing these days where you can get high and where you can't."

"I'll clear it up for you." Patton's voice is quiet anger. I hear it, but I'm not sure if our friends on the screen hear it.

I turn to them, speaking in French. "I'm so sorry about the interruption. Martin has been dealing with some personal issues. He's not himself today... probably needs a day or two off."

I am seriously flailing. I've never met this guy, and I don't know what Patton would want me to say.

The men on the screen frown at each other. Taylor says *Moto-Moto* in a questioning way, and then they speak to each other in a dialect I don't understand. I can only guess it's Malagasy. This can't be good.

When they turn to me again, Rickey, the first man who spoke, addresses me in English. "We're going to need a little more time to discuss the agreement."

Oh, no. They're stepping back from the deal. My chest clenches, and I know I've got to do something to save it. I don't know the investors Patton mentioned, but losing this account so late in the game would not look good to anybody.

"Ah, if you would just give me two minutes." I'm improvising now. "We were all up late last night discussing the new policies we're implementing. We were planning to grandfather in your deal, but we'd have to sign it today in order to do so."

All three men's brows furrow, and they study me a moment. Patton's comment about women knowing their place flickers in my mind, but I won't let it kill my confidence.

"What is this new policy?" Justin asks me.

"Well, starting today, we're implementing a ten percent finder's fee on all new rentals, and the 24-hour premium-level security you have here for free will be an additional fifteen hundred dollars a month." God, I'm making this up as I go. "As it stands, you're set to save almost ten thousand dollars if we close the deal today."

Taylor frowns and leans back, looking over the contract. "I have not heard any mention of premium-level security. It simply says *security*."

"Yes, well…" *Think fast, Rocky.* "Based on client feedback, we've decided to offer different levels of security. Our former service will become premium, with a security guard on site at all times and regular drive-by checks from local police. From there it will go all the way down to basic, which is just the drive-by without the on-site security guard. We'll customize it to meet clients' needs, but as your deal stands, you're getting the top of the line package for free."

Patton returns to the room, straightening his coat and doing his best to appear calm. Still, I can see the muscle moving in his jaw. I know he's agitated.

"Gentlemen, I'm very sorry for the interruption. Our marketing director is a frustrated stand-up comic. I hope you weren't offended by his jokes."

They start to respond, but I quickly lean forward, turning my head so they can't see my wide eyes signaling Patton. "I was just telling them about the changes we decided to make last night to our services, the levels of security and the new fees."

"New fees?" He's taken aback, but I quickly continue.

"I was telling them how we decided to waive it for them on this deal *and* provide our top of the line, 24-hour security at the rate we've already quoted. But only if we close the deal today."

He straightens in his chair, studying me, and I have to hand it to him. Patton is a quick study. I see the wheels turning behind his eyes. He knows I made it all up, but it's working.

"Yes…" He cuts his eyes from me to the screen. "I didn't think we needed to mention these changes, since you were ready to sign. But in case there's any hesitation, we don't want you to miss this opportunity. It's quite a deal."

Rickey lifts the documents in front of him, turning them over and scanning them again. His lips poke out, and he nods. "We like this property. We have already planned the staff and equipment to send. With these additional features…" He looks to the other two men, and their expressions are unreadable.

My stomach is so tight, I can barely breathe. I feel like I'm going to be sick. In my mind, I'm chanting, *Sign the contract… Sign it…*

Finally, he turns to us again. "We'll go forward with the deal today. I'll have my secretary send the signed documents over, and we'll be on site in a week."

The breath I'm holding tries to burst from my lips. I want to jump up and do a little victory booty-shake.

I don't.

I sit calmly, smiling like this is exactly what I expected to happen.

Patton's stacks the sheets in front of him. "If we have no further business, I'll look for the contracts this afternoon."

We say goodbye and the screen goes dark. I exhale and fall back in my chair. "It worked."

The room is silent, and I dare to glance up at my boss. His poker face is still intact, but those dark eyes move from the stack on the table to me. My stomach burns with a low, simmering heat. *Did I impress you?*

He stands without a word, but I can't let him get away with zero feedback. I don't know how to get us there, but I've at least got to get him talking.

I step around my chair closer to him. "What happened back there?"

"What do you mean?"

Is he serious? "Our uninvited guest."

"I'm handling it." Pausing, his dark eyes sear into mine. "Next time you get a bright idea for handling clients, run it past me first."

My jaw drops, but he's not getting away with that. "You seemed to have your hands full."

"You've been here less than two days. You're not ready to take the lead."

Bastard. He can't admit I saved the deal.

He's going to the door, but I'm right there with him. "Are you unhappy with the way I handled it?"

He stops abruptly and turns, and I crash into his rock-hard chest. Strong hands grip my upper arms, steadying me and holding me back. My breath disappears, and that chemistry… that ever-present chemistry flares between us.

I know he feels it. The firm line of his jaw moves, and his eyes roam hot over my face before he releases me. "No."

That's all I get. He turns and leaves the conference room.

The door slowly closes, and I put my hand on the back of a chair, trying to catch my breath, trying to piece together what just happened.

Forget what I told Jerry yesterday. I'm going out with the staff tonight. I want to get to the bottom of this.

CHAPTER Six

Patton

TARON PACES THE ROOM, ARMS CROSSED OVER HIS CHEST, PINCHING the front of his lips. "What the fuck, Marley? You almost lost us Madagascar."

I'm sitting behind my desk with my foot crossed over my knee watching him. If Marley's high, it doesn't matter what we say to him now. He won't remember any of it.

"I drove you home last night… Did you go out again?" It's an easy question, and it'll at least help me locate him mentally.

He sits on my leather couch with his forearms propped on his knees, looking at the floor and not answering.

He doesn't have to answer. I know he did.

Taron doesn't sit. He paces across my office, picking up the framed photo of the four of us in Venezuela. "Do you need to go back to Oak Grove?"

That gets his attention. "Fuck off, Taron. I'm not going back to that place."

Pressing against my knees, I stand and turn to the window. Forcing him into rehab doesn't work. We've tried it, but I'm at the end of my ability to carry him. I can't have him scaring off business—or insulting them… or getting mixed up in some scandal, which is a worse PR nightmare.

Turning back, I temper my tone. "What happened?"

"Nothing happened. Absolutely nothing." His voice is low now, and when he looks up at me, his blue eyes are so tired, it feels like a punch in the gut. "It's not getting better."

Inhaling slowly, I nod. "You want to talk to someone?"

"I just want to live my life. What's left of it."

Taron puts the photo down and takes a halting step toward him. "That's why you need to go back to treatment."

Marley pushes away from him. He'll fight with Taron, but he'll listen to me. I guess it goes back to the days when we were in country. I was always our leader. "You haven't slept since Tuesday. It gets worse when you don't sleep. You know this. I don't have to tell you."

"I dream when I sleep." He finally stands and walks over to my desk, opening the small wooden box and taking out a cigarette. I watch as he lights it up and takes a long pull. "Let's go to AJ's. It's happy hour, and we could have a drink, talk about old times. It'll be like it was."

My eyes cut to Taron, and his expression is stony. We're not making any progress here, but I'm willing to try anything that might get him through this. It's cyclical. We know what to expect. He just needs a babysitter for a little while.

Pulling on my blazer, I loosen my tie and slip it over my head. "I think we could do that." Rolling it slowly, I put it in my desk drawer. "Taron, can you call it a day?"

He studies my face a beat then nods, seeming to understand what I'm doing. "Yeah. I'm waiting on a call back from Dubai, but I booked a meet and greet with Abu Dhabi next week, after the holiday."

Marley blinks up at him. "Holiday?"

Taron narrows his eyes. "If you bothered with regular hours, you'd know Monday is Labor Day."

"Ah…" He waves us away. "Labor Day isn't a holiday."

Leading them out the door, I don't bother arguing. "Sandra? I'm out for the day. I'm expecting contracts from Rickey's firm. Text me if they don't arrive by five."

She stands behind her desk, which is directly across the corridor from my office and holds out a stack of papers. "They're right here."

Taking them from her, I flip to the last page to see all three signatures. *Yes*. My gaze lifts to the closed door of Raquel's office, and the self-destructive part of me wants to invite her to join us and celebrate. I don't like eating crow, but it's possible Taron was right about her. If we can keep everyone in his or her own lane.

I'm the problem this time. I can't stop thinking about her in inappropriate ways. When she stumbled into me in the conference room earlier, I didn't want to let her go. She's so light in my grip, I could've easily pulled her to me and kissed her. The realization tightens my chest and causes my heart to beat faster. I wanted to kiss her.

Inviting her to join us is out of the question.

"Anything else?" Sandra's red lips curl up on one side, and she smirks like she knows everything I'm thinking.

Normally, I'd be pissed, but Sandra started working in this office while I was still in the military. When dad retired and I took over, she fell right in line. She has never tried to go behind my back or talked about how my dad used to do things.

It goes a long way with me.

Passing back the contracts, I shake my head. "This was the main thing I needed. If Hastings or Key calls, text me." Pausing, I lean closer. "It's okay if you want to mention Madagascar is on board, and we're meeting with Abu Dhabi next week."

She smiles big then. "It's all coming together."

I tap my knuckles on her desk and join Taron and Marley at the elevator. Approaching them, I consider this day is the yin and the yang. Good things are happening, but fuck if the problems aren't trying to ruin everything.

Marley lifts a tumbler of scotch. "The three musketeers reunited." He slams it back and winces. "Only D'Artagnan is in fucking Louisiana growing peaches."

Taron eases off his stool with a low groan. We've been at the bar two hours, and I'm on my third drink. Taron's had one more than me, but the pain he's feeling is stronger than the liquor.

We've talked about boot camp, pranks we pulled on plebes, girls Marley sneaked into the barracks, girls Taron sneaked into the barracks. Sawyer's insistence on being a fucking peach farmer, and how much money he's giving up…

"Can you handle him alone?" Taron leans heavily toward me, and I see his expression is pained. "I've got to head out."

"You okay?" The last thing I need is Taron falling apart.

He cuts his eyes, and worry cuts through my gut. "I'm not getting into it tonight."

"We'll talk about it tomorrow."

"With Raquel?" He grins, polishing off the last of his whiskey.

I'm just relaxed enough to throw him a bone. "I'm willing to consider the possibility she might be a good hire."

"Ha!" He's loud and pointing at me. "Consider it? Try believing it. She is good."

"I was impressed today." Something like pride unfurls low in my stomach, which is ridiculous. "Get some rest. We'll talk tomorrow."

I watch him go, and as he passes between the two bars, I hear a loud laugh. Lingering in the neutral space, my eyes roam around the secondary bar, and I see her. She's standing there alone, which surprises me. She doesn't seem like the type to go to a bar alone.

Her head turns, and as if by force of will, her blue eyes connect with mine. Those blue eyes... I feel them in my chest, ticking my heart rate higher, drawing me to her. The fucking invisible current between us grows stronger. I flex against it, but I can't fight it. Her eyes narrow in defiance, and it's like a match to my simmering desire.

She isn't afraid of me.

She should be afraid of me.

CHAPTER Seven

Raquel

My insides were all knotted and warring after Patton left me in the conference room. On the one hand, I was pissed he couldn't even admit the role I played in keeping Madagascar onboard. On the other hand, the way he touched me… He's always so fiercely in control. Would it hurt to thank someone for helping him?

Back in my office, I scoop up my phone and hit Renée's number.

She answers on the first ring. "Sea and Things, how can I help you?"

I'm so giddy, it makes me laugh. "Is that how you answer your phone?"

"What?" She focuses on our conversation. "Rocky? What's going on?"

"What's going on with you? You answered your cell like it was the store phone."

"Did I?" She makes a little surprised noise. "We just got in a big shipment. You caught me in the middle of sorting. What's going on? Are you okay?"

"I'm great! I'm so great, I think I did it!"

The clock ticks, and she finally asks. "Sorry, did what again?"

"Renée! Are you paying attention to me?" I'm walking around my office, my hand crossed over my waist, replaying how it all went down in my mind. I took a big risk, and it massively paid off, whether my asshole boss wants to acknowledge it or not.

"Yes!" She hits the word a little hard. "But you're being so cryptic."

"I think I have successfully impressed Patton Fletcher." I do a little march as I say the words. "Correction! I think I successfully knocked his socks off."

Renée laughs, but it sounds more like disbelief than celebration. "What did you do?"

"You don't believe me! I'm offended!"

"Just tell me what happened."

I run through my story about the fictitious fees and security. "They were seriously quitting the deal, but I made like Sir Mix-a-Lot. I pulled up quick and retrieved it!"

I do a little booty-shake. Renée has no idea what I'm talking about, but she's still encouraging. "I'm very proud of you. I knew you could do it."

"Thanks, sis." Dropping into my desk chair, I exhale all my emotions. "It was so shocking how Martin just burst into the meeting. I've never been in a situation like that before. I mean, I've seen them in movies and stuff, but never in real life. I was totally rattled."

"Is that so?" Her voice goes strangely high.

"Yeah... Did you know him? He kept looking at me like he recognized me." My sister and I don't look exactly alike, but people say we have a family resemblance.

"Ahh... yeah, I remember him."

"His eyes really struck me. They seemed so tired." Turning in my chair, I look out the window, remembering. I start to get sad, but I shake it off. "Anyway, Patton was not ready to give an inch. I practically had to drag an acknowledgment out of him. And it was barely an acknowledgment, let me tell you."

"Well, I'm very glad for you. Now I'd better go, okay? Call again soon, okay?"

Pressing my lips into a frown, I cut my eyes toward my phone. "Sure, sis. I'll call later. Love you."

"Chin down."

"Right."

We disconnect, and I toss my phone on the desk. Whatever.

My feet are propped on one of my drawers, and I'm basking in my second victory in two days working here. I'll be in that old boy's club yet, you just wait.

Smarmy Jerry was thrilled when I told him I'd changed my mind about going to happy hour with them. "Good decision. It's the best way to bond with your coworkers."

He might be right, but I have ulterior motives. I really want to know what the hell is going on with Martin, and maybe I'll find out what the hell crawled up Patton's butt and died.

I might have defended him to Renće, but she's right. He doesn't have to act that way to be the boss. Something else is going on, and I want to know what.

AJ's is a massive rooftop lounge. It has two huge bars on each end, with smaller sitting areas off to the sides. It's rectangular and modern, and the décor is all leather, chrome, and glass.

I'm standing, wedged between Jerry and Sandra. Dean is on her other side, giving me the rundown.

"Oh my God, girl, how cute are you in those pants." He waves his hand over my pretty basic work outfit. "Your chic professional is on point."

I nod, finishing my sip of gin and tonic. "Patton said to lose the cardigan. I'm not eighty."

"And he is so right." Dean shakes his head. "That man has impeccable style. He should be gay."

I want to argue he should not, but that would be showing my hand. Instead, I take another sip of my drink and nod again. "Then you wouldn't be head fashion queen!"

"It's true. He can stay straight. Or not." Dean laughs. "Hell, I'd settle for Taron. They're all so lickable."

"Don't let Patton bother you." Jerry leans too close into my ear, placing his hand on my lower back. "You always look amazing."

"Thanks!" I say bright and loud, doing my best to move away from his hands and face, but Sandra has me blocked. "So what was up with that guy today... Martin? What's his story?"

It's like I uttered the unspeakable word. Their expressions all close. Sandra takes a sip of her white wine, and Dean turns toward the bar. Jerry's the only leach I can't seem to shake.

I start to laugh. "Holy shit, what is he? The Ghost of Christmas Past?"

Sandra leans closer, lowering her voice. "Nobody really talks about it. The subject is very much off limits."

"Off limits?" I take another sip of my drink, getting excited. "Why?"

She shrugs. "They were all in the military together, and something bad went down with Marley. Now they're all very protective of him. Or at least Patton is. Taron is too distracted."

Jerry's voice rises louder. "Taron's back is all fucked up because of it. Marley was in some kind of situation. Now he's shell-shocked." His hand is on me again, and I do my best to maneuver away from him. "He's more a danger to himself than anything—except when he starts losing clients... or other things."

I think about this. Patton was agitated when Marley entered the room. He can't control that one. "I think he was on drugs."

Dean holds up a perfectly manicured hand. "I can verify he entered the office smoking a joint. It was good shit, too. I could tell by the smell."

My voice is quiet. "He actually said *Moto-Moto* to the Madagascar team."

Jerry coughs and starts to laugh. "No, shit."

All our eyes meet, and we all start laughing.

"Tell me he didn't!" Dean cries.

"It was so awful." I shake my head, wiping tears. "It wasn't funny at the time. I was legit freaking out. They almost walked."

"That sounds about right." Jerry's hand returns to my back, only this time it's lower, sliding down to cup my butt.

"Oh! Excuse me." I jerk away from him and almost step on Sandra.

"Careful there!" She lifts her glass and passes it to the other hand.

I'm now between her and Dean, glaring at Jerry. He closes his eyes and polishes off his second whiskey, then turns away to the bartender.

My lip goes between my teeth, and I frown. I suppose it could have been an accident.

Sandra finishes her wine, and gives me a little squeeze. "All's well that ends well. I've got to run."

"No!" I look at my full tumbler. "I just ordered this. Don't go."

"Have to. I unlock the doors at seven-thirty." Hooking her finger in Dean's coat, she gives him a tug. "Time to go, Cinderella."

"Not you, too!" Now I'm really panicking.

"Sorry, babe. Sandra's my ride." He kisses my cheek and does a wave. "Don't do anything I wouldn't!"

I rest an elbow on the bar, threading my fingers in the side of my hair and giving it a pull. I don't have to finish this drink…

Jerry turns back and winks at me, singing, "I like to move it, move it!"

My nose wrinkles, and I look down at my watery, fifteen-dollar gin and tonic. "It wasn't really funny. Patton was furious."

"What else is new?" Jerry puts his arm on the bar and leans closer. "How are you fitting in? Getting adjusted?"

"Sure." I slide back, putting more space between us. "Why is he always so angry?"

Jerry lifts his chin. "Who?" I arch an eyebrow, and he shakes his head. "Patton? Who knows. His father rides him hard. He wants to make a name for himself on his own merit. He feels responsible for everything that happens. Pick a reason."

I think about all of these reasons. "I suppose it's a lot of pressure..."

"You've been in Nashville, what? A week? How about I take you around and show you the sights."

Blinking up at him, I wonder if he even read my résumé. "I graduated from Owen School of Business... at Vanderbilt?"

He grins. "Oh, right. Still, I could take you out, show you the town. It's a long weekend. What do you say?"

"I'm sorry. I promised I'd visit my sister in Savannah. I can't." It's a total lie.

I should just tell him I have zero interest in doing anything with him, but I'm trying to hang onto a few friendly faces in the office. If I can stand it.

"Right. Your sister. How is she?"

"Great! Thanks for asking. Well, I'd better get going, too. Work comes early!"

"Stay and finish your drink." He nods toward me. "I've got to hit the men's room. Be right back."

I watch as he circles the bar moving away from me, and to be honest, I don't mind that he's gone, even if I'm left alone here. Shifting from one foot to the other, I pass my card to the bartender, ready to call it a night. I tap on the Lyft app and order a car, and while I wait, I scan the crowd of young professionals. They're all about my age or just a few years older.

My eyes drift toward the door, where people are coming and going. I'm just about to turn around again when I freeze, sucking in a quiet gasp.

Patton stands in the space between the two bars looking like he just stepped off the cover of *Esquire*. I'm caught in his simmering, brown gaze, and I can't look away.

His blazer is gone, and he's standing there in that thin white dress shirt with the sleeves rolled up to show the ink on his forearm. One hand is in his tailored navy slacks, and the way he looks at me makes my skin hot all over my body.

I want him to come to me. *Come to me*, I whisper silently in my head. As if he can hear me, his lips curl into a cocky grin, and he moves in my direction. I've never seen him smile, and the way he's doing it now makes my thighs press together.

Patton Fletcher is sex on two legs.

He stops right in front of me and gives me a nod. "Are you here alone?"

"No..." I clear the breathlessness from my throat. "Sandra and Dean just left, and Jerry's in the bathroom."

"I see." He lifts his chin, looking around the bar. I take the opportunity to admire the lines in his neck, the scruff of his shadowy beard, the bumps of his Adam's apple. Dean's right—*lickable*.

Fresh soap and citrus surround me, and with him this close, I feel the heat of his body on my skin. I want to lean in and inhale...

The bar is so crowded, he keeps being shoved close then back again like a wave.

I manage to find my voice. "Are you here alone?"

"No." He looks down, letting his eyes move around my face. It's very distracting. "Who are you here with?"

"Marley is at the other bar. Taron just left."

I look across the room and see Marley sitting in one of the square leather chairs. Two women with long hair and slinky dresses are propped on each arm. They look like supermodels.

I take another sip of my drink. *Oh.* I feel my little balloon deflating.

"You're here hooking up?" I don't know what possessed me to say it out loud... Other than I'm dying inside.

His dark brow furrows attractively. "I don't do casual sex."

I love that answer and the way he says it. His gaze is so intense, it prickles down my spine.

"Me either." That's probably TMI.

The bartender interrupts our moment. "Miss? Your card."

I don't move until I realize Jerry is back. "Well, look who's here." He walks up behind me, and again, he puts his hand on my lower back, sliding it down to cup my ass.

"Watch it!" I step forward, right into Patton.

He catches me, those strong hands gripping my upper arms like before, and his dark eyes cut from me to Jerry. I can tell he doesn't know what's going on, but I want to stay with him. I don't want to be with butt-grabbing Jerry. At the same time, I'm not in the mood for Marley's antics.

Oh, shit. I ordered a Lyft already. "I have to go home," I say to no one in particular.

Patton looks down at me, and I look up at him. "You have freckles."

"Since I was a kid."

Again, his dark eyes scan my face, and this time it's like a caress. "You're leaving?"

I hesitate a beat before I give up and nod. "I ordered a Lyft a few minutes ago. It's probably here."

"I'll see you down."

I grab my card, and we head for the elevator without another word to Jerry. It's a short wait, and when we step inside, it's just the two of us. My heart is beating so fast, it aches.

I glance up at him, and he moves closer. "You did good today."

"It's about time you said it."

"You can't just take a compliment." His chin drops, and our breath mingles. It's electric, and the little hairs on my arms and legs stand at attention.

I lean into him. A hint of whiskey is on his breath, and I'm intoxicated by it. I blink up to meet his eyes. They flare, and his hand grasps my upper arm, squeezing as he holds me.

"What are you doing?" I can't tell if he's angry or desperate.

I don't know what I'm doing. I want him to kiss me. I want to know if this thing between us is real or simply fueled by the forbidden. *Kiss me…* the words whisper in my mind, desire tingles on my lips.

The elevator is dropping twenty flights, and my heart is flying through the roof. His eyes move to my mouth. He sways closer, and my eyes flicker shut. I feel the light brush of his nose against mine, the whisper of his breath on my cheek, and I put my hand on his firm chest. *It's happening…*

The elevator dings, and he lets me go.

He walks out of the elevator, leaving me dazed and needy. I watch his broad shoulders, his back, that tight ass leaving me behind in a wilted puddle of lust. I feel like a fool.

Gritting my teeth, I turn my phone over and check the app. My car is supposed to be here—a red Honda Accord. He stops at the curb, looking up and down the street. I don't give him the chance to say another word. I see my car, and leave him there as I hop inside and slam the door.

CHAPTER Eight

Patton

My head aches as I stand in front of my desk, sorting through the papers. We stayed out too late last night. I drank two more whiskeys after she left, and now I feel like shit.

I almost kissed her. *Dammit.*

My lips were right there, ready to push hers apart and take that mouth, pull her hard against me, ravage her tongue. I'd had enough to drink that my inhibitions were down. Who knows what else might have happened if that elevator hadn't stopped when it did?

The door to my office opens and Taron enters looking pained as usual. I'm so fucking sick of it, I'm ready to send them all on a spa vacation. This holiday weekend can't come soon enough.

My voice is annoyed when I speak to him. "Your new hire suggested some changes to our fee structure. I thought you might like to be in on the discussion."

"She's working out better than I expected." He only grins briefly before his expression is serious again.

"Why did we need a new employee again?" It's not like him to bring in someone new without talking to all of us first.

He takes a minute, walking over to the small table in front of my window facing downtown. He picks up that photograph of the four of us in our fatigues. "I've been thinking about my role here... My limitations."

"Have you thought about one of those standing desks?"

He shakes his head and returns the photograph to the table. "I know it's not the best time with all that's going on. I want you to know my plan..."

A light tap on the door makes us both look up. I'm not sure what Taron means, but I'm not about to let him step back when we're about to blow up. This launch is going to be a financial windfall for all of us. It's what I've been working to give them since we got home. It might not make up for what happened, but hell, it's something.

"Come in." My voice is stern, frustrated.

When Raquel appears, my body responds. She's wearing a short beige skirt that shows off her shapely legs and a short-sleeved black top. Her hair is over her shoulders, and her scent drifts to me as she gets closer.

She's so beautiful and so smart. It's a double sucker-punch, and our near-kiss last night is on my mind. It's a memory I do not need right now.

"Raquel, thanks for joining us." I walk around my desk, putting my usual, stern shield in place.

"You summoned me." Her voice is quiet, and she doesn't meet my eyes.

I suppress a grin. Even in deference, she still has that touch of spice. I hate how it taunts me.

"Yes, well, I was intrigued by your ideas in the Madagascar meeting. I wanted Taron to be here so we could discuss implementing them. Have a seat."

She sits in one of the leather chairs and crosses her legs. I blink away from them, and Taron speaks up. "Patton said you mentioned a ten percent finder's fee and levels of security?"

She shifts to face him. "It was all very off the cuff, actually. I based it on the real-estate model. Realtors charge at least six percent on every sale. I thought, why aren't we doing the same?"

Her eyebrows rise, and she lights up as she describes her plan. She's really interested in the business, and she's so damn quick.

I cut in. "Describe the security tiers."

She blinks and when our eyes meet, her cheeks flush a pretty shade of pink. My stomach tightens, and I study her full lips as she speaks, as she follows my orders. She seems nervous today, which bothers me. Did I cross a line last night? It didn't seem like I did. We were very close in the small elevator. She stumbled toward me, and I held her arms. For a moment, it felt like she wanted me to do more...

I didn't.

"It's good." Taron nods, slowly walking around the office.

"It is." I agree. "Where did you learn all of this?"

She shrugs. "Most office buildings have some level of security, and most police forces will send a cruiser to drive by after hours if requested. If they want a full-time guard, we could contract with retired officers or perhaps even military. And we could offer these services at a special rate—or even waive them to make a deal more attractive like we did with Madagascar."

Taron gives me a smug look, but I'm done arguing with him. Even I can't deny how intelligent she is.

"You really saved that deal. Great work." He gives her one of his signature smiles, and it unexpectedly annoys me.

"Thanks." She looks down again. "I've always been pretty good at thinking on my feet."

"I'd like to have all of this on the table for Abu Dhabi and Dubai." He turns to me. "Are we good to go with it?"

"Definitely." I gesture to Raquel. "Get with Sandra and work out the wording on separate addendums we can offer as a menu of options."

She nods and starts to go, but Taron stops her. "I'm heading out early, but you'll be at the picnic tomorrow?"

"I was planning to be there." Her voice is soft, and I don't like the way she's looking at him. I don't like this sudden interest he has in her.

"See you then. Not to talk business, of course." He's still smiling.

"Okay." She grins back at him, but her eyes flicker briefly to mine.

That current is back, and again, she blinks away. Interesting.

She's gone, and Taron is back to smug. "You don't have to say it. That girl is a kick-ass hire. Ten points to Taron."

"What is this? Hogwarts. I said she's doing a good job." I turn to my laptop and type up a brief message to Sandra. "You're leaving early?"

"I can handle my day from my phone. I'm trying to get in some PT."

That's a relief to hear. "Any word from Marley?"

"Haven't seen him." His expression is grim. "You got him home last night?"

"Yeah. I'll hang with him today. See you at the lake."

He limps out, and I rock back in my chair, thinking about lines and crossing them.

"We need more techno in this town." Marley leans back in the square leather chair. "I miss going to raves."

"Yeah, that's exactly what you need to do now." I tilt the tumbler of whiskey back and forth.

We're at a self-proclaimed "world famous lounge," and I'm tired from last night. Still, I'm not going to let him out of my sight. A tall, leggy blonde in a filmy green dress leans on the wooden table between us. "What's up with you tonight, soldier?"

My eyes squint. "You going to let her call you that?"

"Halle can call me whatever she wants." He slides both hands along her hips, and she grins at me.

"I have a friend around here somewhere."

"No, thanks." Girls like her always seem to be hanging around, looking to hook up. In places like this, they're often groupies hoping for a celebrity sighting, but a couple of well-heeled businessmen will suffice.

"I've got something for you." She stands, and he follows her to the restroom.

My jaw tightens, but I'll wait. Wherever he goes tonight I'm on duty, and I'll be sure he sleeps in his own bed. I don't care if a woman is in there with him, but he's going home tonight.

A few minutes later, they're back. Marley's sniffing, and I'm sure they both did a line in the bathroom. "The new Morgan girl is pretty." His eyes are glassy, and Halle sits on his lap.

"She's pretty smart, too." The waitress brings me a fresh drink I didn't order. One's my limit tonight, and I move it aside.

Halle's friend walks to the table, picking it up and taking a sip. "Hey, sailor."

She has bright red hair, and I don't bother correcting her. I'm distracted by memories of a smart, pretty woman I almost kissed last night. I push against these thoughts. As tempting as Raquel is to me, I have to keep it professional.

"That tube top should be illegal." Marley's voice cuts through the noise of the bar. "Sit that fire crotch down by me." The girl makes a loud noise of annoyance, but he keeps going. "Do the drapes match the carpet?"

Halle starts laughing. They're all three laughing when I notice a guy at the bar scowling at Red. Shit. He could be her boyfriend or her husband or just some drunk asshole who thinks she was with him first. I'm not interested in finding out.

Fishing out my wallet, I flag the waitress so we can go before any punches are thrown. I hate nights like this, but we're in a situation. I can't afford any more bad press because of him. I don't want to hear about it from my dad, and I don't want it getting back to clients.

I'll walk him through this valley until we're on the other side.

"Where's a good rave club around here?" Halle is still perched on his lap, but Red is leaning on the table looking at her phone. Neither strikes me as very intelligent.

Halle leans forward. "You want to move it, move it?"

She laughs loudly, and Marley's eyebrows shoot up.

He points at me. "Did you hear that? What she just said?"

Unfortunately, yes. "I hope I never hear it again."

"Ah, fuck 'em. I bet those guys liked it." He looks up at Red. "Moto-Moto."

Her nose wrinkles, and she yells back. "You like *Madagascar* or somethin'? That's my son's favorite movie."

The waitress returns my check, and I quickly sign it, standing and catching Marley's eye. "Let's go for a walk."

I expect him to fight me, but he doesn't. He simply stands, moving Halle into his empty seat and follows me to the door. It's a Friday night, so the foot-traffic is thick. Warm winds push past us, still I shove my hands in the pockets of my slacks. Marley digs in his pocket and pulls out that half-smoked blunt from before, quickly firing it up.

I'm not unhappy about this find. I hope it'll make him sleep. God knows I'm tired, but I'll keep going as long as he does. I'm not letting him slip out on me again.

He hands it over, and I take a pull.

"Remember Mexico?" His hands are free, and he's moving fast.

"I'll never forget it." I pass it back.

"Yeah, looks like I won't either." He inhales deeply, speaking in a strained voice. "They say cocaine kills your memories, but it doesn't kill mine."

Regret flashes in my stomach. When we first got back, they gave us all medals and stuck us all in therapy. I never could let myself off the hook enough to get anything out of it, but now I'm trying to remember what the therapist said.

"The only way to get peace is to find it within yourself." It sounds like bullshit to me, but I've heard it helps people.

"I'll never have peace."

I can't tell him I'll never have it either. Somebody has to be positive, and Taron isn't here, not that I'm sure he's feeling so high on life these days. Still, it's not my style to be Pollyanna.

We're in Cumberland Park, with the bridge to the right and the baseball stadium across from us. Lights flicker off the ripples on the black water, and I want to go to bed, sleep off this shit.

Marley's eyes are fixed on the dark currents, and he stands up on the bottom rung of the metal fence. "Sometimes I wish they'd finished the job."

"That's the lack of sleep talking."

The sound of live music and people on the streets echo around us, behind us. The river silently moves below, deceptively peaceful. It's all so oblivious.

"Sometimes I close my eyes, and that hood is over my head. The torture wakes me up."

I look up at him, and the street lights cast long shadows down his cheeks.

Reaching up, I grasp his forearm. "Get down. It's time to rest."

"I've been hearing noises outside my door at night. Someone's trying to break in."

I'm not sure if it's the cocaine making him paranoid or if he's having sleep-deprivation issues. "Come to my place and spend the night."

He shakes his head. "I've got to get home and make sure all my shit's okay."

I'm frustrated by this, but he's a grown-ass man. I can't force him to spend the night with me. "I'm taking you home, and you're going to stay there. Taron's picking you up in the morning for the picnic."

He nods, looking ahead of us at the pavement. I wish I could take his keys. I wish he hadn't done that line of blow. At least, I guess that's what he did. Who the hell knows?

"Are you going to be alone forever?" He looks over at me, and I pull back.

"While we're on the subject."

"You're never with anyone. I can't remember the last time you were with a woman."

He wasn't watching last night.

Images of Raquel flicker through my mind. I see her pretty smile, her bright eyes. I remember the feeling of her in my arms. I wanted to kiss her so much last night. I wonder if I'll be strong enough to resist her next time… If there's a next time.

I think of how smart she is, how strong. She's supporting herself and her sister now. I wonder if I could take care of her, make things right. I wonder if she'd let me…

Shaking these thoughts away, I focus on the road. We drive the few blocks away from downtown to the high-rise where he lives. Leaving the car at the curb, I walk him inside and make sure he gets on the elevator.

"Taron will be here at ten."

He waves at me and the doors close. I wait as the numbers rise until he's at the top. I wait a few minutes longer until I'm satisfied he's in for the night. I'm dead tired.

Driving home, I know it would be wrong to bring anyone into this life.

This fighting isn't going to stop. These nightmares don't end.

Marley's never gotten over what happened in that Mexico jungle. Taron still carries the scars. We all do.

But I won't let us go down. I won't lose my men. We have to find a way to live with the past and keep going. Knowing our reality fuels my drive and keeps me arm's length from anybody who might be hurt by us…

I have to focus on closing this deal, bringing in this windfall.

I owe it to them. I owe it to me, and we're going to get it.

CHAPTER Nine

Raquel

SANDRA UNFOLDS METAL LAWN CHAIRS AND ARRANGES THEM UNDER sprawling oak trees. "It's going to be hot as the devil's backside by noon."

I do *not* think about Patton's sexy ass when she says this.

Okay, I do, and I swallow a laugh.

"What?" She grins at me, and I shrug.

"That's hot." Saying that makes me want to laugh more, so I change the subject. "What are we going to do out here? Is there an agenda or anything?"

"Oh, it's a fun day. There's drinks... One of the guys will grill hot dogs and hamburgers. Somebody usually rents a boat for water skiing..."

"I've never skied." I make a sad face.

"You can sit on the pier and tan with me." She leans in and winks. "Also known as drinking and watching all the hot guys."

"I can do that!"

"After a few bevs, who knows what might happen."

My eyebrows rise, and I watch as she pulls out a red and white checked table cloth and spreads it over one table. I grab another and help set up under the trees. We're nearly done when Dean skips up in gingham shorts and a pink tee.

"Who wants a Spritz Veneziano!" He hauls out a pitcher of bright orange beverage with ice cubes and orange slices in it.

"What is that?" I take one of the plastic tumblers he's passing out.

"Prosecco and Campari with orange wedges."

He pours us all a healthy serving and then steps back. "Girl, you are putting out some fierce fun in the sun vibes. I absolutely love this little getup."

"Really?" I look down at the white eyelet sundress I pulled over the high-waisted white bikini I'm wearing. "I didn't want to be too revealing, it being my first work function and all."

"You look amazing, and with that hair down over one shoulder. I'm getting so many classic Hollywood vibes, I want to paint your lips velvet red and give you some cat-eye sunglasses."

"Oh! I've got that covered." I reach into my canvas bag and pull out heavy white-framed sunglasses.

Sandra and Dean both let out a squeal. "Yes!"

"Let's get out on that pier and sunbathe!" Sandra is in a yellow cover-up over a red one-piece, and I'm instantly self-conscious.

"Should I have worn a one-piece?" I follow behind her, carrying my own lounge chair. Dean is with us doing the same.

"You look amazing. Relax and have fun."

Before long, we're all camped out on the pier, covered with sunscreen and sipping our drinks through paper straws. It feels like something out of *Mad Men* when I look up and see Taron entering the picnic area under the trees with Patton right behind him.

My stomach does a little jump, when I see Patton's wearing shorts and an unbuttoned short-sleeve shirt over a white tank.

Taron is dressed similarly, but I only have eyes for the devil these days. They place a cooler under the shade, and Taron walks over to the metal grill. Sandra waves from where we are.

"Let us know if you need any help," she yells.

"We're good!" Taron yells back.

Patton's standing beside him with his hands on his hips looking in our direction. With his dark aviators on, I can't tell if he's looking at us or admiring the view of the lake, so I raise my sunglasses. Our eyes meet, and my insides feel all hot and tingly. I bite my lip, hoping he'll take that shirt off and get in the water. I don't even realize he's still looking at me as I do it, but his brow lowers and the corner of his mouth quirks up.

Fire blazes in my stomach. Is he smiling at me?

Just then Jerry comes tromping through the hedge like some kind of raging bull, and I close my eyes, lowering my sunglasses, and lying back in the chair. I turn my face toward the enormous lake and take a sip of my drink.

Jerry is the last person I want to think about today. Him and his grabby hands.

"How about some music, girls?" Dean switches on the radio, and Steve Miller Band drifts up around us.

"Perfect." Sandra smiles, nodding her head up and down. "Give us all a refill, Dee. I've got to get the recipe for this stuff. What did you call it?"

"Spritz Veneziano." He leans over and freshens all our glasses. "It's traditionally made with Aperol, which is an Italian aperitif, but it can be hard to find. Campari works just as well."

"I love it." I take another sip, stretching my arms over my head.

It really is delicious and has me just relaxed enough I don't even mind when Jerry comes straight out to where we're all relaxing on the pier.

"What's happening out here and how do I join the fun?" He

waggles his eyebrows, but I keep my gaze on the kid riding a jet ski on the wrong side of the buoys.

"I figured you'd want to drink beer." Dean squints up at him, lifting his horn-rimmed Ray-Bans.

"I have beer." He trudges back up the hill to the shade and digs a beer out of a white Styrofoam cooler.

Renée would have a cow about how Styrofoam never degrades, how it emits hydrofluorocarbons, which deplete the ozone layer... *Jeez get out of my head, Renée!*

While I'm gazing absently, Patton strolls down to where we're all lounging. "How's the water?"

"How about you get in and let us know." Sandra's teasing him, but I hope he does it. I've been dying to see him without a shirt.

"I'm helping Taron with the grill." He looks back toward the trees. "Any special requests?"

You on a cracker. I cough a little giggle out of my thought, and he looks down at me.

"Did you want something?" His voice is not angry today.

Oh, it's just too easy. "I'm sure whatever you have works for me."

Dean does a very poor job hiding his snicker, but Patton takes it in stride. I don't. I feel my face flushing hot. I might be a little buzzed, but I'm not drunk enough to flirt with him in front of everybody and not be self-conscious.

Patton's brow lowers, and he glances out toward the water "If you do get in, watch out for that kid. He's riding that wave runner in the swim zone."

"I don't think we're getting in the water." Sandra smiles up at him. "But we'll be safe."

I watch through my dark shades as my sexy boss makes his way back to the grill. His ass is so fine in those shorts. Sandra's chuckle snaps me out of it.

"What?" I look up at her, wondering what I missed.

"They could light the grill with the chemistry between you two."

My eyes go wide. "I don't know what you're talking about." I look around quickly to make sure no one is listening.

"Don't worry, everybody has their own problems. My job is to keep an eye on the office, and trust me." She leans closer. "I'm getting an eye full."

I force a laugh. "There's nothing to see. I've only been here three days, and I've been doing my best to learn and catch up—"

"You don't have to be defensive with me. Patton Fletcher is one hell of a sexy-assed man, and trust me, he's noticed you, too. I'd love to see him blow off some steam. I have a theory he needs it bad."

Warmth blooms in my stomach at her words, but I won't admit it. "I'm just trying to do a good job."

She takes a sip from her orange and white striped straw, giving me a wink. "You're doing an excellent job."

The sound of a motor growing louder draws our attention, and Jerry glides up to the pier in a speedboat. "All aboard!"

Dean is off his feet at once, skipping over to the cruiser. Once inside, he lifts what looks like a small surfboard over his head. "Wakeboarding! Let's do this!"

I look over at Sandra, who's getting out of her chair. "Are you going to try it?"

She laughs, shaking her head. "I'll ride on the boat, but I'm too old to risk breaking my neck."

"I don't want to lose my top." Pushing out of the chair, I follow her.

"That would definitely cause a commotion."

As soon as we're all onboard, Jerry steers us out into the middle of the lake. We pass the wave runner still getting too close to the shallows, and I see it's a pre-teen boy. He doesn't even slow down before taking a hard turn and shooting off towards the other side of the lake. He's going so fast, the wave runner looks like it's hovering over the ripples.

Dean prepares to get on the wakeboard, and Sandra takes the wheel while Jerry makes his way to where I'm standing in the back.

"What do you think of your first company picnic?" He smiles and reaches for my waist.

"So far so good." I smile and step to the side, avoiding his embrace.

Why does it seem the guys you don't want to touch you are always so eager to get handsy?

He runs his eyes up and down me, biting his lip. "Classic pinup."

"I don't know if I'd go that far." I look down at my full-coverage, white bikini wishing I'd brought my dress.

"Want another drink? I've got beer here in the cooler." He lifts the lid, and I see Coronas mixed with Budweiser's and Bud Lights.

"No, thanks. I'll just take a water if you've got it."

Sandra calls out from the front. "Hang on! Here we go."

I look back to see Dean in the water holding the line. The side of the board breaks the surface in front of him. I'm still looking back when Sandra floors it, and I stagger into Jerry.

"Oh, shit!" I cry as he catches me around the waist, sliding his hands up to cup my breasts. "Let me go!" I shove at his hands.

"Hey, take it easy. I'm just making sure you don't fall."

I'm pissed now. He knows exactly what he's doing. "Copping a feel is not making sure I don't fall."

He laughs, sliding his hands down to my bare midriff. "You're going to be working with Europeans. You'd better get used to being touched by men."

My forehead is hot, and I want to smack him across the face. "I think I know how to do my job."

Sandra lets off the throttle and looks over her shoulder smiling broadly. "How'd he do?"

"Did you see that?" Dean shouts from the water like a little kid.

I shove Jerry's hands off me and pick my way to Sandra. "I didn't get to see it. Can you go again?"

"See if Dean's up for it!" She has no idea what just happened between Jerry and me, and I'm not interested in returning to the stern. "He can't hear us from here."

Pressing my lips together, I stay low and make my way to the back of the boat. Of course, bending over makes the top of my breasts more visible, and Jerry's right there grinning at me like an asshole.

I ignore him, focusing on Dean. "Want to go again?"

"Yeah!" He gives me an enthusiastic thumbs-up, which I relay to Sandra.

She nods and whips her head around, hitting the gas a little slower this time. Still, the sudden movement throws me off balance, and Jerry is right there to catch me.

He only touches my arm, but I'm still pissed. "Hey, I'm just trying to help you."

"I've had enough boating for one day." I walk over to the side and jump into the water.

At once, I realize my mistake. They fly on, Dean jumping over the wake with the surfboard, leaving me in the deep waters, a good distance from the pier. It only looks closer in the boat.

Fuck, I think to myself and start swimming.

Growing up near the ocean, I swam all the time, but I'm far from the pier, and it's dangerous to be in a lake outside the swim zone. I look up and see that fucking wave runner cutting through the water between me and the pier. I also see a dark-haired figure striding across the boards, his attention fixed on me. *Patton.*

Pushing harder with my legs, I do my best to swim to safety.

The currents are against me, and I'm starting to get tired. Still, I'm making progress when I hear the high-pitched engine growing louder at my side. My eyes go wide when I realize the kids' coming straight at me, and he's not slowing down.

I gulp a large breath of air and dive down, going under just in time for him cut across above me. My heart races in my chest, and I kick, trying to stay down until I'm sure he's gone. When it seems safe, I resurface, but exhaustion is setting in. I've got to swim harder.

Looking up, Patton is on the edge of the dock, and I'm pretty sure I recognize his frown. Then I hear that motor again. Already? Looking up, I see the wave runner is coming back.

Shit. I'm not sure I can swim any faster. My heart is hammering in my chest, and I know in this dark water with my hair wet, I'm practically invisible to anyone on a watercraft.

Panic tightens my throat, then I see Patton strip off his shirt and dive into the lake.

The wave runner skims across the surface, heading in my direction like a rocket. I'm about to go down when a strong arm grips me around the waist like a band of iron. He pulls me to him with such force, and the kid veers away just in time.

"Holy shit!" I squeal.

"Hold onto me." His chin scuffs my eyebrow, and I close my eyes, doing as he says.

My hands are on his shoulders, and my heart is flying. He's a strong swimmer, even with me at his side doing my best to swim along, and he continues toward the shore until we reach a place where he can stand. The water is still a little over my head.

He stops to catch his breath, anger burning in his eyes. "Are you okay? That fucking moron. You could've been killed."

I'm directly in front of him with my hands on his shoulders. My body is pressed against his, and he's holding me securely. I'm intensely aware of his warm skin touching mine. Bare legs against bare legs, his hand on my waist.

Blinking up, I squint into his dark eyes, so full of concern. "Thank you."

His brow quirks as he studies my face. "Why did you jump out of the boat?"

I drop my chin, trying to think of an excuse. I don't want to get into what happened with Jerry, especially not while I'm clutched in his arms like this. But we're too close for me to lie. He'll see it in my eyes.

"Tell me." His voice lowers, and when I glance up, his expression has changed.

"I felt kind of seasick, I guess."

"You guess?"

We're so close. It's like that moment in the elevator, intimate. My heart is beating wildly, and I slide my hand over his bare shoulder. It's broad and strong. His touch is nothing like Jerry's. It's sparkling, delicious heat, and I want more of it.

"I feel better now."

"Good."

Water laps around us, and I'm very aware he's still holding me close. His perfect hand is on my lower back, holding me steady...

"Did you just save me?"

The slightest flinch, and I see the struggle in his eyes. The fight against what's happening between us, this impossible attraction we shouldn't have. I ought to fight it, but I seem to have lost my will to resist.

"You could've been hurt. But you're pretty good at handling yourself."

My lips press together as my eyes linger on his mouth. "I don't think I can handle you."

I should pull away, but it's impossible. I move closer, my fingers curling on his shoulders, my chin lifting, straining for him. I blink up to his dark eyes, and it's a blaze of want and need and barely hidden lust.

"Fuck it," he groans, meeting me in the middle.

His mouth covers mine, and it instantly turns desperate. My hands move to his neck, holding him closer. I kiss him fast, my lips moving in time with his, grasping and pulling.

His hands move from my back, roughly down to cup my ass. He pulls me hard to him, and my nipples tighten. I want his mouth on them. I lift my legs and wrap them around his waist, and the heat of our skin sliding together burns in my core. *God, I want him so much.*

His tongue curls with mine in a sensual dance that circulates fire through my bloodstream. I feel his hard cock against my thigh, and a moan escapes my throat. So little stands in the way of us being together. I could slide my bottoms aside and he could push right in… The thought makes my insides clench, and I lift my chin to gasp for air.

"Raquel…" His voice is strained, and his hands go to my waist then to my upper arms, moving me back.

He sounds as devastated as I feel by what just happened.

"Patton, I—"

"We have to get back to land."

I'm at a place where I can stand, and he takes my hand, leading me to the shallow water. Once we're close enough to walk onto shore, he lets me go and continues on ahead.

"I'll get you a towel."

"Thanks." My insides are trembly from the intensity of his kiss, from the overwhelming desire he provokes.

I watch him move, allowing my eyes to drink in his bare back, to trace the lines down to his tight ass. I admire the shape of his arms, muscular and tanned, the black ink extending up his right arm to his shoulder.

He grabs a towel and his shirt, and *Sweet baby Jesus.*

Just before he jerks it over his head, I see the mouthwatering lines in his stomach, his perfectly sculpted abs. I could feel the ripples of muscle under the water, but he's so beautiful in the wild.

I've been walking slowly, but now I'm standing in front of him, taking the towel he offers me.

"Can I get you anything?" His voice is controlled, as if that wildfire of a kiss never happened. As if the heat raging between us isn't strong enough to burn down the forest.

My eyes squint slightly, and I shake my head. Taking the towel, I turn, walking to the pier where I left my cover up, glancing over my shoulder once more to find him watching me walk away.

CHAPTER Ten

Patton

"Next year we're going to a ski lodge." I crack open a beer and take a long, ice-cold sip, hoping it'll put out the fire inside me.

I was fucking lucky we had a ways to go before reaching the shallower water. It gave my dick time to settle down so I didn't have to emerge from the water with an erection. *Jesus.* I might be able to hide my attraction in the office, in a suit and tie, but there's no hiding what her bare skin against mine does to me here.

Her legs around my waist, her hips rocking against my pelvis, her moans… If we'd been alone, I'd have fucked her nine ways from Sunday. *God, what am I thinking?* What is she doing to me?

"A ski lodge?" Taron is rolling hot dogs around on the hot grill, giving me the eye.

Glancing back to where Raquel is standing, I see the wave runner whip around again, too close to the pier. "Somebody needs to grab that kid by the neck."

"If it weren't for him, you wouldn't be a hero." I don't miss the sarcasm in his tone.

"Where's Marley? You were supposed to bring him with you."

"He was sleeping when I got there, so I didn't disturb him."

I don't like him being alone on a holiday weekend with us all out here at the lake. Still, it was the right call. "At least he's sleeping."

"I'll check on him again tonight. You need a little personal time." He hands me a plate with two hot dogs on it.

"What's this?" I frown, taking it.

"I haven't seen you look at a woman that way since Sofia Vergara." He grins, but it makes my stomach tight.

"Sounds like you need glasses."

"See if she wants to eat something. She nearly got her head knocked off."

His words make my blood boil. "If I see that kid's parents..." I take the plate and walk to where Raquel is sitting in her lounge chair, holding one of Dean's orange drinks.

Sandra and Dean pass me on the way down, and I catch the end of Sandra speaking quietly. "He was touching her. It's why she jumped overboard... Oh, Hi, Patton. Burgers ready?"

She's smiling, but my brow lowers as I think through what she said.

"Yeah." I nod, glancing to where Jerry's tying up the boat.

Raquel is turned away from him, and he trots past me with a brief greeting, continuing up the hill in the direction of the grill.

I stop in front of her. Her eyes are closed behind her white sunglasses. "Are you hungry?"

She looks up at me, and a beat passes before she sits forward. "Is that for me?"

"If you want one. Taron sent them down."

Her pretty lips quirk, and she stands, giving me a look as if she's onto me. "Is Taron giving you orders now?"

I guess she thinks she has some power over me now. Maybe

she does. Either way, I'm pissed. "Did something happen on the boat? Is that why you jumped in the water?"

My voice is sharp. If I find out Jerry touched her... *Fuck*. The anger in my stomach is irrational. Lines are getting blurred, and I'm not happy about it.

"I was feeling seasick. I told you." But she doesn't meet my eyes when she says it. Her cheeks flush, and she focuses on the hotdog she's lifting off the plate.

"But you're hungry now?"

She shrugs. "Jumping in the water cured it."

My eyes narrow. I'm not believing any of it, but I can't force her to tell me the truth. She takes a bite of hot dog and turns away from me as she chews. I take the other one and finish it in three bites.

A wooden bench is on the end of the pier, and I walk over to sit down. Marley said it first, now Taron. I've been so focused on the expansion, the launch, and keeping our shit together, I've lost track of how long it's been since I even thought about a woman. Then this one walked into my office and flipped everything on its head.

She's back in that lounger, stretched out in the sun like a cat. The brim of her large straw hat covers her face, but I see her glossy, pink lips. Her arms are slim and tanned, stretched out on the chair, and her small breasts point up to the sky in her bikini top. Her hair is drying in messy waves.

Only a few inches of her stomach are exposed, but her legs are on full display, shapely and long. I remember them wrapped around my waist in the water, and my mind fills with thoughts of touching her, tracing my lips along her inner thigh, tasting her, circling my tongue around her clit as she moans my name...

"Are you uncomfortable there?" She's staring at me, and I blink away those thoughts. "I'm sure Sandra wouldn't mind if you used her chair."

"I'm okay." I should probably leave.

She pushes the front of her hat up so I can see her eyes. "Are you going to swim?"

"No." I start to stand, but she keeps talking.

"Don't you like to swim?"

"No."

"Then why are we here?"

"They like it." I gesture toward Taron and the other three standing around the grill, talking and joking. "I'd rather be snow skiing."

She laughs, and my eyes cut back to her. "Do you always do things to please others?"

"No. Hardly ever."

"I don't believe you. I think every decision you make is out of concern for them."

I study her face, and her cheeks flush under my scrutiny. She lowers the brim of her hat again and leans back.

"Why did you take the job at my firm?"

Her chin pulls back, and she pushes the hat up again, studying my face. "What do you mean? It was a good offer."

"You could have gone corporate."

"Do you wish I had?"

Do I? "You'd have more options, deal with fewer… idiots." My glance moves to where Jerry is standing beside Sandra, watching us.

She exhales a little hum. "I wanted to stay closer to home for now. And I bet there are idiots everywhere."

When my gaze returns to her, those clear blue eyes study me. It makes me slightly uncomfortable. I want to know what she's thinking, if there's any other reason she's here.

"What happened out there was…" What am I trying to say? What do I want to say? "It's not a good idea."

"That's too bad." Her eyes narrow, and the corner of her mouth rises. "I kind of liked kissing my boss."

"Maybe I should fire you."

"You'd better have a damned good reason." Her brow quirks in a challenge, and I think about the problems it would solve.

Standing, I fold the paper plate. "Don't give me one."

CHAPTER
Eleven

Raquel

THE GARAGE DOORS ARE OPEN AT SOUTH STREET, AND I'M AT A small table with Sandra drinking beer and enjoying the sudden drop in temperature after last night's rain.

"Now will you tell me what happened yesterday?" She's eyeing me over the rim of her pint of beer. "Why the sudden jump in the lake?"

Her husband's still out of town, so she invited me to lunch. "I told you. I was feeling sick."

I'm not sure why I'm protecting Jerry. It's a clear case of sexual harassment, but I don't feel the need to be the office whistle blower on my third day at work. He's not my superior, and I think I can handle him.

She shakes her head, cutting a bite of crab cake with her fork. "You had everybody talking."

"For jumping in the lake?" I take a sip of my beer. "You guys need to get out more."

"For what happened *after* you jumped in." She gives me the eyebrow waggle, and now I'm uncomfortable. *Did she see me kiss*

Patton? I thought we were somewhat discreet, being in the deep water and all. All they did yesterday was stand around and gossip about everybody.

"Why didn't anyone bring a plus one? Is that not allowed?"

"Oh, it's allowed." She shrugs. "Taron's not seeing anybody. My husband's doing shift work. Dean's dating around—"

"And Jerry?" I want to ask about Patton, but I know she's just waiting for that.

"I think he was hoping to make some progress with you yesterday."

My face heats, and I shift in my chair. "He needs to take a hint and keep moving."

"So something did happen between you two?" Her eyes narrow, but I shake my head.

"I just want him to leave me alone."

She considers this a moment. "Let me know if he doesn't."

Leaning back, I exhale deeply. "I can handle Jerry Buckingham. He's not the first guy who wouldn't take a hint."

"Girl, I hear that. The shit we put up with." She lifts her glass and gives me a wink. "Here's to you getting Patton Fletcher to take his shirt off. That was pure heaven."

I take another sip, raising my eyebrows. "It was purely unintentional."

"You're a rockstar damsel in distress, and I thank you."

Shaking my head, I remember sitting alone in my apartment last night binge-watching all the episodes of *Queer Eye* then switching over to *Ally McBeal*. I didn't feel much like a rockstar. I felt like I should have gone to Savannah this weekend.

I glance up at her, wondering if she might know anything about why my sister quit so suddenly four years ago. I don't get a chance to ask before she jumps in her seat and leans toward me.

"Well, look who's here. Seems someone can't stay away."

"Who?" Dread fills my stomach, and I'm afraid Jerry's behind me. Instead, excitement replaces dread when my eyes land on Patton sitting alone at the bar.

"What is he doing…" My voice trails off, and she gives me a nudge.

"Walk over and say Hi. See what he says."

"If I didn't know any better, I'd think you were trying to set us up."

"Girl, it's the first time I've seen him show this much interest in anybody." She gives my arm a gentle nudge. "It can only be a good thing for all of us."

"He's my boss, Sandra. I think he wants to keep things professional." Although that's not what his dick was telling me yesterday in the water.

"You're not afraid, are you?" Her eyebrow arches.

Clearing my throat, I shift in my seat. "Of course not. That's the most ridiculous thing I've ever heard. Why in the world would I be afraid? He simply looks like he needs some alone-time is all…" *Stop talking now.*

I press my lips together.

"Um-hm." She gives me another nudge. "Go say Hi. It's a holiday weekend."

"What difference does that make?"

"Nobody wants alone-time on a holiday."

I'm not sure that's true. Still, I've had just enough beer to do this, even though it's silly. I'm on my feet about to head over when she stops me.

"Take your beer." She puts the pint glass in my hand and my purse on my shoulder. "Just in case."

I give her a little eye roll before casually walking over to where he's sitting. A half-dozen grilled oysters are in front of him along with a pint of beer. This is crazy. What am I doing? I'm turning around to head back, when his voice stops me.

"Following me around now?"

Wrinkling my nose, I turn back and smile, doing my best to joke. "I was just going to say the same thing to you."

His dark eyes slide down and up my body, taking in my short-sleeved navy sweater and denim skirt. "My condo is over on seventeenth, so this is my neighborhood. You're pretty far from home."

"How do you know where I live?" I pretend to be surprised, when I'm really thrilled.

"It's on your résumé."

"Oh, right." So much for that.

"Have a seat."

An open stool is beside him, and I do as he says. Leaning forward, I point toward my old table. "Sandra invited me to lunch."

He turns, and we both see her standing, giving us a little wave as she takes her purse and heads for the door.

"Where is she going?" My lips part, and I turn to him.

"Sandra doesn't live too far, either. We see each other here sometimes."

It was *a setup*. "She suggested I come over and say hello."

"I'm not working you people hard enough," he mutters, lifting an oyster and quickly slurping it out of the shell. My nose wrinkles as he drops the empty shell. "Did you have lunch?"

"No."

"Have one of these." He slides the platter of oysters toward me, but I shake my head.

"Not a fan."

"Your loss." He lifts one and repeats the process. "They're the best."

"I was hoping for hot chicken."

Nodding, he slides off the stool and fishes in his wallet, taking cash and leaving it on the bar. "I know the best place for hot chicken. Let's go."

"Right now?" Glancing back, I take one last sip of my beer and follow him out past the wooden tables filled with reclining patrons to the sidewalk. I get hung up by a waitress carrying a huge platter of food, and when I get outside, he's waiting, lighting up a cigarette.

My nose wrinkles again as he exhales a stream of blue smoke, squinting one eye. "You're something else, you know it? Have you always been a ball buster?"

"I'm not… It's just… It's such a terrible habit."

We're walking up South Street toward sixteenth, and I try to think of something non-ball busting to say. "Are you still considering firing me?"

He takes another pull and grins. "Nah, I think we'll keep you on for now."

"Where is this chicken place? Prince's is in SoBro."

"Prince's is closed on Sundays. We're going to my place."

I stop walking, and he takes a few steps before turning to look back at me. "What?"

"Your place?"

"I played pickup with Donald Prince. I know the recipe."

My arms cross, and I start walking slowly to where he's waiting. "I don't believe you."

"You think I'm luring you back to my place on the promise of hot chicken?"

"I'm not sure what to think."

"Are you afraid to go to my place?"

"A little." That Sandra is one sneaky bitch. "I thought you said this was not a good idea."

His hands are in his pockets. "Hot chicken's always a good idea."

"Is it?" A teasing glint is in his eye, and I feel so curious. "Okay, then. Patton Fletcher cooking me hot chicken? How can I say no?"

"That's more like it." He takes my hand, putting it in his arm. "You don't have to fight all the time."

"You're one to talk."

CHAPTER Twelve

Patton

M Y INSIDES ARE TENSE WALKING WITH HER HAND IN MY ARM like this. It feels dangerous. It feels like we're crossing a line we might not be able to uncross.

I don't really care.

It feels good.

It feels like for the first time in a long time, I can relax.

It feels like a holiday weekend.

We're at my building, and I hold the door as she enters, her warm, sweet scent meeting my nose. Her hair hangs long down her back, and her ass is really cute in that skirt.

As we ride the elevator, I watch her lacing and unlacing her fingers. I think about those fingers on my shoulders yesterday, holding onto me as we swam, pulling me closer when we kissed. My eyes flicker to her glossy lips, and I want to kiss her again.

Her blue eyes blink up, and she seems nervous. "I didn't mean to make you cook for me."

"You didn't fight me too hard." Her jaw drops, and I almost laugh. "It's okay. I enjoy cooking."

"You are a very unexpected man, you know that?"

"Good."

The elevator dings and we cross the foyer to the penthouse. I open the door, and she inhales sharply. "It's gorgeous."

I have an amazing view of the city and the surrounding mountains. She kicks off her sandals and walks across the dark wood floors past the flat screen television and black leather sofa to the balcony.

For a moment, I stand watching her. Her toenails are painted blue, and I like her bare feet on my wood floors. Her skirt shows off her legs, which are quickly becoming one of my favorite features. I want to walk over to her and wrap her in my arms.

Last night, when I got home after our incident in the lake, I sat for a long time looking out at the lights of the city. I thought about Marley's question about me being alone. I thought about Taron's observation. I remembered our kiss and how it affected me. I should be staying away, but I can't seem to do it.

Why did I invite her to come here? What makes her special?

I like the way she looks at me, the way she challenges me and teases me. She's playful and fun. She's sunlight and fresh air. She makes me feel like for the first time in a long time I can let go and simply be. Maybe it's all an illusion, but when I look at her, it feels real.

I don't want her to be afraid of me.

I don't want to hurt her.

Even if I'm afraid it's inevitable.

"Would you like a drink?"

She looks over her shoulder. "Got any whiskey?"

"I do." I walk to the kitchen and pull down a bottle of Jameson, pouring us each a shot in tumblers. "Rocks?"

She walks to where I'm standing and takes the glass, giving me a little clink before throwing it back. My eyebrows rise as I watch her. *Unexpected.*

"Okay." I lift mine and do the same. It burns slightly going down, but it's good stuff. "More?"

"Maybe in a minute. Got any water?"

Digging in the fridge, I pull out two bottles of water, buttermilk, eggs, a package of skinless chicken, and hot sauce. "Come over here and help me."

She takes the bottle of water and twists it open then walks to the other side of the white bar. I place an air fryer in the center of the island and plug it in.

"Healthy."

"Not all my habits are bad."

I can't tell if she's playing with me, but I'm enjoying this, from her tough-girl whiskey shot to her funny attempts at bossing me around. Reaching into the cabinet, I take out flour, black pepper, brown sugar, and the remaining dry ingredients then turn my back to combine them all in a bowl.

"You really do have everything."

"I told you, it's easy to make."

"Why is your back turned?" She skips around beside me, trying to look over my shoulder. "Is it a secret recipe?"

"Back off." I put up an elbow, but she's on her tiptoes, holding my arm.

"I want to see!"

It makes me laugh, and I move around to block her from the final steps. "The Prince family would not appreciate me giving out their recipe to just anyone."

"Rude!" She huffs, stepping back and crossing her arms.

I glance over my shoulder and grin. It makes her blink quickly as her cheeks flush. She's so damned cute. Turning to the counter, I set the dry mixture beside the package of chicken. "Hand me one of those."

She picks it up, and I begin the process of dipping it in the liquid mixture then rolling it in the dry. From there they go into the fryer.

"You really expect me to believe you played pickup with Donald Prince? You?"

"What's that supposed to mean? You think I can't play basketball?"

"I just can't imagine it. You strolled down from your penthouse here all the way to SoBro to play basketball in the park with a bunch of poor kids?"

"I feel like you're insulting me, but I'm not sure." I repeat the process with the remaining pieces of chicken.

"I'm just speaking as a former poor kid. Your kind never played with us."

"My kind?" All the chicken is in, and I hit the button to fry them. Then I switch on the faucet and wash my hands. "That feels very prejudiced against rich kids."

"Puh-lease." She rolls her eyes, and I catch her by the waist, pulling her to me.

She doesn't fight or pull away, and I decide to be honest with her. "I was a pretty lonely kid. I was an only child, my dad worked all the time, and my mom died when I was ten."

Her brow furrows, and she does a little frown. "I'm sorry." Her voice is softer.

I give her waist a little pull. "It's okay. I'd go to the Y and hang out with the kids there. I met a lot of people. Learned things."

"Like how to play basketball and make hot chicken?"

"Yep. And it's where I met Taron and Marley."

"You've known each other all your lives?"

"Pretty much."

Her lips curl into a smile, and the fist in my chest unclenches. Her blue eyes are so pretty. I reach up and cup her cheek with my hand. "What did you do as a kid? Play at the Y?"

"We played at the beach. I didn't even know it was special. It was free, so it's what we did." A dreamy look is in her eyes as she remembers.

For some reason, our voices have grown soft, our bodies relaxed together. I'm still holding her waist, and her hands are on my chest. I lower my face so that my nose is at her temple and inhale gently.

"You smell so good." That heat begins to rise between us.

"My sister made it for me. She makes organic perfumes and things. This one's a body lotion, actually, but I love it. It's coconut and ginger and other stuff. Did I mention she keeps like ten cats and she still lives by the water?" My brow furrows as I try to keep up with her words. Our eyes meet and she blinks, flushing a pretty shade of pink and shaking her head. "I'm sorry. I talk too much when I'm nervous."

"Do I make you nervous?"

"A little bit."

Her confession makes me smile; it makes me think of doing dirty things with her. I move my hands along her waist, finding the skin beneath her sweater. She inhales sharply when I touch her, and I pause.

"I have a confession." My voice is low.

"What?"

"I'd like to kiss you again."

"You would?" She leans closer, her hands moving higher to my shoulders. "You don't think that's a bad idea?"

My face is lower, closer to her lips. "What do you think?"

"I think we work together." Her eyes are fixed on my mouth, her lips seeming fuller as she speaks. "I think it's risky. It could change how we think of each other."

"How do you think of me?" My lips are at her ear, and I press them to the side of her neck. I feel the little pulse beneath her skin beating like a rabbit.

"I haven't decided." She lifts her chin, and I kiss her cheek, making my way closer to her mouth. "I was told you're the devil."

Blue eyes meet mine, and the chemistry between us is alive. "Do you believe that?"

"No." She shakes her head. "When we met, you reminded me more of a tiger, watching for the chance to pounce."

"A tiger?"

She nods, and I can't hold back anymore. Leaning down, I touch her lips with mine. It's a caress, soft and sweet. She tastes delicious, like good whiskey and fresh water.

Our kiss quickly becomes more intense, mouths open, and she makes a little noise when my tongue touches hers. It's gasoline on the fire in my stomach. My hands are under her ass, and I lift her onto the bar. Her legs go around my waist, and she leans closer, devouring my mouth as her fingers thread into the sides of my hair.

"Patton," she gasps. "I don't know…"

I'm about to release her, but her legs tighten around me, pulling our bodies flush. I'm sure she can feel my erection on her thigh. She whimpers, sealing her mouth over mine again. We kiss; I trace my fingers under her sweater, finding the line of her bra. I want to remove it. I want to cover her small breasts with my mouth and kiss, suck, pull…

But I don't want her to be sorry. I don't want her to say later it was all too fast.

Lifting my chin, I find her blue eyes. They're hazy with lust, and I almost can't say the words. "Tell me to stop if you want me to stop."

She blinks slowly. "I don't want you to stop…"

It's all I need to know. Stepping back, I undo the buttons on my shirt, one by one. She sits on the bar with her sexy legs spread, and her lip goes between her teeth as her eyes follow my progress. It's the hottest thing I've ever seen.

When it's open, she reaches for me. I step to her, and she traces her fingers along the lines of the ink on my right shoulder. "What is it?"

I slide my hand from her wrist, to her elbow. Her skin is so soft. "It's several things. A map, an eagle, a band of iron, *semper fi*..."

She looks up at me. "What does it mean?"

"Different things. Our missions, honor, brotherhood, always faithful."

The bell on the fryer dings and we both look at it like it's the end of a round of boxing. The mood shifts, and I walk over to pull out the basket and plate the sizzling food.

Stepping to the side, I grab the hot sauce and a big Ziploc bag. "We'll need to shake it in the hot sauce when it cools."

She grins. "I'm really impressed you used an air fryer."

"Have you ever fried chicken?"

"No." She makes a cute little disappointed face, and I step between her legs again. "It's a big mess. This way it's fast and easy."

"Aren't you the commercial."

Reaching up, I catch her chin and pull her face closer. "Don't be cute." I give her a brief kiss on the lips. "When you live alone, you learn things."

"Your place is so clean. It doesn't look like anybody lives here."

"I have a maid service."

"Lucky."

My hands are on her thighs again, and I'm not interested in chicken. I have a one-track mind and the hard-on in my pants is pointing right at her.

Her hands are on my shoulders, and I feel her fingers touching the ends of my hair at my neck. "Why are you alone?"

Sliding my hands higher, they're at the edge of her skirt. "Work keeps me busy. Keeping up with the guys."

"You must get lonely."

"I live alone, but I'm not lonely. If I want someone, I have them."

"Someone like me?"

My face is in her hair again, and I pull the top of her ear between my lips. She does a little shiver. I kiss along the line of her brow. "What's wrong with you?"

"Nothing you can't fix."

Leaning back, I find her eyes. "What?"

Her nose scrunches briefly. "It's a line from a movie. I know. It's so dumb. You just made me think of it when you said that. It's Bogie and Bacall, and it's really romantic. He says—"

I stop her talking with a kiss, softly at first, pulling her lips with mine, tasting her whiskey mouth. "Stop being nervous."

Her hands touch my face, and she exhales a light laugh. "I can't help it. I've never been with the devil."

I kiss her again, tongues touching, heat centering below my belt.

I want to taste her. I want to be inside her.

My mouth moves to her jaw. "The devil's just like any other man."

"No..." Another kiss. "He's absolutely not."

That does it. My hands go under her ass, and I lift her off the bar. Her legs are around my waist, and I walk the short distance across the living room to my bedroom. Her face is against my neck, and I feel her tongue touch my skin. It's a charge of electricity that shoots straight to my cock.

Lowering her to the bed, I slide my open shirt down my arms. She's lying on her back with those long legs bent and her hair spread all around her.

Be sure... "I want to sleep with you."

Her brow quirks, and a naughty smile curls her lips. "Can we do more than sleep?"

"You said I'm the devil, right?"

"So I've heard."

I catch her bare ankle, pulling her closer. "Then definitely."

CHAPTER
Thirteen

Raquel

THEY SAY THE DEVIL WAS HEAVEN'S MOST BEAUTIFUL ANGEL. Patton Fletcher standing over me, looking down like he wants to devour me, is better than that.

He's the tiger, and I couldn't run away if I wanted to.

I don't.

His shirt's gone, and my eyes trace the strong lines of his broad shoulders to his firm chest to the ridges of his abs. The sleeve of ink following the lines of muscle in his arm is wickedly sexy—it makes my insides clench. I'm so eager, I'm sure I'll burst into orgasm the moment he touches me.

Intense, dark eyes move from my breasts to my legs, and his voice is rich and low. "You have great legs." Instinctively, my knees rub together, and he holds out his hand.

I take it, and he pulls me up, catching the hem of my sweater and lifting it over my head. My black lace bra only covers the bottom of my breasts, and he traces his fingers along the tops of them, causing me to shiver.

His eyes darken, and he dips them inside, rolling my hard nipples between his fingertips. "You have perfect breasts."

My lips part, and the heat surging in my veins has me under his spell. "Thank you."

"Lie back."

I do as he says, and he drops between my knees, sliding his hands up my outer thighs and shoving my denim skirt up to my waist.

"I've wanted to taste you since you wore that skirt on Friday."

Oh, shit. My eyes flutter closed and a moan slips from my throat as he kisses the inside of my knee, tracing his lips higher, along the sensitive skin of my inner thigh.

"Patton..." I hiss as his beard scratches my legs.

He kisses a line, drawing closer to my center, and indescribable pleasure floods my lower belly. With the hook of a thumb, he jerks my thong aside. Cool air touches me just before his mouth covers me.

"Oh, God!" My back arches off the bed at the warm pass of his tongue over my clit.

He circles again, and my hips rock in time with the movement of his mouth over my most sensitive parts. Another pass, and my hands grasp his hair. I thread my fingers as he goes faster, circling, winding me higher.

I'm on the edge, just about to explode into a million shooting stars when he moves his lips to the crease of my thigh, kissing and looking up at me.

"Oh... oh, no..." I gasp, looking down at him.

He smiles wickedly. "You're delicious."

"Please..." I can barely say the words, barely think past the orgasm simmering in my core. "I just need a little more."

His tongue moves over his bottom lip, and he watches me like he's waiting to see if I'll beg for it. I just might.

"What do you need?" A cocky tone is in his voice, and I decide he really is the devil.

"Patton..." My whisper cracks.

I'm about to say *please* when he lowers his face and kisses the crease of my thigh again. I make a desperate noise, and I feel him grin, kissing to my center, covering me with his mouth again and stroking my clit with his tongue.

"Yes," I cry as he continues flicking and sucking.

It's incredible tightness, then... "Oh, God!" The orgasm rockets through my body like fireworks. My heels dig into the mattress, and I lift off, shuddering and pulling his hair, doing my best not to squeeze him between my thighs.

"Oh, fuck," I gasp, pushing against him. It feels so good... too good.

He rises over me, wiping his chin and smiling wickedly.

"I want to be inside you now." The words shoot another thrill through my sparkling core.

I watch with hooded eyes as he unfastens his pants, shoving them down and allowing his massive cock to spring free. I'd felt it in the water, I'd dreamed of it at night, and now it's even better than I imagined.

He reaches over and pulls a condom out of the nightstand drawer, quickly opening it and rolling it on as he watches me.

"You want this?" It's a hungry growl, and my knees rub together again.

I pull my lip between my teeth nodding. "Yes."

My body aches for him, and lust, fresh orgasm, and the remnants of whiskey blend in my veins for a pleasant burn.

"Open your legs." He kneels on the mattress above me, and I do as he says.

Reaching down, he slides the tip up and down before sinking to the hilt in me. He's balls-deep, and we both moan loudly. My eyes are squeezed shut, and we hold, savoring the feeling of fullness, of complete connection.

"Look at me." His voice is soft, and I blink my eyes open.

The intensity is almost more than I can bear. I want to look away, but he won't let me. He's on his forearms above me, and I'm pinned by his large frame, his hands on my shoulders, his cock deep inside me.

"Your eyes..." He leans forward and kisses my jaw, rocking his hips and giving me a gentle thrust. "They were the first thing that captured me."

He gives me another thrust, and ripples of pleasure twist in my stomach. His mouth moves to mine, and our tongues entwine. His hips pick up speed, moving faster, rougher, and I exhale a moan. He kisses me again before dropping his head to my shoulder as he seems to lose control.

His body is hot against mine. Large hands grip my shoulders, and he pulls me down as he pushes up between my thighs.

"So good." His voice is hoarse in my ears.

My knees rise, and the friction of his movements, the force of his thrusting, the sound of his groans all push me to the brink of orgasm once more. I move my hips in time with him, savoring his scent of soap and citrus and sweat.

I press my mouth to his shoulder, tasting the salt there with my tongue. Another low groan, another hard thrust, and he holds, pulsing and filling the condom. I wrap my arms around his shoulders, and for a minute, I close my eyes and memorize this moment, this gorgeous, sexy man all around me, holding me, inside me. It's hypnotic.

Lifting his head, he kisses my cheek once more before looking down at me. "Still hungry?"

A laugh bubbles up inside me, and I shake my head. "You did lure me here with the promise of hot chicken."

"You're the hot chicken."

That makes me laugh harder, which pushes him out.

"Shit." He reaches between us quickly grabbing the condom and disposing of it.

He's out of the bed, and he walks back to where I'm propped

on my elbows admiring the view. His muscles flex as he walks, and that tight ass is so fine. Even at half-mast, his dick is pretty impressive.

"Is it time for the hot sauce?" A smile curls my lips, and he reaches for me, pulling me into his arms and wrapping them tight around me.

I kind of melt a little bit. Okay, a lot.

"Stay the night. I'll take you home tomorrow."

My silly heart rises in my chest, and I feel breathless. *He wants me to stay...*

"Is that a good idea?" I hate even thinking about it, but it feels so dangerous allowing myself to care for him. As if I have much choice about it.

He relaxes his grip, letting me move back. "Maybe not. But maybe…" He leaves the sentence hanging as he goes in the enormous bathroom.

I pull my sweater over my head then bend down and scoop up my thong and my skirt. *Spend the night...* My stomach is so tight, and I suddenly feel like I need to go home. This is crazy. And dangerous.

"Maybe I should head on home."

"What?" He reappears in only boxer briefs, and my resolve tries to fade.

"Yeah, I mean. It's probably for the best." His eyes roam up and down my body. I'm only in my sweater, but I'm holding my skirt over my bottom half.

"If you don't mind, I just need to use the bathroom."

That signature frown returns, and I'm not sure if I'm happy or heartbroken to see it. I scoot past him into his bathroom and close the door, quickly turning the lock. I'm breathing so fast, and I feel like a coward for wanting to cry.

Making a stern face in the mirror, I scold myself in my head. *Get a grip, Rocky.* Yes, it was fantastic sex, possibly the best I'll ever have. But Patton Fletcher is my *boss*. I'm trying to build a successful career, not sleep my way to the top.

Oh, God! I cringe at the thought of this getting out.

Reaching quickly for the toilet paper, I clean up and put my bottoms back in place. I glance again at my reflection to make sure my clothes and hair are straight. My makeup is smudged, and my lipstick is gone. No getting around that.

I'm just at the door, when I pause and see a bottle of cologne sitting on the counter. Picking it up, I give it a sniff. Fresh citrus. It smells just like him. I spray it all over my shirt before heading out the door.

The bedroom is empty, but I hear noises in the kitchen. Looking all around, I spot my purse on a chair and grab my phone out, quickly punching up the Lyft app and scheduling a ride home. The good thing about being downtown is cars are swarming all around my location like ants. I feel the buzz and look down to see "Javier" will be here in a black Cadillac in two minutes.

Patton is at the bar, loading the chicken into a bag with hot sauce. An unlit cigarette is in his fingers.

"Well, thanks again." My voice is high, chipper. "I'm going to head on down. My ride is almost here."

Dark eyes meet mine, only this time they're surprised. "You're leaving now?"

"I ordered a Lyft." I hold up my phone and do a little wave. "I guess I'll see you in the office on Tuesday."

"Raquel, wait." He stops what he's doing and starts to circle the bar, but I'm backing toward the door, praying I don't trip over anything. "You didn't eat."

"No, really, it's better this way. No hard feelings. Scratching an itch or whatnot."

The door hits my back, and I stop, feeling around behind me for the handle. He stops walking toward me, and now he's really frowning. I think he's mad.

"Scratching an itch." He repeats the words after me, albeit slower.

My fingers curl around the handle. "Have a nice night."

I'm out the door, closing it behind me and pressing the elevator button repeatedly praying he doesn't follow me out.

Sweet Jesus, help me. I'll never be able to say no if he comes out and tells me to stay. My eyes are squeezed shut, and my stomach is tight and cringing until the bell finally dings. The doors slide open, and I jump inside, hitting the lobby button and the doors closed button repeatedly.

My breath catches when I see his door start to open, but thank God, the elevator closes before he even makes it out. I slump against the wall clutching my hand over my face.

"Do you know what time it is?" My sister's voice is sleepy when she answers, and I quickly look at the clock.

"It's nine. Are you already in bed at nine?"

"First, it's ten here. Second, it's a holiday weekend, so it's busy as fuck. We open early and work straight through."

I wince realizing she's right. Labor Day at the beach is bananas. "I'm sorry. I just needed to talk to someone who loved me."

She lets out a loud groan, and I hear her flopping around in the bed. "What is it?"

Oh God, can I even say it out loud? To Renée, who cautioned me repeatedly about him?

"Rocky." Her voice is impatient. "I'm tired. Either tell me what's going on or let me go back to sleep."

"I slept with Patton." The words blurt out fast. "Oh, God. I think I'm going to be sick."

"I'm sorry. I think I'm still asleep. It sounded like you said you slept with Patton."

"I know. I know! I know I know I know. You told me not to

fall for him, and I totally fell for him. Oh, God, Renée. What am I going to do?"

She's unexpectedly calm. "What happened?"

I quickly recount the day at the lake, the way he rescued me from the wave runner, then Sandra setting me up at South Street today. "You told me to make friends with Sandra."

"I also told you Patton Fletcher is the devil. Why did you go back to his apartment?"

"He was going to make me hot chicken."

"Oh, Jesus take the wheel." She sounds just like me... only much more sarcastic. "You have got to be kidding me."

Dropping onto the couch, I clutch my forehead. "I know. I'm going to have to change jobs."

Seconds tick by, and it's quiet on the other end of the line. "Did he tell you that?"

"No." I sit up slowly. "He actually asked me to spend the night."

More silence on the other end of the line. I wait as long as I can. "Renée?"

"You know, chicken is one of the worst mass-farmed animals. You really shouldn't eat it."

Blinking, I shake my head. "What?"

"You think I'm fanatical about this, but it's bad karma. You should know how your food lived and how it died before you eat it."

"Renée! I'm not going to stop eating chicken. Tell me what you think I should do."

"I think you should be vegan like me."

I almost scream. Instead I take a deep breath and calm my voice. "About Patton."

"Oh, I already told you."

"Tell me again."

"I told you this job could open doors for you. I told you not to get involved with your boss. I told you not to fuck it up." I can't tell, but I think she's pissed at me, too.

Can anybody give me a break and see it from my side?

My heart feels like it's melting in my chest. I've got the most enormous crush on him. I don't know if I can make these feelings just stop on a dime. Renée at least has seen him, worked with him…

"Why did you quit?"

"Because I hated him."

"Oh." My voice is quiet. I didn't know she hated him.

"Well, I've got to go!" She exhales loudly. "Got to get my eight hours. It's not a holiday for me."

"Okay, well, thanks. I love you."

"Protect your chin."

We disconnect, and I drop down on my couch, pulling my shirt over my nose. Inhaling deeply, with my eyes closed, it's like he's here. I wrap my arms around myself wishing…

I'm so confused and reeling and I still feel like I want to cry, which is silly. I wanted to spend the night with him so bad. I just knew if I did, it would change our dynamics too dramatically. It would change everything.

It would give him all the power.

I exhale a wry laugh at myself. Like he doesn't already have it.

My hand is on my phone when it vibrates. Turning it over, I see a text on the face from a number I don't recognize.

I'm sorry. Tonight was unprofessional and completely my fault. It won't happen again.

As I read the words, I realize it's him. Now my eyes really are wet. I blink, and a tear drops onto my cheek. My inhale is shaky as I lift my phone and quickly save his number as *Sexy Devil*.

I start a reply and delete it. Then I start another and delete it.

I want to tell him it wasn't his fault. I was just as much into what happened between us as he was. Possibly more. Sleeping with him was amazing, incredible. That orgasm was one for the record books. I wish I could do it again and again.

Instead I simply reply, *NP. It shouldn't affect our work relationship.*

Seconds tick past, turning into minutes.

No response.

I fall onto my side and let the tears fall.

CHAPTER Fourteen

Patton

ALL THE LIGHTS ARE OFF WHEN I ARRIVE AT MARLEY'S APARTMENT. "Hello?" I tap on the wall as I walk through the foyer into the living room.

Light streaks across the floor from beneath the drapes covering the balcony, and I go to them, pulling them apart. The space fills with light, and I see full ash trays, empty beer bottles, and twisted off plastic baggies.

"Marley?" My voice is louder, and I move a little quicker, pushing open the bedroom door.

It's musty, and I go to him, giving his shoulder a shake.

"Hey, wake up." My voice is sharp, but his body is warm. *Fuck*. I was worried for a minute. "Hey." I give him another shake. "Are you sleeping?"

He makes a groan and rolls onto his side. "What?"

"It's noon. Get up."

He pushes into a sitting position with another groan. "What the fuck, man?"

"I brought hot chicken. Come eat."

I didn't feel like eating it after Raquel left last night. I didn't know I could feel satisfied and pissed at the same time.

Marley shuffles into the kitchen, where I'm arranging chicken on a plate with a banana. I don't know what he's been snorting or smoking, but I'm sure he could use some potassium.

"Looks good, Julia Child. Did you make it?"

"Yeah." I shove the plate toward him then grab a beer out of his fridge. "Eat it all."

He sits in front of the plate and looks at it a few minutes. Then he puts his elbow on the bar, reaching for the pack of cigarettes.

"What made you decide to cook?"

"Gotta eat."

He takes a long drag and blows smoke over his head. I walk to the balcony and pull the doors open, letting in some fresh air.

"Remember when we'd play basketball at the Y?" He hasn't made a move to eat.

"Yeah."

"It's how we met."

Everything is memories with him these days. It's making me restless. "What did you do on Saturday?"

He shrugs. "Slept. Hung around here."

"Did Taron come by?" I walk slowly to the coffee table and see what looks like heroin in a tight little baggie.

"Yeah, but he didn't stay. Says I'm a bad influence." He takes another drag and laughs. "He's gotten soft."

"He had a hard time getting off the pain meds." I've never used this shit, so I don't know how it feels, but I imagine he took one look and left while he had the chance. "We missed you at the lake."

He bends a knee and rubs his eyes. "Yeah, I don't feel like being in the sun."

Getting off the stool, he goes to the couch and wraps a

blanket around his shoulders. He looks skinny to me. His dark hair is a greasy mess on his head, and he needs a shave.

"We missed you." If missing is the same as concern.

"I didn't want to see anybody." His eyes are on the coffee table, and I want to slip that little baggie in my pocket and flush it.

"Thanks."

"Except that new Morgan girl. She's pretty."

The mention of Raquel makes me pissed again. "She's alright."

"She reminds me of her sister."

"Yeah." I reach for a cigarette now, firing it up and taking a long pull. "I think they have a lot in common." I say it through an exhale of smoke.

"How would you know?" He cuts his eyes at me. "You never liked Renée."

I'm done talking about it. Clearing my throat, I stand. "I'm heading out. Eat something. I want you at work tomorrow." I lean down and pick up the suspicious baggie. "None of this."

He studies it a minute. "I'm not planning to do anything with that."

"Then why do you have it?"

Tired hazel eyes cut up to me, and he shrugs. "Never know."

"Not tonight. You're coming in tomorrow to get with Taron on social media."

I want to take it. I should fucking take it, but I'm not sure where he got it or if he'll just go out and get more. I don't want him going anywhere besides bed.

"It's not that hard. Anybody could do it if I'm not there."

"You're the only one who knows the accounts and passwords. Eat, shower, and be in the office tomorrow."

"Sir, yes sir." He looks up at me, his tone sarcastic.

Still, I feel a fraction better about leaving him. "I'll see you in the morning."

Only Sandra and Dean are at their desks this early on the day after a holiday.

Sandra cuts her eyes at me as I pass her. "How was the rest of your weekend?"

I don't like her tone. I don't like the way her lips curl into a smile like she thinks she's got something on me.

"I want to know when Marley arrives, and tell Taron we need to talk when he gets here."

"Is something wrong?"

There'd better not be. "Just business."

"Okay." Her brow furrows, and I'm slightly relieved.

She doesn't seem to have talked with Raquel, and I'm glad the inner-office gossip mill isn't running. That's the last thing I need right now.

I've just finished sorting through a million emails from yesterday when I hear the tap on my door. "Come in."

It opens, and I spin in my chair expecting to see Taron. When I see who it is, my stomach tightens. I lean back, narrowing my eyes.

"Do you need something, Miss Morgan?" It's not quite a snap, but close.

"I'm sorry to disturb you…" Raquel's voice is soft and high compared to mine. "I wanted to stop by before anybody got here. Except Dean, of course. And Sandra—oh, and I didn't want you to think I'd said anything to Sandra because I didn't…"

She stops speaking and presses her lips together.

She's rambling.

I study her a moment, quietly. She's wearing a low-necked pink sweater and a matching cardigan with a fatigue-green skirt I'm sure shows off her legs.

My gaze remains above her waist, on her pale blue eyes, which are round and worried. "What is it with you and cardigans?"

It's a low grumble, but her pale blue eyes widen. Her chin drops, and she fumble with her clothes... like she did in the elevator. Heat tries to rise below my belt, but I fight it.

"Well, anyway, I... uh, just wanted to see if you needed anything. For Madagascar... or anything."

"You're working with Taron on Abu Dhabi. See him when he gets here." I return to my computer screen, done talking.

She doesn't leave, and I start to get irritated.

Her throat clears. "About Sunday night—" My eyes cut up to her, and she stops abruptly.

"We've said all we need to about that." My tone is final.

She blinks down and nods. "Okay. Sorry." I watch as she pushes a lock of soft brown hair behind her ear then turns and goes to the door. It closes behind her with a quiet click, but the scent of coconut and ginger lingers in my office.

I'm about to go for coffee when Sandra buzzes me. "Taron just got here."

It's not what I asked her to do, and I feel my anger rising. "And Marley?"

"Not yet. Sorry, boss."

If one more person says sorry to me.

Continuing to my door, I snatch it open and stride down the corridor to Taron's office. On the way, I notice Raquel in her glass box sorting through files. Jerry is standing near her grinning like a Cheshire cat, and she seems uncomfortable.

Rumors from Saturday flicker through my mind, and my fists clench.

Knocking as I open Taron's door, I hesitate when I see him with one hand pressed against the wall. "You okay?"

"Don't bother knocking. Just come on in." It's pure sarcasm. No joke.

"How close do you think we are on this Hastings and Key deal?"

He glances up at me, and his green eyes are pained. "If Abu Dhabi comes in, Remi said they'll do it."

"How close are you on that?"

"Should have it in the bag today. We're doing a little meet and greet this evening."

"Will you be able to make it?"

"Raquel's helping me."

My teeth press together, and I look out the door toward her office. Jerry's still there, and she still looks uncomfortable. This is not why I wanted to see Taron, but I'm changing my agenda.

"We're sending Buckingham to LA. Effective now."

"Wait. We're sending Jerry… Why?"

I turn back to him, and Taron's face is scrunched with pain? Confusion? I don't give a fuck.

"I want him there by tomorrow ready to work. It's only 5 a.m. in LA now, right?"

"I think it's six."

"I'll get Sandra to book him a flight. We'll put him up at the Wilshire until he finds his own place. Tell him to clean out his desk."

Taron stops me before I walk out. "Any reason we're sending him to LA so abruptly?"

"We need someone there to scout new properties and see the locations in person." I say it like it should be obvious. "I don't want to waste any time. Pictures only give us so much information."

"Okay." Taron exhales, lowering himself into his chair. "You got a time frame on this assignment?"

"He'll stay as long as we need him there."

Taron's lips pucker and he nods, his eyes going to the desk in front of him.

"What?"

He holds both hands up, and I start for the door, moderating my tone. "I'm going for coffee you want some?"

"No, thanks."

"Watch out for Marley. We need to talk when he gets in."

"You got it."

Instead of coffee, I take a brisk walk around the building and smoke. I feel like a shark that stopped moving—my insides are tight. I'm more relaxed when I get back to my office, ready to run the numbers and see where we stand, when again, my office door opens without warning.

This time, I stand when I see who it is, and my fists automatically clench.

"What the fuck, Patton? LA? Today? I can't just haul off and leave on a moment's notice." Jerry's voice is loud. I'm a little surprised he actually has the balls to challenge me this way.

"Then you can find another job." My voice is calm, my gaze level.

He steps back, doing a mock laugh and throwing out his hands. "Oh, it's like that now. Go to LA or you're fired? What is this? The motherfucking Apprentice?"

"It's my tech-based commercial property rental firm, and I need someone in the new markets finding prestige rentals and verifying they're as good as we say they are. I'm sending you to LA on the company's dime to fill an important role, and you're standing in my office saying you won't do your job."

His flat brown eyes narrow at me, and he tugs on his tie, doing a goose-neck in the process. "I'm not looking to fight with you, Fletcher, but I'm pretty established in Nashville. I've worked here five years."

I sit slowly in my chair, crossing my leather loafer over my knee. "It's a temporary assignment. You could always come back."

The sound of footsteps outside my door draws our attention, and Raquel passes, her long brown hair swaying down her back, ending just above her perky little ass, and I catch a glimpse of those sexy legs.

Jerry's eyes shoot to me, and I blink away the momentary lapse into lust, focusing instead on my computer screen.

He puts his hands on my desk, leaning closer. "You're a real hypocrite, you know that?"

My eyes cut up to him, and my jaw tightens. Now he's looking to get punched. "You'd better make the right decision and get out of my office. Now."

He pushes his hands off the wood and backs to the door. "Sure, I'll take your assignment. I'll go to motherfuckin LA. But don't think for one minute I don't know the real reason you're sending me there."

I don't even rise from my seat. He's out the door, and I lean back in my chair, pressing my fingers together in front of my lips, thinking.

CHAPTER
Fifteen

Raquel

SANDRA HAS HAD HER EYE ON ME SINCE I WALKED IN THIS MORNING. I went to Target yesterday and did some clothes shopping with my credit card, and maybe now I'm the devil. I bought a few skirts. I keep remembering Patton's eyes so dark and full of lust saying he loved my legs. A little shiver moves through me.

"What happened after I left you?" Her voice is quiet, and I'm pretty sure I see annoyance in her expression.

How much to tell her? "Not much. We chatted…"

"And?"

"We went to get hot chicken." That's true enough.

"And?"

"And what?" I look down at the few remaining folders on my table from Taron's banker's boxes. "I went home later and watched *Ally McBeal*. She really does get more annoying as the series progresses."

It's a total *yadda-yadda-yadda*-leaving-out-all-the-good-parts dodge. I don't dare look up at her or she'll see how much I'm omitting.

"I practically shoved you two together." Her voice is exasperated, and she exhales a huge sigh, letting her arms drop. "You can lead a horse to water…"

She's out my door, headed back for her desk, and my shoulders drop. Patton said our work relationship wouldn't change, but I didn't expect him to be exactly like he was before. Hell, he might be even more antagonistic.

When I left him Sunday night, I was so freaked out. All I could see was my future slipping away on one insanely hot, sex-filled weekend. I couldn't let that happen. I had to protect myself.

I've always been a fighter, and I'm a pretty strong person. He just might be a little stronger than I am…

Seeing him in his office this morning, so sexy in that gray suit… His full lips, his glossy, dark hair. My fingers curled at the memory of touching him. Him touching me. Even with his dark eyes narrowed and that frown firmly in place, he's irresistible.

All those emotions flooded my veins, and I couldn't remember why I went in there. I couldn't remember why I left Sunday night.

I said I could resist him.

I was totally wrong.

"Hey, you ready to talk about Abu Dhabi?" Taron jumps me out of my reflections.

"Oh, hey. Sure!"

"Let's chat in the conference room."

I'm out of my chair, shaking off my lustful thoughts and following him down the corridor, when I hear a noise behind me. It sounds like slamming. Looking around, I see Jerry with boxes, packing up his office. I'm not sure whether to do a little dance or be concerned.

Taron continues into the conference room like nothing is going on, and I look back as I close the door behind me.

"What happened with Jerry?" I look up at him, but his eyes are fixed on a spread of papers on the table.

"Oh, he's going to LA."

"He doesn't seem very happy about it."

"What?" Taron looks up at me. "I don't know why. I've heard LA is a fun town, and we're paying for the whole thing."

I'm so confused. "Did he know he was going?"

Is that why he was hitting on me? Was he trying his luck because he knew he was leaving? Not that it makes it any better...

"Patton decided we needed someone out there this morning. He's the logical choice."

My eyes narrow, and I look at the wall that separates this room from the devil's office. *Patton decided this morning to send Jerry to LA?*

"How long will he be there?"

Taron looks at me curiously. "You sure seem very interested. Are you and Jerry—"

"No!" I say it too loud and too fast. "Not at all. I'm just surprised is all. I mean, the two of you hired me, so I thought it was because you'd be around for a while. I have no interest in Jerry. None whatsoever."

Stop talking, Rocky.

Clearing my throat, I press my lips together and smile, blinking innocently.

He shakes his head and laughs, turning back to the sheets on the table. "Okay, here's what we've got..."

We work through lunch preparing for the meeting this afternoon. I hop online and order platters of stuffed vine leaves or dolmas, lamb Kibbeh or meatballs, pita and hummus, dates, and coffee. It's all coming from the Lebanese restaurant, and I'm hoping for the best, being in Nashville.

Taron said our goal is to make them feel welcome, like we're accommodating and elegant so they'll want to commit. I don't remind him my major was international studies.

Looking down, I decide my outfit is fine. Patton insulted my cardigan again, which is ridiculous. I just bought this silly thing. It's very stylish and modest. For a moment, I wonder if that's why he hates it.

We're all set when I look up and see Marley strolling in the office, and my breath catches. Oh, shit. We can't afford a repeat of Madagascar. I have no idea what I can make up at this point to cover him.

Our eyes meet through the glass walls of the conference room, and he gives me a little wave. I'm struck by how resigned his expression seems. I don't know this man, but he seems so haunted.

Less than a minute passes, and he returns, this time with Taron behind him. The door opens, and Patton enters as well. I swallow my sudden attack of nerves and manage a smile.

Taron is the first to speak. "Raquel, you've met Martin Randall."

"Hello." I wouldn't say we've met, but I don't bother getting into that. I will not ramble.

Patton's take-charge voice is next. "Marley's handling our social media accounts and marketing."

"Okay." My voice is quiet, waiting.

"I thought it would be a good idea if you all know how to do this in case I'm not around for some reason." Marley pulls a chair out from the conference table and wakes the giant monitor with the iPad Pro.

He's actually very good at what he does. Two minutes into his talk, I grab a sheet of paper off the back table and hastily start making notes. He walks us through every account, shows us how to update our info, upload photos, set up ads, create audiences, target audiences, then measure the results and make changes. He shows us how to add our contact information to posts and how to check and respond to messages.

"That's pretty much it. If you got that, the rest is a piece of cake." He turns to face us, and his eyes land on me and linger.

Patton inhales and starts for the door. "I hope you two got all that."

I look at Taron, who gives me a tight smile. "People think his job's so easy."

"I didn't."

"Send us a copy of that." He motions to my sheet of chicken scratch and I nod. "I'll type it up."

"I have a doc I'll send you all." Marley leans back in his chair as Taron follows Patton out the door.

"Thanks for the crash course." I smile, not sure what to say to this guy. He's a total mystery.

"You're Renée's sister?"

"Um… yeah." My insides tighten, and I study his face, remembering how Renée asked about him.

His eyes cut away, and he taps on the keyboard, shutting down all the apps. "Do you talk to her much?"

"Almost every day, why?"

He gives me what can only be described as a sad smile. "If she ever asks, tell her I said hi."

Swallowing the knot in my throat, I want to ask him how he knows her. I want to ask him if he knows why she left. I feel like one of those archaeologists who's just uncovered the fingernail of an ancient dinosaur skeleton.

"Were you friends?"

His jaw moves, and I watch as this handsome, deeply troubled man searches for an answer. "I think so." He clears his throat. "I'm sorry… she left. I hope she's doing well."

"She's just down in Savannah. I think she's really happy there."

He nods and heads for the door, leaving me with a million questions.

CHAPTER
Sixteen

Patton

THREE HOURS OF SCHMOOZING, ANSWERING QUESTIONS, SHAKING hands, and Abu Dhabi is in the bag. I'm feeling pretty good right now—ready to go back to Stephen Hastings and slide his UAE requirement under his cynical nose. It would only be sweeter if we didn't need him.

"Did you get anything to eat?" Taron has the contracts in hand, and Raquel is boxing up the few items of food left.

He ate most of the appetizers with our guests, who arrived in an entourage of three CEOs and several bodyguards. Raquel and I were the only ones not eating. I was biding my time, waiting to see if this deal was going to happen. Raquel was running around making sure no one's cups or plates were empty.

"I'll get something at home." She looks tired, and I have a thought as Taron passes me the contracts to put in the safe.

"You never got that hot chicken you wanted." I guess my satisfaction is clear in my voice. She looks up at me as if I startled her. It's also the first time I've spoken to her since this morning, when I might have been a bit irritable. "Prince's is open until ten if you want to go."

She doesn't answer right away, closing the box of grape leaves slowly. "I don't really like grape leaves. Too vinegary."

"Great work, guys." Taron slaps me a high five on the way to the door. "I'm heading home. I'll touch base with Remi first thing tomorrow. We're in."

I can't hold back a smile. Our high five turns into a hand clasp, and I give his shoulder a squeeze to boot. "Good work on this one."

He heads out, and I look over at Raquel, who's lingering over the leftovers. After the way she ran out on me, I'm not planning to ask her twice, but I'm feeling good enough to give her one more chance. "My car's out front if you want to go."

"Okay." She blinks up at me as if suddenly deciding. Still, I can't read her. If she started rambling, maybe I'd know, but she seems to have locked that down.

She puts the few leftovers in the breakroom fridge and collects her things while I secure the contracts in the safe in my office. Then we head down, quiet in the elevator. I remember our first kiss and my eyes go to her glossy lips. I don't move, and her eyes stay fixed on the doors.

It takes less than five minutes for us to be in my car, headed southwest to SoBro. Raquel sits quietly beside me with her hands in her lap. Her skirt is just above her knees, and my eyes drift to them under the passing streetlights.

"I had no idea Jerry was going to LA today." She blurts out the words, breaking the silence. Her tone almost seems challenging.

It's not a question, so I don't respond, downshifting to third. We're almost there, and I'm looking for a place to park my BMW in the light.

"I feel like he would've told me if he knew." She's still taunting me with this Jerry thing.

I find a spot and guide us into it. "I didn't know you had that kind of relationship with him."

"We didn't have any kind of relationship." Her voice goes high like she's offended. I can work with this. "I just thought something like that would've been a big deal. Moving across the country—"

"I can't believe you hooked up with a guy named Jerry."

"I never hooked up with him!"

I hold back a grin. She's so easy to get riled up. I kill the car and hop out, going around to help with her door. She stands in front of me, narrowing her eyes. "You hired a guy named Jerry."

"It was a mistake."

We walk slowly toward the food truck. At this time of night on a weekday, it's pretty slow. We wait behind one person before placing our orders, then step to the side under a young tree with a black grate around the roots.

My hand's in my pocket, and I watch the woman in the window preparing our food. Raquel puts her hand on the small tree and kicks her brown heel along the side of the grate.

"Do you know any of the people here?" She tilts her head and looks up at me.

"No."

"I just thought since you were such good friends with the family." She's teasing, but my frown is firmly in place.

"That was a long time ago."

"You could've brought me some of your chicken."

"I gave it to Marley."

"Oh." She lifts her chin and looks away, toward the bridge. "He's really good when it comes to social media marketing. After that... *incident*, I didn't know what to think of him."

"He does a good job." *When he's sober.* I don't want to think about that right now.

The woman in the truck waves to me, and I step forward, taking our bags and leading Raquel to a nearby picnic table under a lamp. I open them and hand over her chicken breast sandwich with fries and the same for me.

Both pieces are red from the spices, and we dig in pretty quickly. It's a quarter to ten, and I haven't eaten since lunch. I'm hungrier than I realized. I've taken three bites and my lips are on fire. Across the table, Raquel has torn a few strips from the breast of her sandwich and is neatly putting them in her mouth and wiping her fingers.

I stop and sit back, watching her.

Her eyes meet mine. "What?"

"Are you eating it or dissecting it?"

"I'm not devouring it like it's my first meal in a week if that's what you mean." Her feisty tone is back. I missed it. "Oh, look. You can smile," she adds, and I realize my face has relaxed into a grin.

"It's the chicken."

"Oh, sure." She tears off another small strip and carefully puts it in her mouth then wipes her fingers on the napkin. "And you expect me to believe you can make it this good?"

"Maybe not this good." I take another bite, wiping my face with the napkin, and she huffs a laugh.

Our eyes meet, and hers are so beautiful when they sparkle— when she's happy. The streetlight shining down on us makes her hair gleam gold. It shows the freckles on her cheeks. Everything about her is still so appealing to me.

I remember touching her nose with mine, touching her lips, burying my face in her soft hair. These thoughts must be tamped down. She doesn't want that, and I'm her boss.

I put the sandwich down on the paper plate in front of me, wiping my hands. "Why did you study languages?"

She shrugs. "They came easy to me. I learned French then Spanish then Italian. It was like a game. They just... clicked in my brain."

"You're very smart."

"I like to read." She blinks up at me again and smiles.

My hand automatically goes to my pocket for a cigarette, but I stop, shifting in my seat instead. She doesn't seem to notice.

"And you didn't want to go to New York or Chicago?"

"I might've gone to Chicago." She leans back, taking a sip of iced sweet tea. "Not New York."

"I thought all the career girls wanted to be Carrie Bradshaw."

She rips off another strip of chicken and shakes her head. "I don't want to cut my couch in half to get it in my apartment."

"Is it a nice couch?"

"Not particularly. But it's mine."

"Fair enough."

She wipes her fingers and seems to be done. "After my parents passed, I wanted to be close enough to drive to Savannah."

"You could've gone to Atlanta."

Her nose wrinkles. "Have you been to Atlanta lately? It's a mess. The traffic is a nightmare, the people are rude…"

The food truck closes its window with a loud, metallic roar, causing us both to turn and look. I check my watch. "It's ten."

"Oh." Her hand is on her chest. "I guess it's time to head back. My car's still at the office."

She could come back to my place…

We stand and toss our trash before walking to the curb. In the car, she's quiet again. The stereo system plays country music softly, and the streetlights glide in white stripes across her legs and hands. I want to reach over and touch her, but I don't.

My jaw tightens, and I'm frustrated I got so close to her. I'm frustrated she pulled away. I should have been the one to see it was a mistake. Too many people telling me what I should be doing, how I shouldn't be alone. I need to keep my own counsel on these things, especially in view of the past.

"Didn't Taron leave?" Her voice pulls me out of my reverie, and I blink up ahead, seeing his dark gray Tahoe.

"Yes." I parallel park behind it in front of our building then get out and walk around, helping her out and walking with her into the lobby.

Taron is there, pacing, his eyes panicked. "I tried calling you."

Lifting my phone I see four missed calls. "I left it in the car while we ate. I didn't check it—"

"We need to go." He glances at Raquel briefly then pulls me closer. "It's Marley. I got a call…"

My stomach plunges, and I'm moving with him before he even finishes speaking.

"Is everything okay?" Raquel calls from where I left her standing by the elevator.

I pause, remembering how I'd intended to walk her to her car. "Can you get home okay?"

She gives me a small smile. "I've done it every day since I started."

Nodding, I hold up a hand. "See you tomorrow." Then I follow Taron out the door.

We're in his truck, and he does a wide U-turn across four empty lanes of traffic. I'm holding onto the dash, gripping it hard. "What happened?"

"Police called." His voice cracks, and I feel my insides slipping. "And?"

He clears his throat, focusing on the road ahead. "They got a call through general dispatch. A male reported an apparent drug overdose at Marley's address. He gave them my number to call."

"General dispatch?"

"It's like he wanted it to take as long as possible for help to arrive."

"No." It's a sharp groan from the pit of my stomach. My stomach that is turning in on itself, pulling my insides with it. "Is he—"

"They told me to come now." His face is tight. His voice is tight.

The air is tight, and we stop talking. The wheels hum on the pavement on this short drive that feels like an eternity. He parks illegally in front of the apartment building I've left Marley at so many times. Two cruisers are parked along with us, and we both jump out, slamming the doors and jogging into the lobby. Taron punches the elevator button repeatedly until it finally opens.

My heart is beating painfully hard against my sternum. We're rising higher, but it feels too slow. Everything feels too slow. Finally we're at the top floor, and we dash toward the open door where a detective stops us in the entrance.

"Hold it. You can't come in here." He's a shorter man than me, and his hands are in the center of both our chests. He's wearing a white shirt and blue tie and a gun and badges are on his belt.

My insides are coming apart. All I can see is that fucking plastic baggie I should have taken out of here. I should've flushed it. What was it? Heroin? Fentanyl?

"Detective...?" Taron asks.

"Sanchez."

"Detective Sanchez, this is our friend... He's more than a friend. He's a brother. We were in the military together."

Sanchez nods. "Are you Taron or Patton?"

"Taron Rhodes."

"Mr. Rhodes, I'm sorry. Your friend consumed a fatal dose of narcotics..."

A roaring noise fills my ears, and I walk away from the words of Detective Sanchez telling us our friend is gone. My insides are tearing apart. *Until...*

"He's alive?" Taron's voice breaks through.

EMS streams off the elevator guiding a gurney. They push past us into the apartment, where the cops are already wrapping yellow tape over the doors. I guess it's a crime scene now.

"We're taking him to the ER. They'll check him for any physical effects, brain damage, stroke."

They wheel him out, holding us back. A clear plastic mask is on his face, and his skin is gray. He looks dead already. I reach out to touch him, but they don't even stop.

How could he do this? Again? A flash of rage hits me deep in my stomach, turning into burning pain in my chest. I should have done something, a fucking intervention. Anything.

"Can we see him?" Taron asks.

"I'm going to recommend a 72-hour hold. Once he's stabilized, he'll meet with a psychiatrist, who can determine whether an involuntary committal is in order."

Taron looks at me, his face stricken.

"Do we have a say in any of this?" My voice sounds rough.

"Not really." Sanchez looks like he wants me to try and give him a hard time.

He looks like he's bored and disgusted with this whole scene. He thinks we're a band of playboys whose partying has gotten out of hand.

He couldn't be more wrong if he tried.

I reach for Taron's shoulder. "Don't let this get in the media."

He nods, and I head for the door.

I need to get out of here so I can breathe.

I've never lost a man. I've never left any of us behind.

Everything has changed, and we're facing a monster I can't control. This isn't an enemy I can track down in the jungle and blast to kingdom come. Riding the elevator down, my hands are in my hair, my fingers curling into fists.

The fighting never stops for us.

We never escape what happened in that hut.

But I have to keep going. I can't stop until there's nothing left to win.

CHAPTER
Seventeen

Raquel

Only Sandra and Dean are in the office when I arrive. Taron's office is dark, and it looks like Patton isn't here either.

"What happened?" My voice is quiet as I stop at Sandra's desk, not that anyone is around to hear me.

Sandra shrugs. "Marley falls off the wagon. They go running."

"Oh." I nod. Somehow I think it's more than that.

"If you ask me," she leans closer, "he could use a little tough love."

"Maybe." I never know how to respond to that. Tough love has never been a part of my emotional makeup.

Marley is a troubled guy, but he seems nice. I know he's smart and a hard worker. If I were his lifelong friend, I'm pretty sure I'd be there if he needed help, too.

I went running after Renée. I still check on her almost every day.

Still, the way they left last night felt too abrupt. Patton and I had been inching our way back from Sunday, then it all went off the rails when Taron appeared. They were clearly alarmed, and I'm sure it was more than just falling off the wagon.

In my office, I pace around, trying to decide what to do. Yesterday was a huge success landing the two Abu Dhabi clients. When he left, Taron said he'd contact Remi first thing today.

Chewing my lip, I sit in front of my laptop and review the files, reading all of Taron's notes and hoping I'm not overstepping my bounds. Patton's the boss, but they're always saying we're all partners here. *Take the initiative…*

With a deep breath and a little prayer, I type up a letter to Hastings and Key informing them we've landed the Abu Dhabi accounts and Dubai is in the works this week. I play it off that Taron is so busy working our UAE angle, he asked me to let them know. I close by saying we hope to hear from them soon and look forward to doing business with them.

It's perhaps a little too pat and way more ingratiating than Patton would be, but I'm the new kid. I have a feeling it'll be exactly what they need to hear. I hit send and CC Patton and Taron.

That done, I click over and sort through the database of commercial listings Taron showed me. I spend a few hours saving properties that look like what we want to offer—high end, luxury, security guards, and imposing entrances. Our clients are powerful companies, and they like their offices to exude a feeling of power.

I spend another hour reading the trades, looking at Dubai companies expanding or doing business in the U.S. I mark a few that might be in need of temporary office space. It's after lunch when I finally hit the wall.

I'm out of my seat, walking around the office. I was supposed to be working with Taron all week on this, but with him not here and no information on how to proceed, I'm stuck. I've worked both sides of the coin, clients and properties. I don't know what else to do.

"I'm going out for a late lunch." I stop at Sandra's desk and look over my shoulder to be sure Patton's lights are still off. "Call me if the guys come in."

"Oh, Patton said they might not be in today. He said things are a bit dicey."

"That's it?"

"They don't tell me much about these things."

Hesitating, I look back the way I came. "Did they give you any messages for me?"

"Sorry, hon."

"Well... just let me know."

It's a gorgeous fall day, blue skies, no clouds, light breeze. Since it's early afternoon, the lunch crowd is gone, and I decide to stroll down 12th Avenue toward Sevier Park. I'm not really shopping for anything, but it's fun to look in the windows of the boutique stores as my mind wanders.

Last night when I got home, I kept thinking about dinner, our conversation, Jerry. Is it possible Patton sent Jerry to LA because of me? Why would he do that?

He asked me about the incident on the boat, but I didn't tell him anything. Yesterday morning, Jerry was in my office wanting to know what I did for the holiday weekend, which of course, I didn't say. Only Renée knows what happened Sunday night—besides Patton and me.

It's possible Patton noticed how close he kept getting to my backside. I almost couldn't get any work done for keeping my rear end covered. I can't say I'm not glad Jerry's gone.

Inhaling the cool air, I realize I've walked all the way to the "I Believe in Nashville" mural. Patton wanted to know why I stayed in Nashville. I suppose I could have gone to Chicago. I like Chicago better than New York or LA or Atlanta... But being close to Renée was so important to me, and my advisers said this firm would be a great place to get started.

As long as I don't fall in love with my boss.

Seriously, Rocky?

Okay, I'm not in love with him, but I can't deny Sunday was pretty monumental. I've never felt that way... I want to feel that way. He treated me like I want to be treated, and I really wish I could follow up on what happened, what could still happen. I feel it every time we're together.

Exhaling a deep sigh, I stop at a food truck and get a small order of fried okra. My mamma used to make fried okra every Sunday. It was her favorite dish, but fried was the only way I'd eat it. Okra is a hairy, slimy green vegetable shaped like a small penis. But you chop it into cubes and deep-fry it, and you've got a delicious snack.

Taking out my phone, I check for any word from Sandra. I don't see any. I stroll through the park, under the huge oak trees, past the concrete walls covered in fuzzy green lichens. Fresh, earthy dampness is in the air. It's not like the beach, but it's still comforting in the middle of this city.

The sun is starting to set when I return to the office. I need to get my things and head home. Worry has my stomach so tight, I didn't even finish my snack. I really do care about Patton more than I should. But how do I make these feelings stop?

That's something they don't teach you in business school.

Sandra and Dean are gone when I arrive back at the office. I punch in the security code and go inside, thinking I'll gather my things and head back out. Taron's office is still dark, but I see the light shining from under Patton's door.

I hesitate outside it, leaning so close my cheek almost touches the wood to see if he's in there.

I don't hear anything.

Glancing toward my office, I see my light is off, and it appears I've gone for the day as well. I rub my hand over my tight stomach wondering if I should knock or go away. Something in me pushes me forward. Stretching out my hand, I tap softly.

The door opens on its own—I didn't even notice it wasn't closed all the way. Only his desk lamp is on, and across the room I see him. His back is to me, and his hands are spread, palms flat against the back table. His head is hanging forward.

My heart aches at the sight of him. I can't see his face. I can't hear anything, but it's a totally defeated stance. I've never seen Patton Fletcher this way, like he's at the mercy of some invisible force.

He doesn't move, and I know he doesn't know I'm here. I don't want to startle him, but I can't stay away. My feet move of their own accord, and I close the space between us. When I'm close enough, I reach out my hand and gently place it on his back.

His long, lean body stiffens, and he lifts his head. "What is it?"

"It's just me." My voice is quiet. "Are you okay?"

"I'm fine." He clears the thickness from his voice, but when our eyes meet, I see he's far from fine. His dark eyes look so tired.

"Did you sleep at all last night?"

His smile is grim, and he glances down at the papers in his hands. It looks like a letter, and I see a business envelope on the table in front of him with his name handwritten on it. He folds them and puts them in the envelope.

"You must think our office is poorly run."

"Not at all. I'm impressed by how much you're able to do with such a small staff."

"My dad liked to keep it small. He liked to run things tight, like a military team. Strategic. I thought I could do better than him because I actually was on a strategic military team."

His eyes move past me, out the window, and I study the strong lines of his face, his square jaw and perfect nose. He's not smiling, but he's not frowning. I want to wrap my arms around him, but I'm afraid that would be going too far.

Instead, I place a gentle hand on his shoulder. "Are you close with your dad?"

Dark eyes flicker to mine. "Not really. He expected me to run the business just like he did."

"How was that?"

"Focus on Nashville. Keep it small, a boutique service. Keep the money coming in." His voice turns dry at the end.

"Seems like you've done the last part."

"I've spread us thin with this expansion. It should pay off in a big way... If this doesn't break us." He reaches up to scrub his face, and I feel such sadness rolling off him.

"Is there anything I can do?"

"No." He turns to the wall, opening a portrait that hides a safe.

I step away while he enters the code, walking to the window and looking out. "Can you tell me what happened with Marley?"

The noise of clicking and papers shuffling meets my ears. I look up to see him pushing that envelope inside and closing the metal door. He spins the lock and closes the portrait over it.

"I've spent all night and all day keeping it out of the papers." His tone is bitter. "The last thing we need is this getting out now. We haven't even contacted Hastings and Key."

"Actually, we did. I sent them an email this morning and copied you and Taron on it. I haven't checked for a reply, but—"

"What did you say?" He goes to his desk and slides his fingers across the keypad.

My stomach is tight, and I wish I'd checked my emails before telling him what I did. As it stands...

He's silent, eyes focused on the screen, brow lowered. I feel like I'm dying when his expression doesn't change. Finally, he cuts his eyes up at me. "They're onboard."

I exhale loudly. *Oh, thank God.* "So that's one good thing?"

The muscle in his jaw moves, and I'm afraid he's pissed. "He intentionally overdosed. He wanted to die because he couldn't stop the memories." His voice grows rough again. "Now they're placing him in a 72-hour lockdown. We can't see him or talk to him. It'll be like he's right back there…"

His voice trails off, and his gaze going to some distant memory, far away. I go to him, putting my hand on his arm. "You need rest. Let me take you home."

"I can't."

"You can't do anything else. If they've put him in lockdown, all you can do is wait."

He hesitates. I think he's going to tell me no, but when our eyes meet, he takes my hand.

CHAPTER Eighteen

Patton

Raquel moves around my apartment like she lives here. She goes into the kitchen and pulls down two tumblers, pouring us each a shot of scotch. Thunder rumbles outside the window, and the rain starts.

"Rain feels good during tough times." She holds her glass, looking out the closed balcony doors. "Makes me feel like I'm not alone in my suffering."

She's wearing slim blue pants and a striped blue button-up shirt. It's the first time I've really looked at her since she found me in my office losing my shit. As always, she's stunning with that long, dark hair and blue eyes.

Last night was long and hard. Taron and I went to the ER and waited… and waited. Taron stayed as long as he could, but by 2 a.m., his back was giving him too much grief. I sent him home and stayed until the doctors came out and told me Marley didn't seem to have any long-term damage. In view of the circumstances, his past honors and his treatment history—and with a lot of urging on my part—they agreed not to press charges.

It's fucked up to get arrested after attempting to kill yourself, but I get it. He broke the law. He's not supposed to have fucking heroin. I'm not sure whether to be glad or concerned over what he did. I'm glad because the Narcan was able to bring him back.

The problem is I know how Taron struggled to get off that shit, and he wanted to get off it bad. Marley has no such desire.

Raquel returns to where I'm sitting at the bar watching her, and I realize what she just said. "When were you suffering?"

I don't know if she's exaggerating, referencing a broken heart or a missed date, or if she's really had to face hardship in her life. I know she told me she was one of the poor kids growing up, but the way she talks about being at the beach and her sister makes me think they were close…

Another reason I should send her home tonight.

"Oh, you know." She says it through an exhale, taking another, longer sip of scotch. "After my parents were killed things were hard for a long time… I think it's why Renée had her breakdown."

My eyes squeeze shut. "Your parents were killed?"

"In a car accident. It was a long time ago now, but I don't think you ever get over that kind of loss. So sudden…"

"I'm sorry." It's the best I can do at this point.

She blinks up to me, her blue eyes so concerned. Her hair is over one shoulder, rippling in waves over her breast. I can't think of anything I'd rather do than bury my face in it and forget all this shit.

"I guess I should go."

"Yeah." I can't stop her.

Only she moves the wrong way.

She closes the space between us and hugs me, wrapping her slim arms around my waist and resting her cheek against my chest. She feels so warm and caring, it's like a sharp knife to my insides. This simple act of comfort cracks the wall I've erected around my feelings. I lift my arms, wrapping them around her and exhale deeply. *Fuck, she feels so good.*

Holding her unclenches the fist of frustration at leaving my friend in the hands of strangers. The soft scent of her hair cools my rage at him for putting us in this situation. I've done everything in my power to protect him from outsiders, others, himself. Failure is not a concept I have a lot of experience with.

Now this beautiful woman is holding me, caring for me, and I don't understand it. I don't want to let her go.

She lifts her head, and her eyes are heated, vulnerable. "I wish I could stay. You were right when you said it's not a good idea."

"I could still fire you."

"You don't have a reason."

"Tennessee is an at-will state."

A hint of a smile curls her lips, and she reaches up to slide a finger along the side of my hair. "Then I guess it's your call."

Releasing her, I step back, turning to the bar. I think she knows how valuable she is. "Thank you for this, for coming here. I'll be in the office in the morning."

"Tomorrow's Thursday." Her voice is thoughtful. "You should take a long weekend."

"I'd rather be working. Dubai needs to keep moving forward…"

"We're in the perfect position to hit pause. We just landed our backer, we closed three deals… Tell Dubai you had a family emergency. It's not a lie."

She moves closer, beside me at the bar, and I look at her small hand beside mine. It's so slim and delicate, yet she's such a fighter. "My parents have a lodge in Pigeon Forge I haven't been to in years. We used to go there when I was a kid. It's in the woods. There's a waterfall leading down to a small creek."

"It sounds lovely. You should go there."

Looking up, our eyes meet. "Go with me. I'll close the office. Sandra can set up outgoing messages."

Her cheeks flush a pretty shade of pink. "I'd love to go with you, but—"

"Then it's settled. We'll go tonight."

"What about this being a bad idea?"

I reach out and pull her to me again. "I don't know what this is. I don't know if it's a good idea or a bad one. I just know it's right, and you know it, too. We'll sort out the rest when we come back."

CHAPTER
Nineteen

Raquel

Being in Patton's arms makes me forget my good intentions. His perfect hands hold me, and I can't say no. He's in pain, emotions raw in his eyes, and my heart aches for the brokenness I see there.

"I messaged Sandra. The office is closed for the rest of the week." He stands in the doorway to my bedroom watching me pack, and I feel self-conscious.

"I don't have a grand view of downtown Nashville. Just that." I point to the tiny little balcony overlooking the parking lot.

He steps to it. "One of your neighbors left their lights on."

"How do you know it's one of my neighbors?" I tease.

"I was wrong. They went out." He steps back and taps on his phone. "I messaged ahead to the property manager letting him know we arrive tonight. They should have it stocked when we get there. Any special requests?"

"I don't think so. You'll have coffee?"

"Of course."

"Wine?"

"Naturally."

"Those are the main things."

He assures me that by closing down the office, we'll avoid the rumor mill—as if that's the only thing I have to worry about. Patton Fletcher is a white-hot coal of fire that's destined to burn me up, but I can't stop touching him.

"I've never been to a cabin in the mountains. I've never even been to the mountains." I'm standing in front of my closet. "What should I pack?"

He steps up behind me. "Those skirts are good. Any short dresses you have. Heels…"

"Oh, really? Short skirts and heels for climbing up and down mountains? Tramping around in the woods?"

"Throw in a pair of tennis shoes for hiking."

I shake my head, packing jeans, leggings, and one skirt. We're only going to be gone a few days. Once I'm done, he takes my suitcase and carries it out to his waiting BMW.

"What did you tell Taron?"

His jaw tightens attractively. "I haven't been able to get in touch with him. I'll keep trying."

"Are you worried about him?"

"Something's going on with him, but I'm not worried. Taron's never been a loose cannon. He'll do what he needs to do."

Following him out to the car, I quickly type a text to Renée. ***Going out of town for a few days. Will text Sunday. Love you.***

She won't call, and I decide I'd rather say sorry than get permission.

When I look up, Patton reaches for my hand. I give it to him, and he threads warm fingers through mine. It feels so good. Our connection is so real. I don't know why I feel like I can trust him, but I do.

Three hours later, we're pulling onto a four-lane highway with pancake restaurants on every corner in the middle of straight-up mountains.

Looking out the window, I pretend to be thoughtful. "You know what I wish I could have right about now?"

Patton is focused on the road. "A bed?"

"Pancakes!"

His brow lowers, and I grin, pointing out the window. "Oh, look!"

The corner of his mouth curls into a grin and he shakes his head. "Do you really want pancakes?"

"Maybe tomorrow." I really want him, and my heart beats faster the closer we get to his cabin. My stomach is tight, and I rub my thighs together.

We turn off the main highway onto a narrow, two-lane road that seems to go straight up. After a few minutes, he turns again, into a short driveway below a giant cabin.

"Is this it?" I look up at the massive structure. "It's enormous!"

He squints, looking up at it from where he's getting our luggage out of the trunk. "It's about standard for the area."

I follow him up the wooden stairs to a wrap-around porch overlooking the tops of trees. The air is a bit cooler than it was when we left Nashville, and being after Labor Day, the tourist season is over. It's dark and quiet, but I can see the lights of the small town below. I can only imagine it's gorgeous when the sun comes up over the hills. It's impressive now.

The door opens, and I turn, following him into a massive great room with yellow pine floors, walls, and ceilings. The whole place smells like fresh-cut timber.

"This is amazing!" I step inside, looking up and around.

A wall of windows is in front of me, stretching up to a point that follows the line of the ceiling. The room is furnished with a brown leather couch and matching armchair with ottoman, and what looks like a section from a huge tree trunk sits on a sisal rug in the center of the room.

"Why don't you ever come here? I think I'd be here every weekend if it were mine."

"I guess after a while you get tired of it." He's in the kitchen inspecting the contents of the cabinets. A welcome basket is on the counter, and he takes a bottle of wine out of it and puts it in the fridge. "Or tired of the drive."

"I don't know... It would take me a long time to get tired of this."

I walk over to a yellow pine door and open it. Inside is a large bedroom with a king sized bed against the wall. A giant flat screen television is across from it, and another door is off to the side. I walk through and open it to find a modern bathroom with beige travertine tile and a Jacuzzi tub against the wall.

My lip goes between my teeth, and I imagine us in it, our bodies wet and sliding together. I'm here with him, alone... It's going to happen, and it sets my insides humming.

I jump almost a foot when he speaks from behind me. "Glass of wine?"

Turning, I see a hint of amusement in his eyes. He's holding two glasses of sparkling pink rosé, and I take one and take a sip. It's cool and slightly crisp.

"This is good."

He places a hand on my waist, pulling me closer to him. "I'm glad you thought of this." Leaning closer, he hesitates just above my mouth. "I'm glad you're here."

"Me, too." I lift my chin, and our eyes meet.

Chemistry flares between us, and he presses warm lips to mine, melting my insides. I reach out blindly to set my glass on the nearby dresser so I can thread my fingers in his thick hair. His hand moves from my waist down to my ass, and a whimper escapes my throat as he pushes my lips apart and slides his tongue along mine.

Heat floods my panties. My whole body's on fire remembering what he can do to me and how good it feels. He lifts his head and places his glass of wine beside mine before returning to what he started.

"You want this?" His voice is low and rich, like he has to even ask.

I've just driven hours with him to be in this place alone.

"I want it." My voice is soft and high, and he pulls me to him again.

Our mouths collide, and it's like a spark to kindling. We're moving faster, like we've been starving since Sunday. He tugs at my shirt, and I quickly unfasten the buttons. My pussy throbs with every heartbeat. I want his lips on me. I want his beard scratching my skin. I'm tempted to rip the rest of my shirt apart when he catches the hem and raises it over my head. Just as fast, he cups my breasts, which are barely covered by my white lace bra.

"I neglected these last time." His voice is a low murmur, his eyes fixed on my body.

His thumbs circle the rosy areolas just visible through the delicate lace, and my nipples tingle and harden. I reach around quickly to unfasten my bra. His eyes darken as it falls away. My insides clench, and I gasp when his teeth graze my tender flesh.

"So sexy," he says, kissing and pulling at the beaded tips.

Every little nip, every touch, is a charge straight to my glistening core. I feel his erection against my stomach, and I want him so much. I want the weight of his body holding me down. I want to hear his groans of satisfaction as he comes.

In a sweep, I'm off my feet, and he carries me to the enormous, king-sized bed. Gently, he lowers me onto my back, standing tall as he unbuttons his shirt. He doesn't waste time, getting halfway down his gorgeous chest before pulling it over his head, leaving his dark hair in messy waves.

My knees rub together in anticipation. His eyes never leave me, hungry as I unfasten the button on my pants and push them down my hips. Large hands cover mine, and he pulls them off.

"Your turn." I tease, sliding the tip of my toe over the obvious bulge in his slacks.

A naughty grin curls his lips and he catches my foot, holding it in one hand as he unfastens his pants with the other. "I like your bare feet."

"I like your bare everything." I haven't really had enough alcohol to be so sassy, but I can't seem to help it.

His pants fall, and I bite my lip at the sight of his cock pointing right at me. Sliding his hand from my foot to my ankle, he puts a knee on the bed between my legs. My insides are vibrating the closer he gets. His eyes go to where a thin scrap of lace still covers me.

Long fingers slide down my center. He touches me lightly and my thighs quiver. Dipping his head down, he traces his tongue along my belly, kissing my skin, working his way lower. My knees rise, and I squirm at the feel of his beard tickling my insanely sensitive skin. Every touch feels so good, it's almost unbearable.

He's beside me on the bed, propped on one arm at my waist. "Does this feel good?" He traces a finger along the side of my thong.

"Yes," I manage to gasp.

"How about this?" His voice is level, methodical, as he pulls the lace to the side, sliding the edge of his finger up and down my clit.

"Patton…" I moan, my fingers twisting in the sheets.

"You're so beautiful right now. I can't decide what to do with you first."

"Just do something." I want to say *do anything*... Only I'm a little nervous he might take me at my word. How far am I prepared to go with him?

Leaning down, he places his mouth on the skin of my inner thigh. I jump in response, threading my fingers in his hair as he moves closer to the center, pausing just long enough to rip the last of my underwear away.

The first pass of his tongue over my clit has me rising off the bed. "Oh, God ..." I'm writhing, but he holds me in place with his strong arms.

Little sucks, little kisses, and my orgasm explodes through my belly, sending shimmers of pleasure to the arches of my feet.

"Oh, yes..." I gasp, rocking my hips as he continues, drawing my orgasm out impossibly long.

He's gone an instant, grabbing his wallet off the nightstand and quickly rolling on a condom. My knees fall together, my body still shimmering with bliss as I watch the ripples of his muscles, the flexing of his fine ass, the bobbing of that massive cock. I chew my lip in anticipation.

When he turns to me, I reach for him. That simple act seems to change everything. He slides onto the bed beside me, cupping my cheek with his hand.

What can we say? He doesn't try to find the words. Warm lips cover mine, and I open to him eagerly, curling my tongue against his, tasting myself mixed with rosé wine. His lips move to my cheek and to my ear, giving it a nip. My orgasm is cooling, but I ache for him.

Placing a hand on his shoulder, I push him onto his back and straddle him. My stomach is flat against his, and he cups my ass with both hands, guiding me to his erection. Our eyes hold each other's, and I feel him right there.

Heat surges between us, and I lower myself in one swift movement the length of his shaft. He's balls deep, completely filling me, stretching me, and his eyes squeeze shut. I exhale a satisfied moan at the same time a deep groan aches from his chest. It's thrilling, and at this angle, I feel so powerful, like I have some control over this amazing man.

Lifting myself up, I start to rock my hips. My eyes close, and I'm riding him like a champ, circling my hips and massaging my clit as I rise up and down faster.

"Fuck, yeah." He grips my ass, helping me move, lifting me and pulling me down. It's thrilling and sexy, and I'm about to come again.

"Keep doing that," I gasp. "Move me."

He does as I ask, lifting me and driving me down. I watch his muscles flex, until the irresistible tightness shatters in my stomach.

"Oh, yes." My head falls back, and he's still working my hips.

My insides clench and pull, and I feel it when he breaks with a loud groan. His hand rises to my back, and he quickly flips our position, putting me under him and seating himself all the way as he pulses, groaning through his release, filling the condom.

We're both panting and slick with sweat. He holds me to him, kissing my cheek, making his way to my mouth again. Our lips seal together, and this time it's different. We're not desperate or hurried. It's relaxed and confident.

Patton's words are in my mind. I don't know if this is good or bad, but I do know it feels right. I only hope that when it's time to sort it out, I don't end up losing everything.

CHAPTER Twenty

Patton

THE ROOM IS DARK, AND I'M HOLDING HER IN MY ARMS. HER breathing is smooth and rhythmic. Every now and then she makes a cute little noise, almost a snore, but not quite.

What am I doing? For so long, conquering the business world, making my own name in my dad's office were the most important things to me. Making sure Taron and Marley were taken care of was a close second.

A relationship would only slow me down. Not because I don't want one, but because when I find the right woman, I want to treat her right, give her things, take care of her.

Is that what this is?

Shifting in the bed, I fight against the idea. I've only known this girl a week, one week. Sure I knew her sister. Yes, I've read her résumé. We've talked a lot, and I feel like I know her.

It's too fucking soon.

But these feelings won't be denied.

I'm at peace when I'm with her. Even in the face of the nightmare waiting at home, she puts my mind at ease.

With a little snort, she lifts her head, dark hair spilling around her shoulders. Her eyes are closed, but her face is to me.

"What is it, beautiful?" The tenderness in my tone is something new, something I don't recognize. Have I ever been tender?

"Oh!" Her chin drops, and she places her cheek against my skin. "I didn't know where I was for a minute."

"You're with me. Go back to sleep." *I'll keep you safe.*

Can I make that promise?

I feel her cheek rise with her smile, and just as fast, her breathing smooths out again. I lie awake for several minutes longer, before eventually the warmth of her body, the sound of her breath, lulls me to sleep.

Sunlight streaming through the enormous glass windows burns my eyes. Holding up a hand, I climb out of bed and cross the room to pull the heavy drapes closed. I take a brief look at the valley before I obscure it. It's going to be a perfect day.

Walking to the bed, I let my eyes drift down Raquel's body. Her back is exposed, long and smooth, and so beautiful. I open my nightstand drawer and set a condom beside the lamp. Sliding between the blankets, I turn her so her cute little ass is against my pelvis. My morning wood is aching for her, but I'll give her time to join the party.

Her back arches, and she reaches for my face, threading her fingernails through my beard. "Is that a wrench in your pocket?"

A smile curls my lips, and I kiss the back of her neck. "I'm happy to see you in my bed."

"Naked." She does a little hip swish, and I reach behind me for the condom.

It's open and rolled on in record time, and I'm holding her by the waist again. "How did you sleep?" My lips are at her ear, and her shoulder rises.

"Your breath tickles."

Sliding my hand down her flat stomach, I slip my fingers between her thighs. Her back arches again as I touch her gently, circling and massaging her clit before dipping my finger inside to find her wet and ready.

"Oh!" She gasps, and I love the noises she makes when I fuck her.

My fingers are gone, and I take a moment to line up with her before sinking deep into her warm, clenching depths. She's so snug around me. She feels so good. I begin thrusting my hips, and she's backing her ass up to meet me.

Fumbling to her legs, I slip my fingers between her thighs again, stroking and massaging as we rock together. Her long hair falls over my shoulder, and her little cries fill my ears. My cock is aching and hard, and I can't hold out much longer. I reach up to cup her small breast, pinching the tight nipple between my fingers. She lets out another whimper.

"Come for me…" I speak in her ear, giving the back of her neck a little bite, and she shudders.

"Do it again." Her voice is a gasp, and I'm quick to comply.

Truth is, I love burying my face in her hair. My eyes close, and I inhale deeply of ginger and coconut. I trace my lips up the back of her neck, moving them behind her ear, and she lets out a little wail. Her insides break into spasms, and she's jerking and bucking against me.

With a low groan, I let go. It's blinding pleasure, almost excruciating, and I hold her tight to me, driving as deeply as I can as the orgasm blankets my mind.

We're panting, our skin slick where it touches. I lean down to kiss the top of her shoulder, and again it rises.

It makes me laugh. "You're so sensitive this morning."

"Your whiskers tickle."

I hadn't thought of that. "Sorry."

"No!" She threads her fingers in mine. "I like it."

She starts to move away, and I reach down between us to

dispose of the condom. I hop out of bed and only take a moment to clean up and return. She's lying on her side with the sheet draped across her breasts watching me.

A sly smile is on her lips. "Do we have any plans for today outside of bed?"

"We do. Starting with your first request from last night." Her soft brow furrows, and I take her hand. "Get dressed. I'm taking you to get pancakes."

The Fancy Chicken Café is a red and white striped building filled with taxidermied and animatronic chickens. It even has oversized plaster hens and roosters on the roof outside.

"It says more than one hundred chickens sing… I didn't know chickens sang." Raquel looks up at me with wide eyes, and I only shake my head, holding the door.

"You wanted pancakes."

"There are twenty different pancake restaurants on this street alone."

"The one my family took me to closed."

Raquel starts to speak, but a hostess dressed in a red and white-checkered uniform and a white bonnet interrupt us.

"And a Cockadoodley-do-day to you! Welcome to the Fancy Chicken! Table for two?"

We both stare at the friendly girl for a beat.

Raquel is the first one to find her voice. "Yes! Sorry. Table for two."

"And-a right this way!" The girl does a little swoosh of her fluffy skirt and leads us to a booth by the window covered in red and white checked tablecloth. "Your server will be right with you. Can I get you some drinks?"

"Coffee," we both say at once.

She nods and disappears, and Raquel's eyes are wide. "I'm going to need a lot of coffee for this place."

"What are you in the mood for? Sweet or savory?"

A busboy places mugs in front of us and quickly fills them with coffee.

"Pancakes can be savory?" Raquel dumps a small carton of half and half into her mug and gives it a stir before taking a sip. "That's good." She leans back against the seat.

"The Kearny stack has bacon and eggs. They have chicken taco pancakes…" Her nose wrinkles. "Or pigs in a blanket."

"What are my sweet options?" She takes another sip of coffee.

"Funfetti, cinnamon roll, or fruit." Frowning, I read the two outliers. "I'm not sure what to make of pecan or whole wheat."

"Pecan is a rich nut. I'll have cinnamon roll."

"I'll have oatmeal."

Her coffee cup lowers with a little bang. "You will not!"

Leaning close, I speak quietly across the table. "If you eat all those cinnamon-roll pancakes, you'll vomit, and I don't want you being sick when I want to fuck you again."

Her eyebrows shoot up. "This is a family restaurant, Mr. Fletcher."

Sitting back, I give the menu one final sweep. "I'll help you with your pancakes."

Just then the entire restaurant changes. Pink and purple strobes hit the chickens lining the walls, and the lights dim. The animatronic chickens all around us start doing The Chicken Dance in jerky, flappy movements. It's like we're caught on some freakish Disney World ride… Small World gone fowl.

My wide eyes meet Raquel's, and we both start to laugh. "This is nuts."

"You picked it."

"I wanted you to have a memorable experience."

"Mission accomplished."

Our server appears, and we place our orders. The chickens finish their dance and a comfortable lull falls between us.

"Your parents took you to get pancakes in Pigeon Forge when you were little?" She lifts her coffee cup to take a sip. "That must've been nice."

I know she's referencing what I told her at my apartment. "My childhood wasn't all bad."

"You don't say."

"How about you? What did you do as a child? Besides play at the free beach."

She slides her eyes to the side as if she's thinking. "Well... there was something." Then she shakes her head. "I can't tell you that. It's too embarrassing."

"Spill it, Morgan."

She laughs, ducking her head. "Oh, man. It's just... so silly."

I put my coffee down and give her a stern look.

"Okay! Okay..." She holds up her hands. "My dad would take me to see those wrestling matches. You know, the ones John Cena does? And The Rock? Or *did*, I guess."

I was just about to take a sip of coffee, but I have to pause for this. "You went to Wrestlemania?"

She ducks, and her cheeks flush. "I did. My dad even called me Rocky. It kind of stuck. Now all my family calls me that."

"Rocky wasn't a wrestler..."

"Yeah, but I was always trying to fight him."

"You boxed with your dad?" This is better than I expected.

"I didn't box. I tried to wrestle like those guys. It was really just me jumping on his back and making a lot of noise."

I have to sit back and chuckle now. I'm picturing a pint-sized version of the very attractive woman across from me behaving like a member of the World Wrestling Federation.

"So you've always been a fighter?"

Our server appears, placing a huge stack of pancakes covered with whipped cream and cinnamon and oozing with butter between us. We unroll the paper napkins from around our silverware, and Raquel pours the syrup. A sad little side of oatmeal is quickly forgotten next to the golden mound of sugary goodness between us.

"What does that mean, Fletcher?" She speaks around a bite of pancake.

I do the same. "It means you've been fighting since you arrived in my office."

"I'm sorry." She pauses, putting her loaded fork on her plate and looking down. Her remorse doesn't last two seconds before her eyes snap up to mine again. "But seriously, 'Are you going to a funeral?' Really?"

I just shake my head at her poor impersonation of me and grin, taking another bite of the fluffy, doughy dessert passing for a real meal. "Rocky. It's perfect for you."

"Admit it. My suit was very professional." She takes her bite.

"When did all black become synonymous with professional?"

"When New York said it was."

"I'm not sure New York said that. I think some lazy business person started the trend."

"Business *person*? Give me a break, you know it was a man."

"Not this man. Last thing I need is a bunch of undertakers selling me optimism."

Her eyebrows rise, and she nods, giving me a broad smile. "I actually agree with you on this one."

"I don't believe it."

"No, I do! I think you're right." She takes another bite, tilting her head to the side. "Your delivery could use some work…"

"I don't have time to teach you how to think."

"Oh my God." She sits back abruptly, dropping her fork and laughing as she covers her mouth. "She said you'd say that… Or a version of that."

"Who said?"

"It's not important." She wipes her mouth, glancing up to

catch my frown. It gets me another, short laugh. "You really should work on your people skills."

"So I've heard. You ready? I can't eat any more of this, and I have a place I want to show you."

"Sure." She grabs her phone, and I grab the bill our server left on the edge of the table.

The lights go down, and the chickens launch into a rousing rendition of "Rocky Top" as we walk to the register by the door. Raquel is close beside me, and our hands brush. Automatically, I catch it, threading our fingers. It started last night on the drive in—I reached out and took her hand as we drove, and she didn't pull away. It's silly and very high-school-first-crush, but I like holding her hand. It feels good. It feels right.

Those words seem to be my mantra for this little escape. I haven't forgotten reality is waiting for us two days and three hours from here, but I want to put that away for now. I want to enjoy this time and see where it takes us. I want to stop fighting... Only, it seems I've found the ultimate fighter for this venture.

The bill is paid, and we walk out to my car, releasing our hands.

"What next?" She looks up at me smiling. "Dancing goats?"

"We'll save them for tomorrow's breakfast."

I have something special in mind. A place I haven't seen in years. A place I want to see with her...

CHAPTER
Twenty-One
Raquel

WE LEAVE THE CAR AT THE HEAD OF A WOODED HIKING TRAIL that like everything around here seems to go straight up.

Looking ahead, my nose scrunches. "I don't have much practice hiking."

"We'll take the intermediate path. I want to show you something."

We're both in jeans and t-shirts. It's warmer with the sun out, and the temperature is pleasant. Trees surround the path in no particular order, but we're able to follow the well-worn route using the small markers along the way. Patton seems so familiar with this area. I can't tell if he's taking a slower pace for my benefit.

"You must've come here a lot when you were a kid." I'm only slightly breathless.

He pauses and waits for me to catch up. "We came out here… I guess every year for five or six years."

I'm right beside him, and he looks down at me with such a

possessive look in his eye, my insides tingle. "Why'd you stop? I can't believe you just got tired of it. It's so beautiful here."

He nods and looks away. "After my mother died, it felt different. For whatever reason, we felt her absence stronger here. We tried coming once without her, but…"

A knot tightens in my throat, and I try to swallow it away. "I'm so sorry."

Dark eyes return to mine. "It was so long ago. It's funny how her memory still seems so strong here."

Stepping closer, I put my arms around his waist. "I feel bad for suggesting we come here."

His arms go around me, and he gazes down, deep into my eyes. "I'm not sorry. I mentioned it to you. I brought you here." He inhales, releasing me and looking around again. "Somehow it isn't sad now."

He starts to walk again, and I follow, thinking about his words, what they could mean. "You know, Native Americans… or I guess Natives? Anyway, they believed the spirits of their ancestors lived in the trees… Maybe your mother's spirit is here."

"Or maybe I'm just twenty-three years older."

I don't know what to say, and we hike a little ways in silence, me turning these thoughts over in my mind. I don't even notice him leading us off the designated path, until I look up and see we're a good distance from any of the trail markers.

He stops at the top of a ridge and looks down. "We're here."

It takes me a few seconds to walk up beside him, but the closer I get, the clearer I can hear it. Once I'm beside him, I look down to see we're standing at the top of a narrow waterfall descending to a small creek below. It's surrounded by lush greenery and the water is so clear, I can see the multi-colored rocks at the bottom of the pool.

"It's beautiful." My voice is a whisper, and I look all around. "But where does it start…"

"It's a natural stream." He points to our right. "The path steers away, because the ground turns into more of a bog in that direction."

We stand for a minute watching the waterfall, studying how the sunlight glistens in rainbow sparkles off the water, listening to the splashing below. "Come with me."

He catches my hand, pulling me down the left side of the ridge after him. He's moving fast, and it's almost a straight drop through damp, brown leaves with trees all around. I reach out and grab the narrow trunks to keep from sliding, and the scent of damp foliage rises around us, musty and earthy. At last we're standing on the edge of the creek below.

He drops my hand and strips off his shirt. "Let's swim." My bottom jaw drops along with his jeans, and I watch as he wades into the pool completely naked, his tight butt flexing.

When I can speak again, I stage whisper the obvious. "What if someone sees us?"

"We're too far off the path. Anyway, did you see anybody out hiking today?" He stops at the waterfall.

"No, but that doesn't mean—" I look up and around.

"Get in." It's an order, and while my instinct is to argue, I kind of want to be naked with him in this glittering pool.

I watch as he lifts his chin, opening his mouth to take a drink, and the sight of his lined throat, his dark hair hanging in damp waves around his square jaw, is so thrilling. Not to mention his broad shoulders over his muscular torso... His arms—the eagle, the lines of latitude and longitude, a band of iron, and *semper fi*... combined with what I know he's hiding just under the water overrules my hesitation.

Catching the hem of my tee, I lift it over my head. He stays under the waterfall, watching me intently.

I'm self-conscious stripping with him looking at me that way, but I want him so much. My stomach is in delicious knots as I step out of my jeans, leaving me in only my lace thong and almost-matching bra.

His brow lowers, and I hesitate a moment before reaching around to unfasten my bra. My nipples tighten as the thin garment falls to the pile of clothes on the ground, and my thong follows it. His scowl melts into approval, and my whole body is on fire.

I slowly walk into the water toward him. His eyes darken, watching me until the water is at my hips, then he moves closer.

He pulls me into his arms. "You're so beautiful."

It's a low, rich rumble, and my arms are pinned beneath his muscular ones as he looks down on my face. I'm completely at his mercy, and I couldn't be happier.

His wet hair falls in dark waves around his face, and he puts his hand on the back of my head as he studies my lips. I'm electric and horny as hell, my palms flat against his shoulder blades. Finally, he lowers his mouth to mine, sealing our lips together and parting mine in a devouring kiss.

He tastes fresh, like the cool mountain stream, and as our tongues curl together, heat flows through my veins. I exhale a little moan, and he pulls me closer, stepping back, through the waterfall as he kisses me again. He nips my lips, moving my mouth with his. I'm chasing his kisses like the most intoxicating drug I've ever had.

"Rocky..." he murmurs, turning me so my back is against the smooth rock wall. "I want to be inside you."

"I want you inside me." I'm gasping and hot, panting and aching for him.

He lowers me slowly. "The condom is in my jeans."

"Oh..." My brow furrows, and I make a sad face. "Hurry."

He's gone in a flash, swimming across the short space and walking out to where our clothes lie abandoned. I hang out behind the water shamelessly watching his gloriously nude body.

His ass flexes as he picks up his pants, digging in the pocket for the dark square. Reaching down, I stroke my clit, stoking the fire blazing inside me for him as I watch him handling his hard penis with those perfectly elegant fingers before starting back to me, condom in place.

Patton Fletcher's body is the stuff of dreams. His shoulders are broad, his chest is two smooth planes above a landscape of lines on his stomach. Two lines create a V leading down to his cock. His legs flex, strong and lined as he enters the water, quickly closing the space between us.

When he gets to where I'm hiding, he pauses, taking in my posture, my hand between my thighs, moving quickly. I've never this bold, but something in me feels wicked. I think it's the way his mouth drops open. My lips are parted, and heat flushes my body as my orgasm grows stronger.

"Oh…" I gasp, getting closer to the edge.

"Don't stop." His voice is strained, and he turns me to face the rock wall. I put a hand out, steadying myself, then lower my cheek against it as he towers behind me.

Strong hands grip my thighs, moving them apart as he guides his tip to my entrance and thrusts in roughly, all the way.

"Oh, yes…" My voice cracks, and I continue frantically circling my clit as he stretches me from behind.

"Rocky, fuck… You're so tight this way."" His mouth is at my ear, and his beard scratching my skin makes me moan. It feels so good.

My nipples tingle. He pushes me onto my tiptoes with every desperate thrust of his cock. He hits my G-spot again and again until… *Oh, God, yes…* The orgasm shoots through my stomach like a rocket, leaving sizzling streams of pleasure in its wake.

I open my mouth and the noise of pleasure is so loud and low, I sound feral.

Patton's fist grips in the side of my hair, and he turns my face so he can cover my mouth with his. He consumes me, pushing his cock harder, deeper into my grasping core. Our tongues curl, our mouths move, and our lips nip and pull as we try to keep up with each other. My knees are liquid, but I can't fall. He's holding me in his strong hands.

Three more hard thrusts, and his body stills. He holds himself deep inside me, and I feel the pulsing of his cock. His ragged groans are in my ear, and I close my eyes, loving that sound. Loving all of this from the fresh spring waters to the earthy scent of the cave around us.

He wraps one arm around my waist and the other around the front of my shoulders, holding my back flush against his hard chest. I love the feel of his hot skin melding to mine. I reach up and hold his strong forearm, resting my head against his shoulder and closing my eyes.

For several beats of our hearts, we stay that way—the deep feeling of union here under this cascade of water, washing over both of us. All I can think is if this is wrong, if he's the devil, then take me to hell. I'll go willingly.

"I don't know." I take another bite of Patton's secret hot chicken recipe and cover my mouth with a napkin. "We might have to do a taste test. This is pretty damn good."

He sits beside me on a stool in front of the massive, granite bar in the oversized kitchen of his family's "little" cabin in the woods.

Taking a piece, he bites into it, wiping his mouth with the napkin. "This batch is pretty good."

"You say it like they're all different."

That makes him grin. "They are."

"So you don't have the secret family recipe?" My eyes narrow.

"I don't have it written down. I just know what's in it." He takes another bite. "This might be as good as the original."

"Do you remember how you made this batch?"

His dark eyes travel to the dry ingredients still sitting out on the counter.

"You don't know what you did?" I jump in before he can answer.

An attractive grin splits his cheeks. It's more of a smile than I've ever seen on him, and I love that a small dimple appears in his chin. Sliding off my stool, I put my arms around his neck and kiss him, slow and spicy-hot.

"What was that for?" He's looking into my eyes the way I love.

"I don't know. You just seem different tonight." I feel closer to him after our days and nights here, like we've moved to a different place.

I'll find out whatever that means when we get back.

Reaching up, he holds my chin with two fingers. "What's that look?"

"What do you mean?" I tilt my head and smile.

"You're so smart. What are you thinking when you look at me that way?"

"You're so smart," I tease, repeating his question. "What are you thinking when you look at me that way."

"I asked first."

Pressing my lips together, I think about something that's been on my mind since he said it. "What you said about your father… You are a leader. You were there every time Marley needed you. It's not fair to you to say you failed. At some point men have to stand on their own."

He sits back, sliding his hands to my thighs. "He was… injured. Damaged on my watch. It broke him."

I'm a little afraid to ask, but I can tell this is so important. "Can you tell me what happened?"

A quiet moment passes. I'm afraid he'll say no, but he

doesn't. "We were in Mexico on a peacekeeping mission headed to Venezuela, and he was kidnapped fueling one of the trucks. It took us two weeks to find him, and when we did..." He stops and I see him wince. "He's never been able to get over it."

His eyes don't meet mine, but he doesn't have to say what he's thinking. "You think it's your fault he was broken." It's not a question.

"We were all given medals and after that, we all wanted out. We joined the military because we wanted to do good. We wanted to be a part of the solution. After that, well... we were all pretty changed by it."

I slide my hand down his arm until our fingers lace together. "I wish there was a way to show you it's not your fault."

"You'd be doing something hours of therapy weren't able to accomplish." His grin returns, but it's a bit darker, a little more cynical. "What I can do is give them a comfortable life, good jobs, opportunities."

"And when that's not enough?"

"I don't know." Our eyes meet and he shrugs. "It's all I've got."

"I think you've got so much more."

CHAPTER Twenty-Two

Patton

Tomorrow, we drive back to Nashville. Taron texted me they're letting Marley out tomorrow morning, and he wants to meet with me, discuss our next steps. I couldn't agree more.

Rocky emerges from the bathroom wearing one of my tees. Her sexy legs are on full display, and I lie back drinking in the view of her climbing onto the bed, the back of her pink lace panties peeking out.

I've always been a black or red lace kind of guy, but Rocky in her pink and white lace, changed my mind. Rocky… I love calling her that. It's so unexpected and so perfect.

"We never got to use that tub." She flops in the bed beside me.

"I prefer waterfalls." I reach for her waist, pulling her across my lap in a straddle.

"It was beautiful." Her voice is as dreamy as her smile.

Her hands rest on my shoulders, and her words about Marley, my feelings, are in my mind. She was so sad when I told her my truth—that I'll never stop blaming myself for his condition—like it was her problem as well. Why would she think that?

She's doing something to me. From the way she looks at me, to the way she believes in me. I don't know why or how, but the block of ice in my chest that's been passing for a heart for years is starting to thaw.

Leaning forward, I kiss her neck. "I think I'll start calling you Rocky."

Her fingers thread in my hair and she exhales a little laugh. "Join the club."

Straightening, I catch her pale blue eyes. "Did you only ever wrestle with your father?"

"Yeah." Her gaze goes distant. "Renée was never much of a fighter. She and I did not have that in common."

My jaw tightens. I don't want to talk about her sister, but she keeps going, like she's walking down some memory lane.

"She did really well in school, like me. She was really going places, top of her class, passed the CPA exam... Then she just walked away from it all." Her blue eyes land on mine. "Maybe you know why?"

Clearing my throat, I shift under her, moving her to sit beside me on the mattress. "I barely know your sister."

She sits quietly for a moment. I'm on my stomach, my arms crossed under my head, wondering how we got on this topic.

A cool hand touches my shoulder, tracing her finger along the line at the top of my bicep. "So you know my Rocky story... Why Patton? What's wrong with George?"

She climbs over my lower back, putting both hands on my shoulders and starting to massage, and I realize my muscles are sore. "That feels good."

"In addition to being a WWE wannabe, I'm also a pretty great masseuse."

Soft hair touches my back, and she sprinkles warm kisses

between soothing touches. Every velvet touch of her warm lips registers below my belt, hardening my dick. I'm completely distracted and ready to pull her under me when she speaks.

"So tell me."

"I'm sorry... Tell you what?"

She exhales a soft laugh. "Patton. Not George."

Oh, right. "Have you ever found the name George attractive?"

"I never really thought about it." Her hot little core is perched right on my ass, and she slides her hands down the length of my torso, stopping to make circles in my lower back. "To me the person makes the name attractive or not. Like I knew a guy named Thomas once, and he was such a dick. Now I hate that name. But I bet there are lots of nice men named Thomas..."

"When we first joined the military, I was put in charge of our squad. Somebody called me Patton, after the general, it caught on, and I liked it."

The soft flutter of my tee hitting the floor catches my eye, and she leans forward, her taut nipples against my back, her soft lips grazing the shell of my ear as she whispers. "You've been bossing people around ever since?"

That does it. Lifting onto an elbow, I reach back and catch her upper arm, pulling her down onto the mattress. She lets out a shriek of laughter, and I slide my torso over hers, caging her in my arms.

"Yes." Dipping my head, I pull a nipple between my lips and flicker my tongue over it.

She wiggles her hands free and threads her fingers in my hair. "Always so bossy." Her voice is breathless as I move to the opposite breast. "What happens when people don't do what you say?"

Lifting my chin, I look straight in her blue eyes. "I show them the door."

Her eyebrows quirk up, and she smiles. "Does that include me?"

Sliding higher, I cover her mouth with mine, pushing her lips apart and curling our tongues together. I don't know if it includes her. My stomach is tight and my desire is white hot. It's our last night, and I only want to be deep between her thighs, sharing the bliss I've been addicted to all weekend.

Her mouth chases mine, kissing me back with matching fervor. I reach for the bedside drawer, and the topic is forgotten for tonight...

"Will it look suspicious if we walk into the office together?" I glance over at her, holding my hand from the passenger seat of my car.

"No." Taking my hand away, I use it to steer us into the parking garage.

The closer we've gotten to Nashville, the more conflicted I feel. Being with her this weekend was incredible. We talked about so many things, and coming back, I feel less angry than I have in years.

"I think it's going to be suspicious because you never smile." In my peripheral vision, I see her watching me, a grin curling her lips. "Just like that."

When she points, I feel it. I am smiling. "I'm glad Marley's coming home today."

"You wouldn't be smiling about that. I think you'd be more worried. Is he ready to be home? Who's going to keep tabs on him?"

"You have a point." Heaviness tightens my chest, but I still feel the relaxation in my face. Fuck. I'm still smiling.

We're out of the car, waiting for the garage elevator, and she tilts her head to the side, studying my face. "You're handsome when you frown, but you're even hotter when you smile."

"That's the kind of thing that will make people suspicious."

The door opens, and we step inside, hitting the button for the twentieth floor. "Why don't you?"

Leaning against the wall, I think about her question. "Never have much to smile about, I guess."

"And now you do?" She's grinning like she won the lottery.

"I haven't decided yet."

Stepping across the small space, she puts her arms around my waist. Her chin lifts, and she kisses the side of my jaw before whispering in my ear. "I think you have."

She kisses my neck, and it's a mini lightning strike. My hand slides in my pocket to make an adjustment, and the elevator dings. We separate at once. She moves to one side of the metal box, and I step to the other, inspecting my leather loafers as she exits ahead of me.

Taron asked to meet in my office first thing to discuss our next steps, but all I can think about are my next steps with Rocky. She brought up her sister last night, and like a fucking coward, I wasn't ready to have that conversation.

We've got to have that conversation and soon. Especially now that my feelings are involved. How did this happen?

I open my door and go to my desk, lifting the cover of my laptop and sending a quick text. *I'm here. Ready when you are.*

Outside my window, the nonstop traffic pours around the city like a stream around rocks. The pedestrians are already blocking up Broadway, and the sun is making its way up a clear blue sky. I could use a cigarette. My hand goes in my pocket to the plastic pack of gum as a light tap sounds on my door.

"Hey." Taron walks in and my brow furrows I don't like the look on his face.

"What's up?"

"I picked up Marley this morning. He's settled at his apartment. Sandra's working on hiring him a private nurse. A temp is with him now."

"Good work."

"Dubai came in overnight. Sandra's scanning their signed contracts into the system."

"More good news." But his expression is resigned. "Is that it?"

"No." He takes a seat across from my desk, and I'm not smiling now. "We need to discuss this. It's something I've been thinking about for months. I talked to Sawyer over the weekend, and I've made a decision."

"Okay." I slip a white square of gum in my mouth and sit in my leather chair, crossing an ankle over my knee. "Shoot."

"Raquel is doing very well." He slides his palms down the front of his jeans, and I notice how casually he's dressed—jeans and a dark, V-neck tee. "I'm glad she's fit in so quickly here. When I saw the email she sent to Remi, and their response... I feel confident passing the reins to her."

"What are you talking about?"

He lifts his head, green eyes meeting mine. "I'm out. This is my notice. I'm moving to Louisiana, back to the farm with Sawyer. I talked to him over the weekend, and—"

I'm on my feet. "You're not going anywhere. I don't accept your notice."

"It's done, Patton. I can't work here anymore. Not physically... not even mentally. I've got to get out of this place before I... I don't know. Before I turn into Marley."

"You'd never turn into him. You don't have the personality... or the scars."

He pushes to standing as well, meeting me eye to eye. "What do you know about my scars?"

Snatching a piece of paper out of my desk, I dispose of the fucking gum. Who came up with this concept anyway? Chewing gum. Such a bovine activity.

"Is this about your back? We can expense the best physical therapist in the city. Get Sandra on it. Whatever you need."

"It's not about my back." He walks to the window. "At least, not entirely. My back started the wheels turning, but it's more than that."

"What is it? The girl?"

His eyes flash at me, but I lower my brow. "You did what you had to do, Taron."

"Yeah. Marines killing little kids. What a fucking cliché I am."

"That is *not* what happened." My voice is sharp. I will not let him rewrite history this way or torture himself for doing his duty. "That young woman would have cut your head off if you hadn't done what you did. She would've killed Marley and possibly wounded Sawyer."

"Maybe."

"Have you forgotten how we found him? What they did? She was in on it."

"Or she was kidnapped just like him. She could've been left there, confused and afraid."

"You don't know that."

"You're right. I don't." He picks up the photo of us again, like he always does in my office, as if holding it has the power to send us back in time, to right past wrongs. "What I do know is I need to get away from this place."

"From me?"

"From Marley. I can't watch him spiraling. I can't pretend like it doesn't bother me, like it doesn't make me want to…" He puts the photo down and goes to the door. "Sawyer needs help. It's honest, hard work. I'm going to see if I can find peace. I'm sorry, Patton."

"Sawyer needs help. You're leaving me short-handed in the middle of our expansion."

"Raquel is more than capable of helping you. Jerry's in LA… You got this." He pauses at the door, looking down. "You don't need me, brother. And I need to go."

He's out the door, and I collapse into my chair. I want Taron to be happy. I don't want to force him to stay somewhere that makes him miserable. But damn, it feels like a kick in the gut for him to leave.

CHAPTER Twenty-Three

Raquel

"SOMETHING HAPPENED." SANDRA IS IN MY OFFICE, SITTING ON the corner of my desk and grinning like she had a hidden camera in Pigeon Forge. "Patton looks like he just got back from some kind of spiritual oasis."

"As if Patton would go to a spiritual oasis." The very thought makes me want to laugh.

"He was smiling." She leans forward. "Smiling!"

I dig in the new banker's box I just inherited from Taron. He stopped in this morning to say it was his last day. I had a small panic attack, but he was strangely calm. He said I did such a great job communicating with Hastings & Key and supporting him last week with Abu Dhabi, he was passing all his files to me. He vaguely mentioned having something else lined up, but he didn't elaborate. I didn't feel right pressing for details.

Long story short, I guess I'm the new Taron in the office.

The door to Patton's office opens, and my stomach tightens. My insides buzz in anticipation of seeing him again, but only Taron walks out. My shoulders fall, and I return again to the banker's box.

Sandra laughs, looking from me to Taron. "Are you disappointed?"

"I don't know what you're talking about." Shaking my head, I keep my eyes fixed on my work, even while my cheeks grow hotter.

A light tap on the door draws my attention. Taron's there, and I can't help thinking he's such a handsome man, I'm sure he'll land on his feet wherever he goes. "Sorry to interrupt…"

He steps inside, and I stop what I'm doing. "It's okay. I was just looking through the new files."

"I know it feels like a lot all at once, but it's really all maintenance. You can call me if you have any questions or if you need a sounding board." He glances over his shoulder. "I know Patton isn't always the most approachable."

A relieved smile breaks across my face. "Thanks. I really appreciate it." He pats my arm and heads for the door. "Good luck with… your future endeavors."

That seems generic enough.

"I'll see you around."

Sandra hops off the desk and follows him out. "I've got those forms you wanted…"

They're gone, and I sink into my chair, my head spinning. I can't imagine Patton is happy about Taron leaving, especially with Marley in such a fragile state. Still, Dubai is onboard. We're in a really great position for me to figure out my place here.

Sandra has been on me like white on rice trying to figure out if Patton and I are more than just colleagues. I cannot let her find out I slept with him… repeatedly—especially not now that I've been promoted to Number 2. If that's what I am.

I'm about to get back to work when my phone buzzes. "Rocky, I need to see you in my office."

My stomach jumps. Patton sounds pissed, but he called me Rocky… that has to be a good sign, right? Picking up my phone,

I walk down the short hall to his closed door, ignoring Sandra along the way.

Knocking softly, I open the door and step inside, closing it behind me. Patton's in his chair with his back turned, looking out the window.

He doesn't move, so I clear my throat, speaking quietly. "You wanted to see me?"

I hear him exhale, and he puts his foot on the floor, turning to face me. His eyes are on the papers on his desk, and I notice something new.

"You're chewing gum?" Disbelief is in my tone.

For someone who despises all black, I can't imagine chewing gum is acceptable behavior.

Dark eyes cut up to me, and he is not smiling. "It's nicotine gum."

I hold my expression steady even though my insides are doing a little happy dance. "Is it helping?"

"Not really." He holds out a cream card with black calligraphy engraved on it.

I take it, quickly scanning the words of the invitation. "What's this?"

"Big investor's gala. They have it every year in New York. This year it's in LA. I want you to go with me."

Now my insides are really jumping. "But... Isn't Jerry in LA?"

"Jerry can attend, but he's not representing me. This is a very big event."

"Okay." I nod, studying the date... this Thursday. "Won't the office be short-staffed if I go with you?"

"You'll only be out two days. Anyway, I need you in case I need a translator."

"If it's a gala in LA, I'm sure everyone will speak English."

"Are you saying you don't want to go?"

Am I? I think about this a moment. I think about Sandra's

obsession with finding out what we're doing. I think about our weekend in Pigeon Forge, and my toes curl. We came so far. We shared so much.

The answer is really easy. "I'd love to go. I just wanted to be sure—"

"We'll leave Wednesday afternoon." He lifts the cover of his laptop and starts to type. "I'll RSVP for both of us."

The muscle in his jaw moves as he types, and I hesitate before speaking. "I'm sorry." Confused eyes look up at me. "About Taron. I know you must be unhappy he's leaving, and I just... I'm sorry."

He blinks back to his computer screen. "Taron is free to do what he wants."

I'm sure he's more upset than he's showing, but I have to let him come to me in his own time.

With a nod, I start for the door when he stops me. "Are you staying at my place tonight?"

"No." I look at him confused, my voice lowered to a whisper. "Patton, we can't—"

"Wednesday, then." He continues typing. "It's formal. We'll find you something to wear once we're out there."

My brow lowers, and his dark eyes cut up to me. A hint of a grin curls his lips. "Don't fight me on this one."

"Patton, I really don't think it's appropriate for you to buy my clothes."

"Can you afford the type of dress you'll need for this event?"

"I don't know. I'm not even sure what type of event it is."

"Exactly. I'm not buying your clothes. It's a business expense. You're working."

"Working." My voice is pure skepticism.

"Of course. If I wanted to take you to LA for sex, I'd take you to LA for sex. The investor's gala is work."

Such a typical Patton response. I want to point out this is not what I consider sorting out our relationship. It feels like muddying the waters even more, but he picks up his phone. "I'll see if Jerry can set up a few meetings with our west coast brokers. Maybe we can see a few properties on Thursday."

When he puts it that way, it does sound like a business-only trip. Still, I know it's going to be more than that.

"Jerry? Rock... ah, Raquel and I are coming out for the gala." I pause at the door, glancing back as he speaks. He puts his hand over the receiver. "Read up on our LA clients over the next few days. Let me know if you have any questions."

He returns to the phone, and I step out into the hall. Looks like I'm going to LA for a gala. I need to call Renée. Only I'm a little scared of what she's going to say. I left her advice so far behind, I can't even see it anymore.

Just before I close the door, I glance back at his square jaw, his dark eyes focused on the computer screen, his hands quickly typing... I've fallen for the devil, and there's no turning back now.

I've always heard Los Angeles is a big smoggy mess of traffic and fake people, but when we touch down at LAX on Wednesday evening, I couldn't be more excited. The sun is shining and the sky is clear and blue. We left Nashville at the same time as we arrive, which slightly messes with my head when we disembark after a three-hour flight.

"Time zones..." I muse, but I don't feel tired at all.

"I'll see if our car is here." Patton takes my hand, lacing our fingers.

The minute we stepped on the plane, his demeanor changed. All week, he's been very professional in the office. Almost too professional considering how close we got in the mountains. Still, I've been sleeping at my place and reporting for work like we're strictly coworkers. He's been following suit.

Now it's like we're on another mini escape—even if he's

calling it business. It's my first time in the city, and I can't wait to walk around downtown and hopefully see some of the famous Los Angeles landmarks. Leaning into the window of our black Lincoln towncar, I look up at the skinny palm trees clustered in the breaks on the Interstate.

"We're on our own for dinner tonight." Patton is checking emails on his phone with one hand, my hand still clutched in his other. "Tomorrow we can head down to Rodeo to find you a dress."

"Rodeo Drive?" I feel like Julia Roberts in *Pretty Woman*... without the whole prostitute thing, of course.

"Jerry will meet us at the gala. He's bringing a plus one." His voice goes down, and I think the same thing. *Great*. "It's being held at the Griffith Observatory."

"Oh, yay!" I jump around in my seat. "That's in *La La Land* and *Rebel Without a Cause*..."

"Didn't you read the invitation?" He chuckles at my enthusiasm. "I showed it to you."

"I guess not." I wasn't able to focus on anything Monday. My head was still spinning from our weekend. Kind of like it is right now.

"We're staying downtown." His face turns thoughtful. "It didn't occur to me you might want to sightsee."

"I didn't know if we'd have time."

"What do you want to see?"

"I'm not really sure. The only things I know about LA are what I've seen in movies. But I don't know where these things are or how long it takes to get there."

"Like what?" We're weaving through traffic, winding through the downtown area past tall skyscrapers mixed with tall, skinny palm trees.

"The Hollywood sign?"

"You'll be able to see that from the Griffith Observatory."

"And the stars on the sidewalk—"

"The Walk of Fame. Not too far from Rodeo." He's still holding my hand, and I'm starting to get excited.

"Venice Beach, Santa Monica, Mullholland Drive... I guess we don't have time to tour any celebrity homes..."

"The Hollywood sights are pretty close together. We'll be right in the middle of it tomorrow. The beaches are probably too far for this trip."

I make a sad face, and he lifts our clasped hands, kissing the back of mine. "We'll have to come back."

My breath catches at his words. *Have we reached the point of making future plans?*

"Okay." The word comes out on a breath.

"We have offices out here now. We're going to have to make an effort to be on the west coast more often."

Oh, right. Duh, Rocky. Cool your over-active imagination.

He looks out the window, and I feel like a naive little girl. This actually is a business trip. We have clients here we need to meet with and solidify our relationships. This isn't a sex trip to LA as he so delicately put it back at the office.

The car pulls up in front of the Ritz Carlton, passing the Grammy Museum and the Staples Center on the way, which I excitedly point out. I step out, looking all the way up to the sky before Patton drags me through the doors into an expansive, beige-stone lobby.

It's bright and open, and elegantly dressed couples mix with couples wearing long shorts and too-tight tees with flip flops walking from the bar to the elevators. I wait by the complimentary cucumber water while Patton checks us in.

"They're sending up our luggage." He takes my hand and leads me to the gleaming elevators. I'm still looking all around like I've never been in a nice hotel before. Actually, I'm hoping to have a celebrity sighting.

Patton leans toward my ear as if reading my mind. "The stars stay up in Brentwood."

"How far away is that?"

"Far enough."

The elevator dings and we step inside with a few other couples. They're not celebrities, and I feel Patton's eyes on me. Glancing to the side, he's got a mischievous grin on his face. It makes my stomach feel tight. I'm instantly thinking about our moment in an elevator not too long ago and wishing we were alone. That man has the most talented tongue...

Eventually, it's just the two of us going higher, and I study the panel. "What floor are we on?"

"The penthouse suites are on the fifty-first floor. Here." He hands me a plastic card. "You need it to take the elevator to the top."

My chest squeezes. "Sandra put us in a penthouse suite... together?"

"She booked you a regular king room, but you're staying with me."

A soft tone sounds, and the elevator stops, opening to a small foyer area with four large, brown doors spaced out and leading to individual suites.

Patton exits the elevator, and I follow him slowly, trying to decide how I feel about this. "I don't get a say in where I stay?"

He swipes the door open, and holds it, looking back with that same grin. "Come inside and tell me what you think."

Marching across the short space, I'm planning out my comeback when my breath is stolen by two walls of windows with a view of the whole city and the San Gabriel Mountains hazy in the distance.

"Oh..." It's a breathless sigh as I walk across the dark wood floors covered in beige carpets to kneel on the sofa in front of the window. "Look at it."

The door closes, and I hear Patton chuckle as he goes to the kitchen and takes two bottles of San Pellegrino from the fridge.

"I remember the first time I saw that view." Cracking one open, he hands it to me. "I thought you might prefer it here to a smaller room farther down."

"You're right." I cut my eyes at him, unable to hide my smile. "It's incredible. So much bigger than I realized."

"It's the second largest city in the U.S." He takes a sip of his water, going to the door.

I'm unable to move from my spot looking down at all the houses and buildings. To my left are more high-rise buildings, but we seem to be on the edge of them. We have an unobstructed view of the scenery.

Looking over my shoulder, Patton tips the bellman and rolls our luggage down the narrow hall to what I assume is the bedroom. The suite is long and narrow with matching beige furniture, brown wood tables and soft leather chairs. The bedroom is behind a wall with entrances on both sides. I climb off the sofa and go to where he's hanging his suit and tux.

The wall of windows extends the length of the hall into the bedroom, which is gorgeous. It's decorated in soothing shades of sand and cream, and the bed looks like it's floating over a rectangular base. A thick white duvet is on top with a soft, knit blanket in the center.

"I think you'll like this." He turns and catches my hand, leading me past another wall to an enormous bathroom with a stone-lined jetted tub near the window-wall. "This time, we'll use it."

A little thrill zips through my stomach at his words. "I bet it's beautiful at night."

"We'll find out, but first, dinner. Are you hungry?"

"I'm starving."

"I'm sure you are." He catches my hand, leading me back

down the hardwood hall to the entrance. "Your body is two hours ahead here."

We hop in the car, holding hands as usual. It's almost like we're afraid to let go, lest one of us slips away. Five minutes later, he's helping me out in front of a large square with a brown sign reading Grand Central Market. It's crowded with pedestrians, but it seems we're a bit ahead of the regular dinner rush. He leads me to a white-tiled counter with Wexler's Deli painted on the front.

We wait in line, and I scan the menu. It's typical New York deli fare. The woman at the register smiles expectantly.

"Two MacArthur Parks and two Cokes." As far as I can tell, Patton never even looked at the menu.

She rings it up, and he hands over the money. It's like I'm not even here.

"You know what I want?"

He passes me a paper cup, and two guys behind the glass barrier get busy slinging rye bread, pastrami, swiss cheese, Russian dressing, and cole slaw.

"It's the best pastrami in the city." He takes his change and takes a pause. "Okay, the best pastrami in the city is Langer's, but this is a very close second."

They're done, handing us a white paper bag, and he leads me to a table. I'm sipping my drink thoughtfully as I watch him.

"How do you know so much about LA?" We unwrap our sandwiches, and I confess, it smells delicious. "Do you visit here a lot?"

"When we're talking to potential clients, it helps to know about the citics, the best and the worst, to get them to sign."

"Makes sense." I take a bite, considering how much additional homework I need to do when the smoky, tangy flavors hit my tongue. "Oh my…" I sit back, covering my mouth. "This is so good! How did you know I'd like this—"

"This isn't our first meal together."

I'm amazed and a lot thrilled that he pays so much attention to my interests. We chew quietly for several minutes. As usual, he's nearly finished in five bites.

"You should slow down and let your stomach catch up."

He seems confused at first, then nods. "Habit."

"You have a habit of eating like it's a contest?"

"Saves time."

I finish half my sandwich and wrap up the other, putting it in the bag. My stomach is tight and my heart is beating so fast, I'm not really hungry.

"That's it for you? I thought you were starving."

"I'll have more later. Let's walk around."

He leads me out, and we stroll down Broadway a little ways. "It's about two miles back to the hotel. LA isn't really a walking city."

A park is on our right with paved steps and trees clustered around a fountain. A wall of art is in the middle, leading out to a pool of water. We walk a few more blocks, and I notice the sky is growing dim. The sun is setting here, but to my body clock, it went down hours ago.

I can't help a yawn, and Patton sees it. "Here…" He reaches out, hailing a cab, and we hop in. "We'll head back and get some rest. Tomorrow's going to be a long day."

The thought of returning to the hotel with him tightens my stomach, waking me up again. "Good idea."

CHAPTER
Twenty-Four

Patton

"It's so beautiful." I watch as Rocky walks ahead of me into the softly lit suite. The sun is just setting over the mountains and the lights of the city are blinking on.

Being here with her is like seeing it all again for the first time, and I want to lay her on the bed and be inside her.

Instead, I go to the kitchen, open the fridge, and uncork a bottle of Mumm Napa. "Start the water. I'll meet you in the bathroom."

Blue eyes flicker to mine, and she smiles in a way that stokes my anticipation. Holding the wine and two flutes, and I pause at the control panel to turn on the music. Soft singing fills the air, but it's not too distracting. I want to focus on her, my little fighter.

She always wants to argue with me, but I appreciate when she lets me win. Like, for instance, with our accommodations. Of course, who could resist this view? I put the wine on the beige counter holding a large, flatscreen TV and remove my blazer. I hang it in the closet and toe off my shoes. Reaching in my pocket, I take out a condom and place it on the bedside table, then I grab the wine, ready to find my girl.

I don't even pause to reflect on me... Patton Fletcher thinking those words. I'm too distracted by the trail of clothes leading to the bathroom. A pink sweater followed by a lacy pink bra has my blood heating. Dark jeans and a black thong have me setting the wine on the vanity and pulling my dress shirt out of my slacks.

The low hum of the jets fills the air, and I see her fully immersed with her hair tied up in a bun on top of her head. Her body is obscured in the water by white foam.

"They have bath bombs." Her eyes are full of delight, then she laughs. "Don't look so disappointed. It smells amazing."

"I was more interested in seeing than smelling." Getting closer, it's the earthy smell of lavender. "I prefer coconut. And ginger."

Her lips press together and she shakes her head.

I pour two flutes of wine and hand one to her. She takes a sip, her eyes fixed on me as I unbutton my shirt halfway and pull it over my head. As usual her eyes heat, and desire is plain on her face. It raises my semi to full hard-on.

My pants drop, and her lip goes between her teeth.

"Like what you see?" I can't resist teasing her.

She blinks quickly, tearing her eyes away from my cock and tilting her head toward the window. "I do—it's really a gorgeous view. You were right."

"That's not what I meant." Stepping into the warm, swirling water, I clink my glass against hers. "And I'm always right."

Her nose scrunches adorably, and she takes a sip. "Is that so? You're always right?"

I take a sip and set my flute aside, setting hers aside as well and reaching for her waist. "Always."

She's on my lap in a straddle, and our lips meet, parting as our tongues slide along each other's. Her hand goes below the water, fingers wrapping around my cock and slowly moving up and down. It makes me groan, and I don't want to stop. I want to slide right inside her now.

"If we're going to keep doing this, we should get tested." I'm tired of having to break for condoms.

She's on my lap, her lips right at my ear, kissing my skin and making it harder to resist her. "I've always been safe."

"I have, too." It's been so long, I barely remember the last time.

Her voice is a sultry purr. "I want to taste you."

We've only just gotten in the tub, but she stands and grabs one of the plush robes off the hook on the wall. She taps the button to turn off the jets and carefully steps out, pulling the soft terrycloth over her shoulders and holding out a hand to me.

"Come on." She doesn't have to ask twice.

I stand, taking the other robe and pulling it over my body. It absorbs the water from our skin, and I take her hand as she walks me to the California king-sized bed. It's lit on all sides with small yellow lights, and track lighting illuminates the floor around it, making it seem to float.

We step onto the fluffy beige carpet and she turns, dropping to her knees. I'm just about to speak when her hands slide up my thighs, grazing my balls with her nails and guiding my aching erection to her lips.

"Rocky..." My large hands catch the sides of her head, and she pulls my tip between her pillow lips.

Round, blue eyes gaze up at me, and she flickers her tongue all around, sucking as she slides her hand up my shaft to meet her mouth.

I groan loudly as she takes me farther down her throat. It feels incredible. My knees are weak, and I can't stop watching her moving faster, taking me deeper. I'm about to shoot down her throat when I reach down to lift her by the arms, moving her onto her stomach on the bed.

Snatching the condom off the night stand, my fingers shake, I'm so close. I roll it on quickly then step to her, ripping the robe up and exposing her creamy, heart-shaped ass.

Yes, I want that. Grabbing her hip, I pull her to the edge. I'm lost in a haze of need as I line up my tip and shove balls deep into her clenching, wet pussy.

"Fuck, yes." It's a low, guttural groan, and I thrust faster.

She moans, lifting her hips up to meet me, chasing her own orgasm. I'm too far gone to help. I'll make it up to her in just a few... more... *Jesus*... I come so hard on my last thrust. Her ass bounces as I slam into her, and my eyes squeeze shut as I fall forward, gripping her waist.

I'm breathing hard, and her face turns to the side, searching. I cover her mouth with mine and kiss her long and full, tasting the bitter tang of the wine on her tongue. She kisses me back with matching need, and I slide my hand between her legs, finding her clit and circling as I rock my hips slowly, still deep inside her.

A whimper aches from her throat, and I reach down to catch the condom, holding it as I pull out and quickly tying it off and tossing it into the trash. Then I flip her onto her back placing my mouth right between her thighs and kissing her there, sucking and pulling her clit with my tongue and teeth.

It doesn't take much before she's bucking against my face. Her fingers thread in my hair, and she moans so loud. I keep going until she's pushing away from me, writhing in the blankets and begging me to stop.

Rising up, I climb onto the bed beside her and pull her against my chest feeling satisfied and so damn good.

We were supposed to sort out this thing between us when we got back from the mountains, but between Taron leaving, following up on Marley, and preparing for this gala, it seemed easier to fall back into our work roles.

I know there are conversations we need to have. Two very important conversations in particular. Still, in this moment, with this beautiful woman in my arms, I can't imagine willingly taking us into difficult situations. At least not yet.

What happened in the past, what's coming in the future, none of it will change if we wait a few hours more. One more day. We've come this far, after all.

These thoughts are drifting quietly through my mind when I notice her breathing has turned into that soft, rhythmic sound of sleep. I kind of love that sound.

My eyes are closed, and I follow her to that place of rest, where there is no fighting. Where we can simply be together, safe in each other's arms.

"We'll be late if I don't call the car now. Are you ready?' The room phone is between my shoulder and my ear, and I polish off my scotch.

After a day of walking up and down Rodeo Drive, checking out the Walk of Fame, Warner Bros studios, driving on Sunset Boulevard with the Hollywood sign to our left and the Griffith Observatory to our right, I had worried she might be too exhausted for the gala. I was wrong.

My little fighter insisted on getting ready in her own room tonight, much to my annoyance.

"Almost done." I can hear the sounds of movement on the other end of the line. "Head on down to the lobby bar. I'll meet you there in five minutes."

"I'm calling the car, so don't be too long."

We disconnect, and I put my glass in the sink. Jerry checked in and let us know where he'd be tonight. I'm tempted to avoid that part of the building, but I can't ignore my senior account exec, especially since I sent him here to get us established in the city.

Or at least that's what I said.

That motherfucker had better not put a finger on Rocky if he knows what's good for him.

The elevator opens to the bustling lobby, and I make my way through a mix of appropriately and inappropriately dressed guests.

The things people put on to wear in public amazes me—men in particular. I receive a text the car is out front, and when I look up, my surroundings seem to fade.

Rocky steps off the elevator and takes my breath away.

She's dressed in a floor-length, slate-blue dress with a halter top held up by thin spaghetti straps that crisscross over her shoulders down to her waist leaving her beautiful back exposed.

Her hair is swept over one shoulder, and the way the top is cut, it gives a teasing glimpse of the curve of her breasts on the sides. The full effect is tantalizing. It makes me want to blow off the gala and take her upstairs…

Clearly, we can't do that.

She closes the space between us, her blue skirt moving in filmy waves around her legs, and her lips curl into a sly grin. "You look like you've been struck by lightning."

I'm pretty sure I have.

"You're stunning." Reaching out, I slide my hand around her waist to the soft skin of her lower back and lean forward to kiss her cheek, just beside her ear.

A shiver moves through her body, and *damn*. I really do want to blow off this gala. "We should just call it and head back upstairs."

She starts to laugh, taking my arm and turning me toward the door. "I thought we were here on business, Mr. Fletcher. This gala is a very important event, and you don't want Jerry representing you at it."

The mention of his name is a boner-killer, and I put my hand over hers. "It's true. We might have to make a pitstop in the lavatory when we get there. I don't know how much longer I can look at you in this dress without ripping it off."

Her eyebrows rise, and I suppose I am being a bit forceful.

"This is a very expensive dress, Mr. Fletcher." She keeps calling me that. It's unexpectedly erotic.

"I should know. I bought it for you."

Our driver waits, holding the door, and she kisses my cheek, giving me a teasing, doe-eyed glance. "When we get back, you can do what you want with it."

I climb in the car beside her, and I lower my gaze, giving her a heated look. "Don't worry, I intend to."

A line of limos and towncars blocks the circular drive leading up to the observatory. We inch along at a snail's pace for several minutes. The sun is setting, and the air is cool. The sky is a gradient of deep red at the horizon to orange to yellow, and Rocky pulls my hand.

"Let's get out and walk."

I hesitate a moment, looking down at the delicate, strappy heels she's wearing. "Are you sure? It's a little ways…"

"I'm sure." She smiles warmly, and I lean forward to ask the driver to stop.

Waiting by the door, I hold her hand as she emerges in a swirl of blue. The color of the dress makes her pale blue eyes seem to glow. She's difficult to look away from.

"You should wear this color more often." Even I can hear the amazement in my tone, and her cheeks flush a pretty shade of pink.

"You might not get any work done…" She's teasing me, and I pull her hand into the crook of my arm.

"I'm very good at multitasking."

We walk up the slick, concrete drive toward the three-domed observatory. When we get to the astronomer's monument out front, she turns, looking out at the view of downtown. We walk farther up, and we see the Hollywood sign.

She hands me her phone from her wristlet. "Take my picture."

We did this all morning, but it is the best view of the sign. She stands in front of the railing, and I tap the button. With the orange glow behind her and the blue of her dress, it looks almost like a painting, and I quickly tap the buttons to send it to myself.

"What are you doing?"

"Texting it to my phone."

"No... wait—" She reaches for the device, but it's too late.

I've typed enough numbers for mine to pop up as saved. "Sexy devil?" My eyes cut up to her, and her cheeks are vibrant red now. "Is this me?"

"Give me that." She reaches for her phone, but I hit send before she can take it away.

My hands are in my pants pockets and I watch as she shoves the device back in her wristlet. "It's rude to read someone else's phone. Hasn't anyone ever told you that?"

"You gave it to me to take your picture. I was just sending a copy to myself."

"Next time I'll take a selfie."

Chuckling, I catch her around the waist. "Why are you embarrassed? I feel like now I need to change your name in my phone.

"My name's in your phone?" She blinks up to me.

"You bet it is. Saved as PITA. Pain in the Ass."

"Oh!" She pushes my arm and walks quickly toward the building.

I laugh, catching up to her and taking her arm. "I'm only joking. You're saved as Raquel, but I think I'll change it to Sexy Fighter. Or maybe FILF, fighter I'd like to..."

She shakes her head, and I thread our fingers again, leading her to the growing crowd of attendees waiting at the door to have their invitations checked against the master list.

We're just at the front when I hear a voice that makes my neck tighten.

"Patton? Is that you? Patton! Raquel!" Looking around, I see Jerry bobbing in the line, midway back and waving.

Rocky moves away from me, sliding her hand out of mine. An acute sense of annoyance filters through my stomach. I'm not smiling when I turn to find him moving through the crowd to where we're waiting.

"I'm not sure it's kosher to cut in line," I murmur when he reaches us, shaking my hand.

"It's good to see your frowning face," he laughs, turning to Rocky. "Hey, Raquel, you look great as always."

He starts to move toward her, but she moves back. Instead, he quickly changes directions, pulling forward a blonde with a short pixie cut and a bright red dress. Angelique Johnson is our go-to realtor on the West Coast.

"Angel," I lean forward in a brief hug, and she air kisses my cheek.

"Patton, so good to see you again."

"Let me tell you, she truly is an angel." Jerry motions between the three of us. "Angel, you obviously know Patton. Raquel here is one of our new account executives. She's a real whiz-kid."

The woman smiles broadly. "It's so nice to meet you. I hope you're enjoying your visit."

"Thank you." Rocky smiles. "It's so nice to meet you."

Jerry jumps in again. "In the short time I've been here, Angel has introduced me to most of the bigger real estate groups in town. She's a real door-opener, if I can say that."

They both laugh at his corny joke, and Rocky forces a light titter. I look at her strangely, and her cheeks flush. Then her hand slides up the back of my arm and gives me a tiny pinch. My eyes narrow, and I smile, but it's a warning. Somebody wants to get spanked.

Rocky returns to the other two. "Isn't it a beautiful night? It's so breezy, and the view of downtown is breathtaking."

"Is it your first time in LA?" Angel takes her arm as we arrive at the front of the line.

I hang back with Jerry showing our invitations and waiting for them to check the lists.

"I say, I was surprised you brought Raquel with you." Jerry's studying me with an intensity I don't care for.

"You heard Taron resigned?"

He nods, "I did, although I can't say it was entirely unexpected."

I didn't expect it. "Raquel is moving into his position. She's here to meet the clients and get a feel for our new market."

Anger flares in Jerry's eyes, and he takes a step back. "You're moving her into Taron's spot? That should be my promotion."

My jaw tightens, and I turn to face him, matching his tone. "What gave you that idea? Taron hired Rock... Raquel to take over his accounts."

"His international accounts. I helped him develop all our domestic partners. She's too young."

"You're in LA now." My tone is final, but he's turning my decision into a snub.

"Temporarily. You said I'd be able to come back—"

"You're here to grow the West Coast branch. It's as important as what Taron did in Nashville."

"But it was *in* Nashville." Angel and Rocky stroll back to where we're speaking in low, heated tones. "She's too young and inexperienced."

"She's young, but she's proven her ability."

The ladies are back with us, and Rocky smiles, meeting my

eyes. Our chemistry is strong, and I wait too long before blinking away.

"I see." Jerry's tone is cynical. "It's like that."

"Like what?" Angel blinks between the two of us, but Jerry's eyes are fixed on me.

He's grinning like he just figured out some new angle, and I don't like it.

"Let's get some drinks, Ang." He starts to go, but pauses after a few steps. "Oh, I was able to set up meetings with Keller Martin and Shelldrake tomorrow. We can talk more about what we're going to do then."

As far as I'm concerned, the conversation is closed, but I'm not in the mood to deal with him right now. "We'll see you then."

"Yes, you will. We can also discuss my new terms for staying tomorrow. Now that things are changing so much."

My eyes narrow, and I try to figure out what he's planning. Rocky is at my side, so I'll let it go for now, but this asshole better not think he's going to push me around. "Tomorrow, ten."

CHAPTER
Twenty-Five

Raquel

"So far this is shaping up to be my favorite business trip." We've slipped out to the narrow walkway along the outside of the observatory, overlooking the city. We've somehow managed to be alone, and it's magical... like a fairytale.

I'm here in this beautiful dress at this elegant ball. A glass of wine is in my hand, and the music from inside is loud enough to be heard. Patton holds my hand as we stroll.

"You seemed to hit it off well with Angel." He glances over at me.

"She's nice." We take a few more steps, and I look up at the sky.

The yellow, orange, and red has transformed to pink, blue, and deep purple, and I exhale deeply, pausing beside the wall. Patton's warm hand slides across my bare back, and it feels good. I lean my head against his shoulder.

"Too bad we're heading home tomorrow." I think I've fallen in love with this city.

He exhales a laugh. "I thought you were worried about leaving the Nashville office shorthanded."

"I didn't know what I was missing."

We're quiet, watching the twinkling stars, the lights of LA spread like a glittering blanket below. I get to thinking. "What was going on with Jerry back there?"

The two of them seemed to be having a heated conversation when Angel and I returned from our stroll, and they've been scarce ever since.

"Nothing. Shop talk."

"It seemed like more than shop talk to me."

He pushes off the wall and starts to walk again, holding my hand. "Jerry tends to get ideas in his head... he thinks he has more of a say in my decisions than he does."

Fear tightens my throat. It's the one thing able to burst my dreamy bubble. I wouldn't put it past Jerry to try and make something out of Patton's and my relationship. I've worried before about the wisdom of sleeping with my boss. Too bad wisdom always seems to take a backseat whenever Patton's sexy ass is around.

"He seems to be doing very well for himself here." I try to calm my nervous thoughts. I'm probably misreading the situation. Why wouldn't Jerry be happy here? It's a great place. He's his own boss.

"He's doing something." He stops, turning to face me. "I don't want to talk about Jerry. I'm glad you're enjoying the trip. I've enjoyed it more having you here with me."

"It's still a business trip, right?" I blink up briefly and give him a smile.

A heavy brass door bangs open, and we drop our hands. Two party guests stumble out into the night and I take the opportunity to return to the party.

We've spent the night swapping business cards and shaking

hands. Remington Key is here, and he greets Patton, introducing himself to me. He's very friendly and congratulates me on taking over Taron's old spot.

Shaking hands with Patton, he smiles. "I'm sorry I won't get to chat with Taron as much anymore, but I'm sure Raquel and I will find something in common."

"I look forward to working with you... Remington." My forehead scrunches, and he grins.

"You can call me Remi. Everyone does." He's handsome and clearly wealthy. His suit is very fine, and I see a Rolex watch peeping from beneath his sleeve.

"Okay, Key, you don't have to land our business twice." Patton puts his arm around my waist and moves me to his other side, away from our financial partner.

Remi laughs. "I hope this is a change for the better. It'll be nice to see you smiling more on our conference calls."

Patton puts his hand on his shoulder. "We're taking off. Give my best to Hastings. I'll give you both a call next week."

"I'll be in Seattle for a few days, working with our software designers. I'll let you know when I'm back in the office."

Patton nods. "We'll chat then."

"Nice to meet you, Raquel." Remi smiles, and I do a little wave as Patton takes my arm and leads me to the door.

It's late as we stroll out to the car, and I'm feeling the time difference again. Still, I pause for one last look at the valley below, the Hollywood sign above, and the flickering stars. It truly is unforgettable.

"I'll take the lead when we meet with Keller Martin and Shelldrake." Patton's voice is pure business. It's how he's been since we saw Jerry at the gala last night.

I'm sitting in the passenger's seat of a rented Audi coupe.

Based on our day yesterday, I'd expected things to get crazy when we got back to the penthouse. Instead, he was distracted. He spent some time working on his computer before joining me in the bed. We made sweet love, but I quietly hung my blue dress neatly in the closet and slipped into one of his tees.

Nothing was torn or wild—not that I'm complaining. Being held in Patton's arms while he kisses me gently and fucks me hard is about the best thing I've experienced since I graduated from business school.

"I wouldn't even know where to begin to take the lead in this meeting."

"Good. You'll learn more by listening."

I don't think he's trying to start an argument. I think this is more of his distraction, but my old nature wants to point out how much I've done and learned since I joined Fletcher International, Inc.

Instead, I let it go, choosing to watch his square jaw flex attractively as he chews another piece of nicotine gum. I haven't seen him with a cigarette in days. It's a little victory, but a victory all the same. Another Round goes to Rocky, and this win fills me with happy warmth.

Truthfully, I'm a bit distracted myself, thinking about Renée. I haven't checked in with her since my text before Pigeon Forge. It's the longest we've gone without talking, and it has me uneasy. I feel certain Hazel would call me if she had any trouble, still, I don't like to go too long without hearing her voice.

Patton pulls into a parking space in front of a mid-rise glass office building. "Our flight's in two hours. I don't expect this will take long. We're primarily putting faces to names."

"Okay." I smile and follow him into the building.

We step off the elevator into a modern, stainless steel and concrete interior. It's all white with sparse furnishings. It seems to be the trend in West Coast design these days. Minimalistic, or monastic, depending on who you ask.

Jerry is alone when we enter the conference room, and Patton is immediately annoyed. "Where are the realtors?"

"They're on the way. I figured this would give us time to chat about my promotion before you cut out early."

My throat tightens, my eyes cut to Patton. Jerry's trying to set him up, and even I know that's a bad idea. Patton only gets fiercer when he feels cornered.

"Is that right?" Patton's grin is relaxed, and he pulls out a chair, taking a seat. "You've decided you deserve a promotion?"

"As a matter of fact, I have. And I think you're going to agree with me when you hear what I have to say." Jerry's smile is conniving, and my hands are clammy.

"Should I wait outside?" My voice is soft, and Patton gives me a reassuring smile.

"You're fine. Have a seat."

"Yes, please stay, Raquel. Some of this concerns you as well." I don't like the sound of that.

I pull out a chair at the other end of the table, closest to the door, and try to calm my galloping heart.

"Let's hear what you have to say, Buckingham." Patton leans forward, propping his forearms on the table. Black ink peeks out from the cuffs of his shirtsleeves, and it calms me slightly.

Patton is a badass devil. Renée told me so herself. I'm pretty sure he cares about me, and if anyone can handle a slime ball like Jerry it's him. My stomach starts to unclench.

"First, let me be sure I've got my facts straight." Jerry sits in the chair directly across from Patton, and even though I'm confident in my man, I don't like how gleeful Jerry seems. "You're promoting Miss Morgan here into Taron's role as VP of client development. Is that right?"

Patton's voice is level. "That's right. She has the credentials, and she's proven her ability in the office."

"After only a few weeks, whereas I've been with Fletcher

International five years, and I've been exiled to the farthest reaches of the country."

Patton laughs, leaning back in his chair. "I'd hardly call heading up our West Coast division exile. Some people actually like it out here."

"We've already had that conversation." Jerry's brow lowers, and I decide he might be a devil himself. Only not the tall, dark, and sexy kind like Patton.

Jerry's the short, red, spiteful kind.

"I assume along with Miss Morgan's promotion, she'll be getting a salary increase and an increased share of the company, not to mention a stronger voice in our administrative meetings?"

"Of course." Patton says it like it's a given, and my eyebrows rise.

Wow. It all happened so fast, I haven't really thought through all of the details of taking over Taron's old job. Patton and I haven't had the opportunity to discuss it. Now I wonder if it also means I'll get one of those massive corner offices.

I'm starting to feel pretty good about myself until Jerry continues.

"You're going to promote me to VP as well, and I expect to be paid a salary commiserate with my level of experience and the clients I've developed during my years with this firm."

"Is this really how you're going to handle this?" Patton's voice is quiet calm.

I'm not saying a word.

Jerry smiles. "There's nothing to handle. You're going to give me what I deserve, or I'm going to go public about what's happening behind the scenes at your father's company."

"What you deserve?" Patton's jaw tightens and the small hairs on the back of my neck start to rise. "Fletcher International is *my* company. It's a private company. Going public with anything will only make you look like a sore loser—and you lost to a woman. Is that the kind of limelight you want to have on you?"

"Limelight?" Jerry's voice is dangerously calm. "Limelight..." He repeats the word in a way that makes my fingers tremble. "What about the kind of limelight that sweeps sexual assault under the rug? You bring up women, what about the kind of limelight that drives out aspiring young female employees to protect your friends?"

My throat tightens, and I feel like I'm having trouble breathing.

"Are you trying to blackmail me?" Patton's voice is fierce. He's the tiger, ready to maul.

"Blackmail? Oh, no, I simply think it's an interesting contradiction. Tell me, when you're finished sleeping with Miss Morgan here, will you make her look insane like her sister? Will you drive her out of Nashville as well?"

I'm having trouble focusing. I feel like the air is being sucked out of the room. "Patton?" My voice is small. "What is he talking about?"

"I did nothing wrong." A crack is in his voice. "Renée had issues..."

"Yes," Jerry chuckles and keeps going. "Issues she brought to you to fix. Issues that threatened your old boys club."

"You hypocrite." My voice cuts through the thick tension. "You're mad because you grabbed my ass repeatedly and Patton sent you here to avoid a lawsuit."

Jerry's eyes flash to me. "The hypocrite, Raquel, is your boyfriend. Why don't you ask him what he did to your sister when his beloved Marley set his sights on her. He sent me out of town? He drove your sister to the nuthouse. Then he ruined her reputation with all his CEO friends. She couldn't get a job in Nashville if her name was Dolly Fucking Parton."

My heart is beating out of my chest. I want to stand up and

shout at Jerry to shut up and stop talking about things he doesn't understand. Patton would never do that. Only...

Renée's words, her strange silence when I told her I was sleeping with him. Her withdrawal. *I hate him... He's the devil...* These are things my mild-mannered sister never says about anybody. *Oh, God, please say it's not true.*

The nausea in my stomach tells me I'm afraid it is.

Patton's eyes are flinty. "Clean out your desk. You're finished here."

"With pleasure. I got a better offer anyway—with Braden."

Patton's jaw flexes. "Then why...?"

Jerry leans close, spitting the words. "Because this time, you don't get away with it." With that, he turns on his heel and strides to the door. "Oh, and no realtors are coming. I cancelled our meeting first thing this morning. Good luck establishing your West Coast division."

He slams the door, and silence falls over the room. It's so silent, I can hear the second hand ticking on the clock above the door.

I feel like I've been hit by a freight train. I'm breathing fast, trying to make sense of everything Jerry said. "Patton?" My voice breaks.

He doesn't answer immediately. He's silent, and his silence speaks volumes.

"Please explain what he said about my sister."

Dark eyes rise to mine, and I see guilt in them. "I didn't know how to have this conversation with you. I didn't know what to say."

"What did you do?" I'm shaking uncontrollably, but somehow my voice is level.

"I protected my friend."

"From what?" Protective anger twists in my chest. "A young woman?"

I think about my sister and what a bright, aspiring college graduate she was. I remember her getting this job and being so excited to join corporate America. Then I remember her eighteen months later, hiding in her apartment, refusing to return to work.

"She never filed a formal complaint. She asked me to talk to him, to make him stop..." He looks at the table as if he's replaying the scene in his mind. "I'd only been CEO a few years. I was still fighting with my dad for control. The last thing I needed was a Marley scandal."

I feel the blood draining from my face. "He raped her?"

"No." His eyes cut to mine, and then he blinks down like he can't hold my gaze. "God, no. I don't think it went that far."

"You don't *think*?" I'm on my feet, my voice growing louder.

"There were no witnesses... It was all very unclear."

"It seems crystal clear to me. You protected your friend at the cost of breaking my sister. Then you destroyed her career."

"Jerry exaggerated. I don't have that kind of power." His hand flexes on the table. "I simply let her go. That's all. I didn't destroy her career."

I take a step back, giving him an incredulous look. "You made it so she couldn't explain an eighteen-month gap on her résumé. She couldn't use you as a reference. You could make her look crazy if she accused him publicly, if she tried to explain why she left here. You say you don't have that power, but you know you do. You ended her professional life." Shaking my head, I know what I have to do. "I'm leaving. When we get back to Nashville, I'm turning in my notice."

He's on his feet at once, crossing the room to me, reaching for me. "Rocky, please."

Holding up my hand, I back away. "Don't touch me."

I storm out the door before I start to cry, but he's right on my heels, catching my arm. "Stop and let me explain..."

My voice is savage as I jerk my arm away. "Stay away from

me." My eyes flash. "I knew you were broken. I never thought you were cruel."

"You've seen how he is." Patton's voice is soft, pleading. "I had to protect him. I was young—"

"Renée was young. You were old enough to know what you were doing." I'm looking at my phone typing in my destination address.

"What are you doing?"

"I'm leaving you."

His voice drops. "I won't let you."

"You won't let me?" My voice is a whip. My eyes flash, and that fight deep inside me rises to the surface. "That's not your call, George."

My phone buzzes, and I look up to see Javier in a red Honda Civic arriving to take me to the airport, the pink Lyft logo glowing in his windshield.

"Rocky, wait." He tries to reach for me again, but I pull away, stepping into the car.

"You hurt a defenseless person who came to you for help. You hurt my sister." A tremor is in my voice, but rage is boiling away my tears. "I never want to see you again."

CHAPTER
Twenty-Six
Patton

"**Y**OU NEED TO GET YOUR SHIT TOGETHER AND GET BACK TO work.**"** I'm standing in Marley's living room watching him drink a Red Bull in pajama pants and a threadbare Phish tee.

He makes a sarcastic face. "Haven't you heard? I'm suffering from exhaustion."

"Don't start that shit with me." My voice rises, and I take a cigarette out of my pack. Lighting it, I inhale a long pull and exhale the stream of smoke slowly. "We had to say something to keep it off the gossip sites. How long do you think Hastings and Key would stick with us if they know what you did? What about Abu Dhabi? Dubai? Those guys avoid scandal like sand fleas." I add under my breath, "Not to mention my dad." That asshole. I don't even want to hear what he'd have to say.

"Well you fucked up." He reaches for his own cigarette. "Everyone knows 'exhaustion' is code for drug overdose."

A fist of rage is in my chest. It's been like this since I got back from Los Angeles. Rocky walked out, and it all went to hell.

Stalking to his balcony doors, I pull them open, studying the Nashville skyline. My mind trips back to standing with her in my arms, studying the view of Los Angeles. I push that memory aside. I was a fool to think I could have her after everything that happened. She's right. I'm broken and cruel, and I injured the only family member she has left.

I take another long pull off my cigarette, blowing the smoke out the doors. "How's it going with the therapist?"

"You mean am I going to do it again?"

As pissed as I am, what he did still hurts. Turning my back to the doors, I look directly into his eyes. "Yes. That's what I mean."

He shakes his head, breaking eye contact, seeming defeated. "I don't think so."

It's not good enough. "I need you back at the office. You know Taron left."

"I know what Taron did." He takes another pull off his cigarette. "I know what he wants. I hope he finds it."

Whatever that means. "Rocky put in her notice."

His head snaps up at that, and his brow furrows. "But… she was really good. Why would she do that?"

I want to say 'because of you,' but that would be a lie. She left because of me, and I know it. "She has her reasons. What it amounts to is I'm short-handed, and you need to get out of this condo. Work will do you good, give you something to occupy your mind."

He shakes his head, exhaling a cloud of smoke. "Bring Jerry back from LA."

"I fired Jerry."

His eyebrows shoot up. "Good."

I'm surprised. "What's that supposed to mean?"

"It means I hated that guy. He was a conniving backstabber willing to step on anybody to get to the top."

"That would've been fucking good information to share with

me." I still haven't figured out how he knew what happened with Renée. I didn't even tell Taron why she resigned.

A bitter chuckle scrapes from his throat. "You're so focused on conquering the world, you can't see what's in front of your face."

My jaw tightens, and my patience is done. "I'm focused on taking care of my men. Everything I've done has been for all of us, to make us comfortable and secure."

"Did it ever occur to you we might not want it?"

"No." My voice is flat. "I expect you to be in the office in the morning. On time, in a suit, and ready to take over Taron's job."

Grinding out my cigarette, I scoop up my phone and my keys and head out the door. I'm back in my office by noon, and Sandra's at her desk, typing away. Our eyes meet, and she shakes her head.

"She hasn't been in all morning."

Glancing toward Rocky's office, I see her lights are off, but the books and photos she brought in are still on her desk. She wouldn't leave those behind.

"Any hits on LA?"

"I only put the posting on the job boards an hour ago. Give it some time."

"Tell me if Rock… Raquel comes in. I'd like to see her before she leaves."

Sandra shakes her head. "It doesn't make any sense to me. She seemed like she really liked it here." Hazel eyes cut up to me in accusation, but I turn and go into my office.

Dropping into my chair, I want another cigarette. Instead, I pull up the office flowchart. I've lost three people in as many days. Marley is more than capable of taking over Taron's accounts, especially with the way Taron left them.

We could hire an intern to keep our social media presence going. Hell, it might be a better use of resources, considering how adept college kids are with that shit. Los Angeles is another story.

Rocking back in my chair, I reflect on my solo plane trip home from the West Coast. Despite what she said, Rocky is still a smart business person.

My mind trips further back in time, four years ago, Marley was in my office sitting on the couch confused. He told me how sweet Renée was. He told me how she liked helping little animals and she was always telling him about some cause or the other she wanted to support.

He told me how beautiful he thought she was. He told me he couldn't stop thinking about her. I'd never seen him act that way about any woman. Usually he treated them like they were disposable, use them and lose them. I told him to leave her alone.

As usual, he didn't listen.

Not that I'm any better. I was stupid to let myself pursue Rocky the way I did. I got greedy. I was lonely, and I let my guard down. Admitting this weakness makes me angry. It makes my throat tight. I should've known better. Love isn't what I do. I don't give anyone that level of power over me…

My phone buzzes, and I snatch up the receiver.

"She just walked in, boss." Sandra's on the other end. "She's moving fast, so don't waste time."

I hang up as the last word comes out of her mouth. Straightening my coat, I take a beat before opening the door. Seeing her is like a kick in the stomach. It's been three days since she left me in LA, and I think she's even prettier.

She's wearing ripped jeans and a khaki top with beige heels, and Sandra's right. She's moving around her desk like the building's on fire. I close the space between us quickly and tap lightly on her open door.

"What?" When she looks up and sees me, her lips tighten. I think she's clenching her jaw at me.

"May I speak to you a moment?"

She looks away and continues putting her few possessions in the canvas bag on her desk. "There's nothing to say. I gave Sandra the laptop. I've taken all my information off it." She reaches into her purse and pulls out a business-sized envelope. "Here's my official letter of resignation."

A tremble is in her hand, and I wonder what it means. Is she nervous? Is she sad? Is this killing her as much as it is me?

"You're required to give two-week's notice." Her blue eyes flash, and I shrug. "It's in your contract."

"You can figure out a way around that."

The last of her things are in the bag, and she pulls the straps over her shoulder. She takes a step toward the door, but I step in front of her, closing it behind me and putting my back against it.

"Just give me a minute to run something past you."

"I've given you all the time you get from me." My hands go up, and hers do the same. "What do you want, Patton?"

That's when I hear the crack in her voice, and I know. This isn't as easy for her as she's trying to make it seem. I might have a chance.

"You haven't been here long enough to quit. It won't look good to future employers. You don't deserve that."

She rocks back, crossing her arms. "You did not just say that to me."

"I'd like to send you to LA." I pause a moment to let the idea sink in. "Would you be willing to take Jerry's place launching our West Coast division? It's a great opportunity, and it won't hurt your résumé."

"It would help you, too." Her voice is terse.

My hands go in my pockets, and I nod. "It would help me, but it's also helping you… And you won't have to see me."

A weight is in my chest as I say it. I don't want to send her to LA. I want her here. All of this is fucking bullshit. If she would just listen to me…

Blinking quickly, she turns her face toward the window. Her throat moves with a swallow, and my eyes trace the line of her jaw, the sweep of her golden-brown hair, her soft neck.

Clearing my throat, I move away from her door. "Take the week to think about it. You can let me know on Monday." I turn the envelope in my hand and slide it into my breast pocket. "I'll hold onto this until I hear from you."

She inhales slowly then cuts those pretty blue eyes to me. The freckles on her nose make her seem so young. *What will it take to win her back? Is it even possible?*

"Can I go now?" Impatience is in her tone, and I step to the side, allowing her to pass.

She leaves me in a swirl of coconut and ginger that gets caught in my throat. She's so beautiful as she walks out the door.

CHAPTER
Twenty-Seven
Raquel

RENÉE ISN'T ANSWERING HER PHONE.

Since I got home Friday night, I've been pacing my small apartment trying to reach her. I spent Saturday in bed and let myself cry. Sunday, I got up and took a shower. I forced myself to walk around the block, to go to the grocery store and buy food.

It was all I could do before it started again. I'm not sobbing crying, but I can't stop the tears streaming down my cheeks. I don't even know why I'm crying. He doesn't deserve my tears.

But my heart is broken...

Of course, Renée isn't answering her phone. I've been over here sleeping with the enemy, betraying her with every story I tell.

At the same time... she didn't tell me anything. She could have warned me a little better instead of just issuing cryptic suggestions. "Don't fall for him," she said. "He's the devil," she said. *Really, Renée?*

I'm so frustrated, I start packing my things. Seeing Patton in the office today almost broke me. I waited until I was sure he'd be at lunch—of course, he wasn't. It was all I could do to stay focused, to not fucking cry, to keep my hands from shaking. To act like he didn't hurt me with his lies... his omissions.

Dropping to sit on my couch, I put my face in my hands. Fuck these stupid tears! Why does he have to look so good? His eyes were so open and pleading asking me to go to LA. As much as I hate to admit it, he's right about me quitting. Future employers won't know what a conniving bastard he is. They won't know how he destroyed the life of my sister without even looking back.

All they'll see is I landed a plumb job straight out of business school at one of the top firms in Nashville, then I quit less than three weeks later. They'll think I couldn't hack it. Or they'll think I'm a problem employee... In any case, it's a red flag.

Exhaling a big sigh, I grab my suitcase and head for the door. I'm going to make Renée talk to me, and I'm going to force her to tell me the truth. I deserve to know what happened.

It's almost nine when I'm pulling into Savannah. Following the old, familiar roads, I wind my way down through Wilmington to my parent's old home in the tiny neighborhood where I grew up.

So much has changed since I was a child here. Most of the smaller, older homes are gone, replaced by million-dollar mansions and country club estates. Savannah has become a dream destination, as my sister keeps telling me, and the population is steadily growing as more people relocate closer to the coast.

I miss the days when it would be just us kids, running around the marsh lands, playing along the old piers, fishing with cane poles... Going with my daddy to WWE matches.

More tears are on my cheeks. I can't help thinking how

Patton had started calling me Rocky. It feels so long ago since we were in the mountains, since he held me in his arms, and all I could think was how good it felt, how much I wanted him.

No. I push those thoughts away. He doesn't deserve my fond memories. He lied to me the whole time. He knew what had happened to Renée, and he never said a word about it—even when I asked him point blank.

He said he didn't know how to tell me. Guess what? He could've told me the night I asked him. Shifting the car into park, I pause in front of the posh home in front of me. I have to double-check the number above the door.

Yep, it's my parents' old place, but it looks... different. *Good* different.

I'm out the car, and the grass is cut and the neat sidewalk runs around the front like always. But now I'm walking up new wooden steps to a pristine wrap-around porch. The exterior, which was formerly vinyl siding is now stucco, and large, dark-brown shutters line the long windows across the front, making them seem more like French doors.

Going to the life-sized ceramic sea turtle on the corner, I pat his head. "Hi, Crush." Then I flip him over and shake, hearing the familiar clinking of the key hidden inside him.

When I get the front door open, I'm even more amazed. The wood floors have been redone. The wall that divided the kitchen from the formal dining room we never used has been removed, and now it has a big, open floor plan.

Our three tiny bedrooms are still down the small hall directly across from me, but to the left, an entire room has been added with a large television and couches and chairs. Dropping my small suitcase, I walk around the new kitchen, taking a glass from the refinished cabinets and filling it with ice and water from the new Viking refrigerator.

"Renée?" I call, but I don't get an answer. I'm starting to get worried until I walk down the hall to my bedroom, and I hear the sound of a shower running.

It looks like the bathroom my dad started off his and mom's old bedroom—the one he never finished—has been finished. I go into my room, which now looks like a fancy guest room straight out of Pottery Barn and put my small suitcase on the bed.

A card on the dresser lists the wifi address and password, which makes me frown. Now I'm not sure what's going on here.

Stepping into the hall again, the noise of the shower has stopped, and a voice is on the other side of the door singing "People Are Strange" by the Doors.

That is my sister.

Knocking on the door, I open it as I say her name, and I jump almost a mile in the air when she closes her eyes and screams bloody murder.

She screams so loud, my ears pierce. I wind up screaming as well out of pure shock. Once we stop, I fall back against the wall, clutching my chest.

"Jesus, Renée! You almost gave me a heart attack!"

"I almost gave *you* a heart attack?" Her voice is loud, and she's gasping, clutching a towel to her chest. She's wearing gray sweats and a long-sleeved pink tee. Her brown hair is wet, and it's getting her shirt wet.

Then our eyes meet, and she starts to laugh. My nerves are completely shot and my emotions are so strung out… I start to laugh, too. We both laugh. We laugh so hard, I'm crying again, and I step forward to give her a hug, holding her a minute as she pets my head.

She steps back, squeezing the ends of her hair with the towel. "What the heck are you doing here? Aren't you supposed to be working? Or whatever you're doing in Nashville these days?"

Touching the tears from my eyes, I don't miss the accusation in her question, but I'm past all that.

I simply shrug, acting casual. "I missed you. I haven't heard from you in a while, and I wanted to check on you. Why haven't you been answering my calls?"

She hangs the towel on a hook inside the bathroom and calls over her shoulder. "I'm sorry! I've been absolutely exhausted. I rescued two neonatal kittens, and oh my lord, Rocky. I have to feed them every two hours around the clock... I have to stimulate their little butts to make them go to the bathroom. The last two weeks have been intense."

"You rescued baby kittens? What happened to them?" My eyes heat, and I feel so stupid. My emotions are so fragile. I'm going to cry over kittens?

Stopping in front of me, her face scrunches with a frown. "Why are you crying? What happened?"

"Oh, Renée..." My throat aches, and when I close my eyes, two tears hit my cheeks. Nooo... I don't want to cry anymore, but my eyes have a mind of their own these days. "Everything is wrong. I had to come home and see you. I just... I just needed to see you."

It's so late, and I'm so tired. I don't know what I want to say to her, but I can't do it tonight. Instead, I hug her again, placing my face against her shoulder.

"Did Patton Fletcher hurt you?" Her voice is not scolding. It's protective and warm, just like a big sister ought to be.

How long has it been since she was able to help me like this?

I don't even care.

"No... I mean, not directly." Lifting my head, our eyes meet. Her hazel ones are so full of concern, I want to talk to her about this, but I can't do it tonight. "It's really complicated."

"Let me make you some tea. I have a special blend for when I'm feeling down. I call it gogo-gi. It's made with gogi berries and rose hips, lemon oil, melon, and hibiscus. It'll make you feel right as rain."

I don't bother reminding her I don't like hot tea. I'm too tired, and honestly, with the way my insides are, I'm willing to try anything if it helps me feel less devastated.

Following her into the kitchen, I sit at the long table across from the bar as she fills the kettle.

Looking around at the modern appliances, I can't hold back any longer. "What happened to the house?"

She pauses, seeming confused. She follows my eyes around the room then returns to me. "What do you mean?"

"It looks amazing. When did you do all this work? How could I not have known?"

"Well… I guess I should have told you." Her lips press together as she clicks on the gas stove. "But I was pretty confident this would work out, and it was clear you weren't planning to come back here to live any time soon. So I did my research and crunched the numbers… And you were so close to finishing business school. I didn't want you to worry."

Listening to her explaining makes me smile in spite of myself. Renée rambles just like I do when she's nervous. It's soothing being with her, feeling our family connection so strong.

"It's okay, I'm not mad. It really looks great, but how?"

"I got a loan from the bank about a year ago—"

"Another loan? Renée!"

"Now just hang on…" She takes down two mugs from the cabinet and two shiny silver steepers from the drawer. "It was a small-business loan. I renovated this ole place, and now I have it up on Airbnb."

I put my elbow on the table and drop my head against my hand. "A concept I'd like to put out of my brain for a few days."

"I got the idea from Fletcher International, and you wouldn't believe it. I made almost five thousand dollars a week last summer!"

I sit up quick when she tells me that. "What the hell?"

Nodding, she puts two scoops of tea in a silver infuser and places it in a mug. Then she takes another canister and repeats the process with a different tea.

"Let me get this straight… You rent the house to people visiting the area, and what? When they arrive you all sleep back there together? Isn't that sort of crowded?"

"Oh no, I stay with Ms. Hazel when guests are here. I let them have the whole house. That's how I'm able to clear so much money."

"Why have I been worrying about you being able to make ends meet?"

The kettle starts to whistle, and she laughs, shaking her head. "I don't know. I tell you every time you call I'm doing fine, not to worry about me."

It's true. She always tells me she's fine, but I never believe her. I've been living in fear she's going to have another breakdown when the reality is, she's putting her accounting degree to work and making a buttload of money.

Walking to where I'm sitting, she puts the mug in front of me. "Now only let that steep for two minutes or it gets bitter."

"Okay."

"The best part is I've got the small-business loan completely paid off, and I've been doubling up on my student loan payments. I'm really making headway on getting out of debt."

My silly eyes heat, and I almost start to cry again. "You're doing so well."

Her brow furrows, and she reaches over, taking the steeper out of my mug. "Rocky, that's not something to cry about. What's the matter?"

Shaking my head, I look down at my mug. "I'm just so happy for you."

Her lips tighten, and she takes the strainer out of her mug, watching me closely as she sips her tea.

Inhaling a shaky breath, I do the same. Then I pull back quickly. "This is good!"

"It's the quality of the tea leaves and the flowers. Oh, and the metal steeper. I had no idea how much of a difference it makes compared to those paper tea bags you get at the grocery store. My goodness." She shakes her head like it's a travesty.

I take another sip, and I don't know if it's the warmth of the liquid or the relief of finding my sister okay and thriving... Or if it's because I just drove almost eight hours today after not really sleeping for three days... Or if it's my broken heart. "I'm so tired, sis. Would you be offended if I went to bed?"

"Come on." She stands, placing our mugs on the table and taking my hand. I let her lead me back to my new and improved room, and she gives me another hug, stroking the back of my head. "You just curl up and sleep now. We can talk about everything tomorrow. Okay?"

I nod, feeling like I'm eleven years old again. She goes to the door, and I toe off my shoes. I don't even remove my jeans. As soon as I hit the mattress, I'm asleep.

"Now hold its little head like this." I'm standing beside my sister with my arms over a five-gallon fish tank filled with blankets and a heating pad as she holds the head of a kitten so tiny it's little eyes aren't even open yet. It's the size of my palm.

"I'm afraid I'm going to hurt it," I whisper.

My hands shake, and my heart is beating too fast.

"You're not. Now come on, we need to get this done, so I can do the other one." I watch as she uses a Q-tip to swab the tiny thing's eyes with antibiotics. "When I found Binky, the fleas were just eating her alive. I cleaned her up, and she's been growing like a weed ever since."

She takes the kitten from me and puts it back in its chenille-blanket cocoon inside the incubator. Then she takes a teeny black kitten and hands it to me. I watch as she repeats the process. "I almost couldn't see Midnight, it was so dark. You know, I think the lord just brings them to me. He knows I'll help them."

Placing the small animal back in the incubator, she closes the lid and watches them. "They're too much work for the shelters to keep them." Straightening, she heads for the door of her small shed. "We'll have to feed them again in about four hours. Every week I get to add an hour between feedings. When I first found them, it was every two!"

I hesitate a moment, watching the little creatures bob their tiny heads before burrowing down and falling asleep again. "They're so cute."

"They're so strong." She waits for me at the door, and I walk slowly to where she's standing. "I learn so much from them. It's so healing."

I follow her out to where two bikes are waiting near the gate. "How do you know how to do all of this?"

"YouTube." She throws a leg over her bike, and I do the same.

"You've got to be kidding me."

"I'm not. You can find out how to do just about anything on YouTube. It's amazing. I even got some tips on making my Airbnb listing more desirable."

She pedals faster, and I pump to keep up. So far, since I got up this morning, after a quick breakfast of yogurt and fruit... and coffee. I insisted she let me make coffee, and we've been making the kitten rounds... or cat rounds. We fed all ten of the cats that live at Ms. Hazel's sprawling old place. These neonatal kittens are new, but Renée insists they're not as much work as they seem.

"Can we go out to the beach now?" I call from behind her.

"Just for a little while. I have to work a shift at the store this afternoon."

"Why are you working at the store if you make almost 20K a month with Airbnb?"

Her laugh floats back to me on the salt breeze. "I don't make that much every month. That's only in the summertime. Once Labor Day passes, it all dies down."

We pedal down the familiar lanes, past towering oak trees with their black trunks and dark green leaves hanging low over the roads. We bump over wooden bridges and quiet two-lane highways. It's just like we used to do as kids, running to the beach to spend the day.

Finally, we're out to the path that crosses Bull River. We abandon our bikes on the brown sand and jog out to the water. Renée's white skirt whips in the breeze, but I'm in skinny capri pants. The tide is out, but the sand is wet, and the wind blows our hair back. It really is like we're kids again. We did this every single day when school was out, playing on the beach like mermaids who'd just been given legs.

When we're out of breath, we start to walk, side by side, headed nowhere in particular. After several minutes of silence, my sister glances at me sideways. "Are you ready to tell me what happened?"

Am I? I don't know.

I take a deep breath that does little to ease the pain of the hole in my chest. If anybody can help me, it's the person walking beside me—and not just because she's a key factor in what happened, but because she knows me better than anyone.

"Why didn't you ever tell me why you left Nashville?"

Her chin pulls back like she's surprised by the question. "I don't know. I didn't want to talk about it."

The wind blows both our hair around our faces and we walk quickly, leaving matching footprints in the sand.

"Will you tell me now?" My voice is quiet. I need her to tell me.

"Oh, Rocky..." She looks up at the sky. "Why does it matter? I was a different person then. I was trying so hard to be a part of a world where I didn't belong."

I'm chewing my lip thinking about this. "It seemed like you belonged there. You graduated at the top of your class. You passed the CPA exam on your first try—"

"Yes, I knew how to do the work. I was good at it..." She looks away. "But the longer I was there, the more I felt like my soul was suffocating."

Scrubbing my fingers against my forehead, I don't know what to make of this new information. "I thought you liked accounting. You told me you were so excited when you got the job at Fletcher. You were joining corporate America."

"I was," she nods. "I was excited to be out of school. I was thrilled this amazing firm hired me right out the gate. I loved feeling like I was part of something big. It was like something out of a movie... Until it turned bad."

We walk a little more. She crosses her arms over her chest, and I briefly hug her waist. "What made it bad? Was it Marley? Did he hurt you?"

Her brow furrows, and she studies me. "Is that what he told you?"

"No." I shake my head. "He never told me anything. I just heard things."

We walk several more steps. The only sounds are our feet squeaking on the sand, the wind blowing around us, and the seagulls crying overhead.

"I didn't tell you because I felt so overwhelmed. It was like I started something that snowballed until it was completely out of my control."

"Were you sexually assaulted?"

"You mean like... raped?"

I nod, and she shakes her head. "Marley's not like that."

"Were you sexually harassed?"

Her brow furrows, and she chews her lip. "That's the part that gets kind of... fuzzy." She looks out to the horizon then back to me. "Marley and I were friends. After a while, we started having lunch together, then he started buying me little things. One week he stopped by my office with an ice cream cone or the next week he'd say he bumped into a guy selling flowers, so he bought me one... That kind of thing. It was sweet."

"Okay..."

"Then we went for drinks a few times after work. Only... it wasn't just the two of us. Everybody would go."

"They still do that..." I'm doing my best to understand. It all sounds pretty harmless so far.

"One night he kissed me." She drops her chin, and her cheeks turn pink. "It was a really great kiss. I guess that's when I started thinking of him as more than just a work friend. Then it got to where we'd slip into the break room or the supply closet at work and make out..."

She blinks quickly, shaking her head like she's embarrassed.

"But you were into it?"

"I was into it." We walk a little farther, and she's quiet.

I feel like I'm about to burst. "But...?"

She shrugs, holding her hands out. "He started trying for more when we were together. If I'd wear a skirt... well, you know."

"And you told him no?"

"Well... not exactly. I told him I was worried."

"Because you were coworkers?"

"Because the rates of STDs have been skyrocketing in recent years. Have you heard about this?" Her eyes are round, and I'm confused.

"No?"

"The CDC has reported a rise in the number of syphilis cases... Syphilis! Not to mention herpes is rampant. And the medicines have terrible side effects..."

Holy shit, and I thought I rambled. "Renée... Stop for just a second." We stop walking, and I hold her arms. "What are you saying? He wouldn't take no for an answer?"

"He wouldn't get tested. He said he'd just use a condom, but I said what happens if the condom breaks? What happens when he's pulling out? A drop of semen could escape and—"

"Renée. Did you want to have sex with him or not?"

Her head tilts to the side and she starts walking slowly. "I don't know. Everyone's so quick to jump into bed these days. I liked being his friend. I liked kissing him… I hoped Patton might talk to him for me. They were practically brothers. I hoped he would tell him to stop with the pressure."

"Instead he fired you. He ran you out of town." My jaw is set.

"I don't think he understood what I was saying." A line pierces her forehead, and she hugs her waist. "He was just so *evil* about it."

Anger burns in my stomach. "What did he do?"

She squeezes her eyes shut. "It was more what he said. I'll be the first to admit making out at work is unprofessional, but Patton made it sound like… He looked at me with those black eyes and asked me how much I wanted."

"How much… what?"

"Money. He thought I wanted money. I guess he thought I was trying to blackmail him or something… I don't know. He said if I tried to turn it into some kind of scandal, he'd bury me." Her voice breaks. "But I didn't want a scandal. I liked Marley… He seemed so sad, but sweet. I still think about him sometimes."

Her chin drops, and I put my arm around her waist. "I'm so sorry, Ray."

My stomach cramps. *Bully* doesn't even cover how Patton treated her.

She clears her throat and seems to come back from that memory. "I don't know." Her eyes meet mine, and she smiles. "Forgiveness is a gift you give yourself, right? It was the last red flag I needed. After that meeting with Patton, I knew I didn't belong there."

We're at the bikes, and I think about this. "Or maybe you just crossed paths with the devil. Another firm might be completely different."

"No." She shakes her head. "I'll never go back to that life. I'm so much happier now. And... Oh my goodness, look at the time!"

She hops on her bike, pushing the pedals. "I've got to get to the store. I'll see you there or back at the house."

I wave, watching her growing smaller the farther she rides down the path.

I'm glad she's happy. I'm glad she's found a life that works for her. She says I can stop worrying about her, and I see she's right.

Only... now what?

Rubbing my forehead, I try to figure out what I'm supposed to do. Should I go to California? If she's okay, I can at least protect my career... and I won't have to see him.

Pain like a knife twists in my heart. An image of me pinned naked against Patton's bare chest under a waterfall, his strong arms over mine, his hands in my hair, his possessive gaze...

I won't have to see him.

Fresh tears flood my eyes.

Why does that feel even worse?

CHAPTER Twenty-Eight

Patton

"Taron left things in good shape." Marley is in my office, and I'm staring out the window thinking of dark hair and blue eyes.

Seven days, and I still can't shake the feeling of her in my arms. I can't stop remembering a brief moment in time when I felt good, a moment when I could stop fighting. A moment when I let go, and the past didn't matter.

"These accounts practically run themselves." He keeps talking. "The building managers take care of the details, and we collect our share of the rents. It's pretty brilliant."

Cutting my eyes to him, I smirk. "Are you just figuring out how our company works?"

He leans back grinning. "This part of it."

We made it to Friday, and I'm gratified he looks happy. "How's it going at home? How are you sleeping?"

"Good. Getting the full eight hours."

"Let me know if that changes."

"I will." He stands, walking to the window. "So back to Taron… While he's got everything running, what now?"

My brow furrows, and I think how Rocky knew exactly what to do. One day in, and she never let us miss a beat. "You read the trades. Make notes of which companies are doing short, eighteen-month to three-year deals in the states and where. Then you cold call. Or cold-email, I guess."

He makes a noise. "Sales."

"What about it?"

"I've never sold a fucking thing in my life."

"Time to start."

"Come on, Patton." He leans against the windowsill. "Send me to California. Raquel is way better at this kind of work than I am. It's not my gig."

I wish it were that easy. "Speaking of, we still need to hire someone." I flip through the résumés Sandra put on my desk, handing half to him. "Help me sort through these. I was thinking an intern for social media—"

"That right there's a mistake. Your social media marketing is your most powerful tool. You should give it to someone who knows this company inside and out and cares about it as much as you do."

My eyes flicker to his. "You?"

"Damn straight."

"I need you for more important things."

"You're not hearing me. Nothing's more important—"

"Having clients who need office space, having elite properties for clients, putting the two together. That's more important."

He shakes his head, exhaling an impatient breath as he flops down on my couch. "You're missing the big picture..." Then he holds up a résumé. "Mary Jones. She's perfect. MBA from Kellogg, four years in—"

"Not another woman." I flip through the ones I'm holding, discarding the females. I can feel his eyes on me, but I don't care how it makes me look in my own office with just the two of us present. "See if you can find an Arab man."

Marley gives me a confused look. "An Arab man? That's very specific."

"It's good to have diversity."

"You care about that?"

"Yes." No more women... *Dammit.*

"Okay..." He keeps flipping. "Here's one. Alex Whitehead... unappealing last name, but he's a homeboy—got his MBA at Owen. Not Arab, sorry. At least not that I can tell..."

"Give me that." He leans forward, and I take it, quickly scanning the sheet. "How did I miss this?"

"See, I'm good for something."

Reaching out I tap the button on my phone. Sandra's voice rings through the line. "What's up?"

"Hey, get me this Alex Whitehead in for an interview. As soon as possible. Work it into my schedule."

"On it."

We disconnect, and I think about what he said. "Don't do that. You're good for a lot of things."

"A lot of things that fuck up your life." He's back to flipping pages, and I study him a moment.

Marley is more than a fuck up. The thing with Renée, well, I've gone over how that situation broke down in my mind so many times, I can't do it anymore. I was inexperienced at being a CEO, I thought you could handle an office the way you handle a group of Marines...

Renée didn't argue with me. Hell, she barely spoke. I asked her what she wanted, how much money it would take, and she wilted like a flower.

Then Marley went off the rails. At least for now, it seems he's cut back on the partying. If only he'll stay on the wagon. Nobody falls off quite as spectacularly as my friend.

He grumbles at me. "Whoever we get has to be better than Buckingham."

"Who hired that guy?"

"You." He looks at me, and I lean back in my chair with a groan.

"He took a job with Braden." I wonder how long he was courting them behind my back. Jobs like that don't just appear overnight.

"Good thing we locked down Hastings and Key." He slaps another résumé to the side. "I can't imagine that bastard holding the purse strings on us."

Stephen Hastings is no walk in the park. At least he'll let us run our business.

A knock on my door draws my attention. I look up to see Sandra standing there with a puzzled expression.

"What's up?"

"First, Alex Whitehead is a woman."

I cut my eyes at Marley, and he only shrugs. "It's a gender-neutral name."

My gaze returns to Sandra. "And…?"

"She'd like to withdraw her application. She said she was unaware of the 'toxic work environment' when she submitted her résumé for consideration."

Sandra does little air quotes, and now I'm really frowning. "What the hell?"

"Problem solved." Marley slaps another résumé down on the side table.

More like brand-new fucking problem. "What the hell is that supposed to mean?"

"Your guess is as good as mine." She crosses her arms. "It's not like we have a lot of turnover. Yes, Taron just left, and you fired Jerry, but—"

"On the record, Jerry accepted a position at Braden Investment Group."

"Off the record?" Sandra gives me a pointed look I don't particularly like, considering she's my secretary.

"Off the record is nothing you need to worry about."

"You've told me not to worry before. I think it's time you started letting me in on some of this stuff. I can keep an eye on the job boards and keep you posted on the scuttlebutt."

"What are you talking about?"

"She's talking about social media gossip. The stuff you think is so unimportant." Marley's moved to lying on his back on the sofa, sorting through résumés. "I think I found another guy."

Sandra's still waiting, and I glance up at her. "Off the record, Jerry tried to extort money from us. He objected to Raquel being promoted over him, and when I wouldn't change my mind, he threatened me then quit."

"Oh my God!" Sandra gasps.

Marley only mutters, "Told you I hated that guy."

"Yeah." I study the stack of papers in front of me. Remembering how that all went down. Remembering the shattered look in Rocky's eyes.

I want a drink. Or a fucking cigarette.

Slipping my hand into the pocket of my blazer, I pop another white square out of the blister packet and put it in my mouth.

Sandra's eyebrow cocks. "In all the years we've worked together I have never seen you chew gum."

"Few things are less professional. It's that nicotine shit."

Her eyebrows shoot up. "Really… Is it working?"

"No." I toss the résumés aside. "See what you can find out about this toxic office whatever—"

"Toxic work environment," she supplies.

"See if you can find out what that's about and let me know. Also, see if this Ryan Daniels can come in for an interview tomorrow." My eyes go to Marley. "Can you drink? I need a whiskey."

"I'm on a cleanse, but I'll be happy to sit beside you while you destroy your liver." That's just perfect. Standing, I grab my phone. "Whatever—just don't join a cult."

"I have been looking into Buddhism…"

Waving my hand, I nod. "Buddhism is fine. No cults."

Friday night at AJ's gets more crowded as the evening wears on. A live band plays a mix of country covers and what I assume are originals. We are in Music City, after all. Marley and I are sitting at a high top table on the patio overlooking the skyline.

"So Jerry tried to extort us." He's sipping an O'Doul's Amber. "Sounds like there's more to the story. What did you not tell Sandra?"

I'm on my third whiskey, so it's less painful to talk about it. "He dragged up that business with Renée. Really stuck it to me… right in front of Rocky."

"Rocky?"

"Raquel, sorry." My eyes are fixed on my glass, but I'm seeing her eyes fill with tears. The things she said… *Broken and cruel*. Two whiskeys, and it still hurts.

"Rocky?"

"It's a family nickname." She used to wrestle with her dad… I've got to stop this now.

He's strangely quiet, and I glance up at him.

"What?"

"Nothing. It's cute." He takes another pull of the tawny near beer. "She's a fighter."

"Yeah." I polish off my drink as the waitress approaches and order another, anything to stop the flood of images tormenting me.

Marley waves that he's fine for now, and we both fall silent. The band's not bad, but I'm not in the mood to feel good. I've never felt like this about a woman, like I'm not sure how I'll put her out of my mind.

"She really made an impression on you." Marley holds the empty bottle, turning it in his hands. I can't answer that, and he adds under his breath. "Lost opportunities and missed chances... they suck."

My phone buzzes, and I take it out of my breast pocket. A text from Sandra's on the face: *Jerry's running his mouth.*

She sends me a link, and when I tap on it, it takes me to a brief in *Nashville Notes*, a rinky-dink online journal run by the Nashville Association of Business and Industry. I scan it, and the more I read, the hotter my blood gets.

"What the fuck?"

"What?" Marley leans closer to check out what's on my screen. "Area business leader and CEO Patton Fletcher throws hush money at sex scandal?"

Obvious click-bait.

His brow furrows, and he studies my face. "Sex scandal? Is this about..."

My hand tightens on my fresh glass of whiskey, and I read aloud. "Shake up at Fletcher International. Less than a week after senior partner Martin Randall was hospitalized for exhaustion, the tech-based corporate realtor vying to be 'the Airbnb for business' has lost three senior staffers in as many days.

'Taron Rhodes, VP of client development, Jerry Buckingham, senior account executive, and Raquel Morgan, the newest member of the Fletcher team have all left the building.

'According to Buckingham, CEO Patton Fletcher paid hush money a year ago to keep Renée Morgan, former Fletcher CPA, from going public with sexual assault allegations against Randall...'"

I can't read any more of this bullshit. Tapping the number in my contacts, I wait as it rings.

Marley's face is pale. "Sexual assault? I didn't assault her..."

A gravelly voice finally answers my call. "NABI, this is Hank."

"Hank, Patton Fletcher here."

Shuffling on the other end, and he clears his throat. "Patton. I was expecting a call from you."

"I hope it's because you're preparing a retraction. Since we're old friends, I thought I'd give you a chance to correct yourself before my lawyer does it for you."

I use the term *friends* loosely.

"Aly's got her facts straight, Patton. I checked them myself before approving the story."

"Her facts are not straight. Taron took a leave of absence and Ms. Morgan has been offered a promotion."

"That's not what Jerry told us…"

"Jerry Buckingham is a dick, and I fired his ass for insubordination. What you're printing is his sad attempt to strike back."

"So you're saying this business with the CPA never happened?"

Fuck. I hesitate… which looks bad. "You misrepresented the facts."

"Jerry provided documents showing you gave her money a year ago—"

"I didn't give her money. I never even spoke to her."

"But you did personally secure a small-business loan on behalf of Ms. Morgan?"

Shit, I should not have called Hank. I need to hang up the phone before I make matters worse. This is PR Crisis Mismanagement 101.

"You'll be hearing from my lawyer." I disconnect and consider slamming my phone against the table. Repeatedly.

Marley's face is twisted. "What now?"

Fire is in my veins. "You got a cigarette?"

"You're not supposed to smoke here."

"I don't give a damn."

He fishes in his pocket, and I fire it up. I'm going to hell anyway. Slamming back the fourth whiskey, I'm on my feet, grinding my jaw. *Nashville Notes* is a shitty little gossip rag that every business leader in this town reads. Hell, anyone doing business in Nashville reads it.

"Fuck…" I growl louder.

"Stop pacing." Marley's voice is low. "The waitress is coming. We'd better go."

He's on his feet, putting an arm across my chest.

"Sir, you have to take that outside."

"We are outside." I've had too much whiskey.

"I mean off the premises. Please don't make me call security." Her smile is flinty, like I'm not the first belligerent smoker she's encountered.

"Come on, Patton. Let's go, man." Marley's pulling on my shoulder, and my eyes flare.

The waitress's expression turns to fear, and she takes a step back, doing a little wave toward the bar.

"Colleen, is it?" I read her nametag. "Some little worm is trying to fuck with me."

"Hey, we're just going. No worries." Marley smiles and then steps to me. "Don't make things worse. Let's. Go."

A big guy is headed in our direction, and my first thought is *I can take him*. My second thought is my fucking dad.

Clenching my fist, I take one last drag then drop the cigarette in my drink. " Sorry, Colleen. We're leaving."

She puts her hand on the bouncer's arm, and says something quietly. I'm behind Marley heading to the door. Pinching the bridge of my nose, I close my eyes as we descend, trying to stop my fury. Trying to think this through.

"They're eight hours ahead of us in Dubai… Abu Dhabi… I need to call David."

"Our lawyer?" Marley's lost in his own thoughts. "Did Renée tell you I assaulted her?"

"No." His words fan the anger in my chest. "Don't even address that."

A tone sounds, and the silver doors open.

Everything shifts.

Right in front of us is Jerry with his stupid head thrown back in a laugh. On his arm is a blonde, and I see he's with Chip Braden. The two see me at the same time, and while Chip looks smug, Jerry's face goes white.

My fist clenches, and it's too late for clear thinking. Lunging forward, I catch Jerry by the collar as he tries to run.

"Patton!" His voice breaks on a scream as I punch him in the face.

Damn, that felt good is quickly followed by screaming pain. I might have broken my hand.

I don't give a shit. I'm pulling back to hit him again, harder, when Marley has me around the bicep, pulling me back.

"Patton, stop." He's right in my ear, and I see the crowd gathering, all with phones out taking photos.

Struggling against my friend, I glance down to see Jerry on the floor holding his face. "You're going to pay for that, Fletcher."

"Then I'd better make it worth it." Marley's not strong enough to hold me, and I'm going in for another punch when two men grab me, hustling me from the lobby out the doors.

"That's enough, Tough Guy." The big one holds me outside as Jerry's crew quickly files onto the elevator. "Don't let me see you back here tonight, or I'm calling the cops."

This guy's the size of the Rock, and even though my insides are on fire, I back down. Marley has his keys, and I follow him to the car. He studies me like I might go off again. Hell, I might.

I breathe slowly, doing my best to calm my wrath. The worst thing I could do tonight is get arrested.

"Take me back to the office. I've got to try and fix this."

CHAPTER
Twenty-Nine

Raquel

"ANOTHER MERMAID... NO, WHAT IS IT?" RENÉE HOLDS UP A pearl-glazed mermaid statue. "Oh! It's a lamp."

I'm standing behind stacks of boxes holding a price-scanner gun. "Hand it over." She holds the base toward me, and I zip it. "Inventory is fun!"

She gives me a look. "That's because you've got the counter gun."

I point it at her. "Drop your weapons. I said drop 'em!"

"Stop quoting *Star Wars* and keep scanning."

We're in the small storage closet at the back of Ms. Hazel's store. It's Saturday morning, and all week I've trailed Renée on her daily rounds.

Every day we do our cat care... Every night, too, with the tiny kittens. I feel like a new mom getting up every four hours to help her bottle-feed Binky and Midnight. After breakfast, we ride our bikes out to the beach and walk around, then we do whatever Ms. Hazel needs at the store in the afternoons. Today she has us doing inventory to get ready for the holiday rush.

Renée and I have talked about everything except why I'm here.

I know she's waiting. I'm waiting. I'm afraid if I start talking about Patton, I'll start crying again, and thankfully, the water works have stopped.

I've only heard from him once since I got here, a lone text sent late on Wednesday night, after I'd gone to bed.

None of this works without you.

Reading it made my heart beat too fast. It made the tears start again. I cried myself to sleep and was late to help her on that day, and now, just remembering it, my chest aches.

I still haven't decided what to do about California, and my time is almost up. I've got to do something. Can I honestly work with him when I still feel this way?

"I love getting ready for the holidays." She pulls out another mermaid lamp and holds it to me to scan before arranging it on what is now the mermaid shelf. "We get to order tons of new stuff, and when it all starts coming in, it's like Christmas morning."

Speaking of boxes, I open a new one that's filled with crinkled paper and bubble wrap. "What's this?"

Reaching inside, I take out a glass vase that's deep purple on the bottom and blue on the top.

"Oh, those must be our pieces from SCAD." She walks over and takes the vase, turning it side to side. "It's blown glass."

"It's beautiful. It looks like it's made of water."

"The art students send us their best pieces to sell. I love seeing what they make."

She pulls back more paper, and we both gasp. Inside are blown glass balls with swirls of colors through them. Some are rainbow, some are blue and white like the ocean, some are amber and green like the sunset.

"We need to price them and put them out." She digs farther into the box.

"How do we do that?"

"Here." She hands me a sheet. "These are their suggested prices. If you think they're right, go with it. Or price it whatever you think will sell."

"Me?" My jaw drops. "I don't know how to price original art."

"Then just go with what they suggest. Unless you think it's too low... We can always run a sale." She reaches for my gun. "Give me this."

I slant my eyes at her, and she laughs. "It's my turn!"

For several minutes we work in silence. I neatly write the prices on the tiny tags attached to the art.

After a while, I feel Renée watching me and glance up. "Am I doing it wrong?"

She only smiles. "I was just thinking how nice it's been having you here. I'm going to miss you when you go back to Nashville."

Blinking down to the list, I know what she's doing. She's letting me know it's time to tell her what happened. *Am I ready?* I suppose I have to be.

"I'll head back tomorrow, I guess." Just saying it flushes me with nerves.

"You can stay as long as you want. The only possible conflict is if the house rents, but we can figure that out."

"Thanks, but I can't hide forever."

She scans a few more bar codes, and I make a few more price tags.

Her voice is gentle when she asks, "Why are you hiding?"

I take a vibrant orange and yellow vase from the box and stare at it, feeling the pain fresh as ever. "I didn't protect my chin."

Her eyes soften. "He got you on the ropes?"

"I went all the way down."

She's around the box, pulling me into a hug at once. We stay that way several minutes while I do my best to calm my breathing, not to cry.

I can feel her stroking the back of my hair. "You know, those wrestlers always got back up and started fighting again. Even when they spun around like a top."

She catches my eye and winks.

I do my best to smile back. "It was all fake. You don't get up so fast from a real knockout."

Picking up the gun again, she returns to the shelves of stock. "I was afraid this might happen when you said you'd slept with him." She starts scanning bar codes. "I've never met anyone as dark as Patton Fletcher in my life."

I think about him cooking me hot chicken, holding me back from seeing the secret recipe. I think about that crazy place where we got pancakes in the mountains. "He wasn't all dark. He could be really funny sometimes."

"That's something I can't imagine." She digs on a bottom shelf and pulls out a stack of starfish clocks. "The Patton Fletcher I knew never laughed. Nothing mattered to him except closing the deal."

Chewing my lip, I think about it. "Marley mattered to him…" My voice trails off as I remember the mountains… His mom mattered. *I think I mattered…*

"I don't know. I walked away and never went back." She keeps scanning.

I'm almost to the bottom of my box. I pull out a blown-glass Christmas ornament and study the red and green lines.

"That's my problem. How can I work for a man who treated you like he did? You're my sister."

Her brow furrows, and she stops scanning. "Is that why you're here? You're thinking of quitting your job?"

"What else can I do?"

"But I'm okay, Rock. I'm better than okay—I'm happy. And you were happy there. I could hear it in your voice. Don't ruin your career for me."

"You're happy now, but you were not happy when you left there. I don't care what you say."

"I told you—"

"I know what you told me, but I also know you wouldn't return my calls. You stayed in bed for who knows how long." My stomach hurts remembering her that way. "You had a real crisis, and it was his fault."

She puts the gun down and walks to where I'm standing. "It wasn't his fault. Yes, he was a bastard, but I was glad to leave Fletcher International. I didn't return your calls because I didn't know what I was going to do. I didn't know what I was going to tell you. That's why I hid."

"You can always tell me anything."

"But I felt like I let you down." Her chin drops, and I see the guilt in her eyes. "We lost Mom and Dad. You needed me to be strong, to take care of you…"

"I just needed my sister."

Our watery eyes meet, and we hug again. "You've always got me. I'll do anything I can to help you." She squeezes tighter, exhaling a little sigh as she releases me. "Even if it means giving Patton Fletcher another chance."

Blinking away the mist in my eyes, I look at the ornament in my hand. "I kind of fell in love with him."

The side of her mouth tilts down in a little half-frown. "Then go back. You're the fighter in the family. Make him prove he's worth your love."

She gives me a nudge, and we head to the front of the store. Ms. Hazel is with a customer, so we smile and walk outside to where our bikes are waiting. We pedal slowly back to the house, and I look around, memorizing the scenery.

"I won't wait so long to come back for a visit next time."

"Then maybe you'll know what's going on around here." She's teasing, but I pull my bike up beside hers in the garage.

"You need to tell me more."

She waves a hand, and I follow her inside, watching the hem of her skirt sway as I think. Renée has always been more of a girly-girl, wearing skirts and beads. She likes drinking tea and not wearing makeup. Suits are not her style.

Thinking of her in Patton's office, keeping up with their corporate lifestyle… Of course she felt like a fish out of water.

We go to my room, and I take out my small suitcase and place items I'm not going to use tonight inside. I'm picking up my makeup when my phone starts to buzz on the dresser. I don't recognize the number on the screen.

"Telemarketer?" I look at Renée, but she's inspecting my toiletries. With a shrug, I slide my finger across the face. "Hello?"

"You have to be careful with these exfoliants. They contain microbeads." She holds up the tube of facial scrub.

"Hello, is this Raquel Morgan?" I don't recognize the female voice.

"Yes, can I help you?"

"They go straight into the ocean and end up in our fish… then in us." Renée's eyes are stern, and I hold my hand over my phone.

"Tell me the good ones, and I'll get just those."

"Sorry?" The female says.

"I'm sorry. I was talking to someone else. What is this about?"

Renée is still going. "Just check the ingredient list for polyethylene or polypropylene… these things should not be in your facial cleansers."

"Okay… I'll do that." I'm nodding as I step into the bathroom and close the door. "Sorry, what did you say your name is?"

"This is Aly Walden. I'm with NABI, Nashville Association of Business and Industry?"

"Oh, right. I think you spoke at one of my classes. At Owen Business School?"

"I sure did!" Her voice gets friendly. "I'm also a reporter for *Nashville Notes*."

"I'm not really familiar with—"

"It's a local business publication. Did you say you're out of town? I don't want to bother you if you're busy…"

I didn't say I was out of town, and she kind of sounds like she does want to bother me. "I'm actually just heading back to Nashville. I have to get back to work."

"At Fletcher International?"

"Yes…"

"Ms. Morgan, are you related to Renée Morgan?" The way she says it has my antenna up.

"She's my sister."

"Are you aware that Patton Fletcher paid your sister hush money a little over a year ago to keep her from going public with allegations of sexual assault at Fletcher International?"

I look at the closed door, frowning. "I was not aware of that. I'm pretty sure that's completely false."

"How sure would you say? Ninety percent sure? Eighty-five?"

This feels like she's fishing. "I'd better go. I'm sorry."

"Is it true you left because you were having sex with Patton Fletcher?" She speaks fast, clearly trying to get one more question in before I hang up.

Her question shocks me, and I quickly answer. "No. That's not why I left."

"So you did leave?"

"Ah, gotta go." I hit end before she can say another word. Then I stand staring at my phone. "What the hell?"

Grabbing the doorknob, I whip open the bathroom door to see my sister sitting on my bed with my toiletries sorted on either side of her while she holds up the organic lotion she made for me.

"I sorted them for you. These over here are bad bad bad.

These over here are not bad at all." She looks up and smiles sweetly. "Good work, sis!"

"It was purely accidental, I assure you."

"You're still using the lotion I made for you."

"I'm running low. Can you send me some more?"

"Sure!" She hops up like she's going to do it right this minute, and I fly through everything Renée has said about Patton this week—as well as what I know about Renée.

My sister is not sneaky. I'm one hundred percent sure she wouldn't say all the things she said about Patton if he gave her a bunch of money. Heck, I'm more sure she wouldn't take hush money if she had decided to say something... which now I know wouldn't have been anything, since Patton is a bastard, but he's not the reason she walked away from her promising career.

Her words, blended with mine.

She collects the "bad" tubes from the bed. "You know there are more than three hundred *thousand* plastic beads in a tube of facial scrub?"

"Renée. Listen to me a minute." She discards a tube of my favorite exfoliant and blinks at me. "Did you take any money from Patton Fletcher last year?"

Her head jerks back, then her nose wrinkles. "Take money? I haven't even spoken to Patton Fletcher in almost five years."

Pressing my lips together, I quickly pull up the Internet on my phone, searching for *Nashville Notes*. I don't have to dig. The second the site loads on my phone, I see the headline and teaser text at the top of the scroll.

"Oh my god..." My voice is quiet as I read the first few sentences. "Ray, I'm going to have to head on back now, I'm sorry."

I'm already moving, collecting my clothes and the acceptable toiletries into my small suitcase.

She's watching me, concern lining her brow. "Is everything okay?"

"I don't know. What I read is bad." I give her a tight hug. "It's possible, depending on how this is handled… Patton could lose his company."

"So you're running to help him?"

I hesitate, and it hits me what I'm doing. I lower my arms and look at her. "I guess I am." My insides are tight. I'm so mixed up right now.

Renée puts her hand on my arm and smiles. "It's your life. It's where you belong. Go."

Stepping forward, I give her another hug. "I love you."

"Protect your chin this time."

"I'll try."

CHAPTER Thirty

Patton

"You need to consider turning yourself in." I've been on the phone with my attorney, David Worth for almost an hour. "If he goes to the police ahead of you and files a complaint, you'll be cuffed and stuffed and trust me, the press will be all over that shit."

"Jerry's not going to go to the police." My swollen hand is under an ice pack Sandra prepared this morning. "He's done all the damage he needs with that fucking story."

"The video is on YouTube. It's clear you hit him without provocation."

"Without provocation?"

"We don't hit. We use our words." He's speaking like I'm in preschool.

"I've got a few words for that bastard." Words they won't print in *Nashville Notes*. "I need to see that video."

Tapping on my keyboard, I wake my laptop. It might make me feel better about not getting in that second punch. I can watch it on repeat.

"I talked to Hank as soon as I got your email. I apologized for your call, but I said it was understandable in light of the situation."

"Thanks." It's a sarcastic response.

"I told him if they didn't correct the parts of the story that are untrue, they would face litigation for slander and defamation. Apparently some of it is true? I'm your lawyer. You need to tell me these things."

Groaning, I push back on my chair. "There was some inappropriate conduct between Marley and the CPA, but it was not assault."

"You need to let him go. A public parting of ways would go a long way—"

"That's not happening. Marley means more to me than this fucking bullshit."

David exhales long. "Well, if you continue to employ someone who is clearly a liability, you'll keep me in paychecks."

"Congrats on the job security."

David chuckles. "I'm here if you need me."

"Thanks." He's here at $450 an hour.

It's a Saturday, and I've been in the office since the sun came up—busted hand, hangover, and all. Sandra has been screening my calls from realtors concerned about our clients, clients concerned about our realtors, media wanting more information.

So far, our expansion seems to be intact. I was able to convince our new UAE guys the story is typical U.S. tabloid gossip—all hearsay from a disgruntled former employee trying to make us look bad. Those guys were all too familiar with such matters, and to my pleasant surprise, they were willing to take my word a retraction is in progress.

That just leaves Hastings and Key.

I'm sure Remi is back from Seattle by now, but I can't tell if the story has legs. It's possible, if I shut up and leave it alone… and stop calling publishers or punching assholes in the face… it might blow over.

Leaning forward on my desk, I put my face in my hands. I'm tired, and the only thing I can think about is Rocky. Does she know about this? I haven't heard from her since she walked out.

I sent her one text this week, one night after a few drinks, and she never replied. Lifting my phone, I look at it now. ***None of this works without you.***

Shit, I cringe when I read it sober. I'm never that open with people.

The strange thing is, I want to be that open with her. She made me want things that never appealed to me before. I don't work without her. I don't care about any of this. The expansion, proving myself, what good is it if I'm alone?

"Jesus," I hiss, rubbing my forehead. I'm going to lose my mind if I stay in this office one more minute.

I'm about to walk out when my desk phone buzzes.

I hit the button for Sandra to speak. "Your dad's on Line 2."

Of course he is I've been waiting for this call all morning. "Thanks." We disconnect, and I take a beat before hitting the button.

"Patton here."

"What's going on down there, son?" The condescending tone in his voice makes my skin crawl.

"Oh, you know." I make my voice casual in spite of it. "I had to let Jerry Buckingham go, and he made up a bunch of sh-stuff and told it to the press. Not even the press, it's that crap NABI posts on the Internet.

"That everybody reads. This is tacky, George. A sex scandal?"

I'm pinching the bridge of my nose and counting to ten. "I'm handling it, dad. I just got off the phone with David. We're going to get them to post a retraction."

"Which no one will read. Do you need me to call Hank? He and I go way back."

"David already called him." I'm not about to say I called as well. "I appreciate the offer. You don't have to worry."

He breathes deeply, letting me hear it on the receiver. "I'll be keeping an eye on this."

"I really need to take this call." It's a lie. "Take care of yourself, Dad. We'll talk soon."

I disconnect before he can get another word in, and I'm out of my chair, out of my door. "I'm walking to get some lunch. Want anything?"

Sandra stands, pulling the strap of her purse over her shoulder. "I've got to pick up Ralph from the airport. If we're all done here…" She raises an eyebrow, and I hold up my hands.

"We're done. Thanks for coming in on a Saturday. I can manage the remaining fires." I hope.

"Wanted to be sure I had a job to come back to on Monday."

"Right." Nice vote of confidence. "Have a good weekend."

She hesitates at her desk as I keep going. "You know I remember how Marley was with that girl… Renée." This makes me pause to hear her out. "It was the one time I thought he might be okay. He was calm with her. He talked to her. No pretense. She seemed to like him, too…"

"Are you saying there's a silver lining out there?"

"If there is, it's still a ways off." She bends down, clicking her mouse to log off. "But I'm rooting for you."

Walking on the street helps me put everything in perspective. It's a cool fall Saturday in Nashville, the tourists are out *en masse*, and my problems feel small by comparison. I'm a corporate guy in Music City.

Nashville is about dreams and country singers, it's about having fun and then crying in your beer. It's the place where an appliance salesman can walk into a recording studio and walk out the Man in Black. I should take comfort dreams come true here, but I can't stop thinking about her.

I walk until I run out of road. Standing on the banks of the

Cumberland River, I remember the night I pulled Marley down from the railing. I should have known then what was coming, but I was too blind to see it. The brown water rushes by, and I watch the currents, thinking about what comes next. He hasn't been in the office today. I didn't call him. He needs to rest, and he did enough last night, saving my ass from jail.

David says I need to fire him, but I'd never do that. At the same time, he isn't happy here. He doesn't want to do this work any more than Taron does. I tried to make a place for them, but I've got to let them go.

It's what I do.

Don't hold onto people too tightly, that way they can't hurt you when they go.

There's only one person I'm holding onto, and it hurts like hell.

She's gone, and I have to let her go and get back in the game. But how do I go back to what I was before? How do I make myself only care about my work again? I've got to figure it out. I've worked too long and too hard for this.

The office is dark when I return. The sun is setting, and I don't even know why I walked back here. I should go to my empty penthouse.

Yeah, that sounds appealing.

Dropping into my chair, I swipe my computer to wake it up, checking to see if David's had any luck with Hank. I should watch that YouTube video again. Watching me punch Jerry in the face, seeing his stupid face as he hits the ground, is about the only thing that makes me smile right now.

My office phone rings, and I stare at it a moment. Sandra's not here to screen it, but only a handful of people have my direct number. I place my hand on the receiver and let it ring once more before picking up.

"Fletcher speaking."

"Patton, it's Stephen." At the sound of his voice, I'm on guard. Stephen Hastings doesn't make casual calls.

"I take it you saw the article?" No point in acting like we do small-talk.

"I saw it." His tone is clipped.

I don't really like waiting, so I don't. "Well?"

"Is it true?"

"The majority of it is false."

He exhales deeply. "Which minority is true?"

"Marley and our CPA had a... thing about five years ago. He developed a crush, I guess. I couldn't tell if it was reciprocated..."

"Jesus, Fletcher, that's the worst part. Turnover is understandable. All businesses deal with it, but sexual assault? You should have fired him."

"There was no assault." My voice is stern. "He kissed her a few times. I believe it was mutual affection."

"Then why the hush money?"

It's something I've been wondering all day. *How the fuck did that get out?*

"It wasn't hush money. I secured a loan so she could start a small business. As far as I know, she's ignorant of the entire deal. Her lender contacted her previous employers, and when they said she was going to be denied, I asked what it would take to approve it."

"Why?" His tone goes low.

Now I exhale deeply. "I wanted to help her. I felt... I wanted her to be okay."

The line goes quiet. He's thinking whatever the fuck he thinks. I think about that day in the office when I told the bank I'd cover her loan. It was a change for me, helping someone outside my family. Renée had been a ditsy young woman, but Marley had loved her. I wanted to make amends.

"I believe you." Stephen's voice is different. "I've been in situations like that myself."

"Okay." I sit a little straighter.

"We're going to stand by you, Fletcher. You and I butt heads, but I know you're better than what they're saying. I'm going to give Chip Braden a call as well. I think he'll be interested to know what kind of a man he's hired."

I don't know what to say, so I keep it professional. "Thanks, Stephen."

"Don't mention it."

We hang up, and I feel a strange mixture of relief and sadness. Is it possible I might survive this? Do I want to without her?

Standing, I walk to the window, looking out at the lights of the city. I try to think of anything I can do to change things between us. I already extended an olive branch, albeit a secret one. Perhaps if I went there and apologized in person…

Taking my phone off the desk, I slip it in my coat pocket. I'm just about to grab my keys when a figure enters my office. She's quiet, dressed in all white, and I want to rub my eyes. I want to be sure I'm not asleep.

"Rocky?"

"Hi." Her voice sounds so good. "I came as soon as I heard."

"You heard about the article?"

"Yeah."

"You were worried about me?" The tiniest flicker of warmth sparks in my stomach.

"I thought you might need backup. I'm pretty good in a fight."

God, I love this woman. "It's been a bit of a shit show these last twenty-four hours."

"But you're smiling. Does that mean you came through it?"

"For now." I walk around my desk, closer to her. "It's possible we might have survived."

Her eyes go to my hand, and her lips part. "What happened to your hand?" She closes the space between us, touching me gently. It feels so good. "Is it broken?"

"I don't know. I haven't had a chance to get it checked." She turns my hand over and tries to move my fingers. "Ahh…" I wince, and worried blue eyes snap to mine.

Such pretty blue eyes. My stomach tightens, and I want to trace that hair off her cheek, push it behind her ear.

She's here.

Ginger and coconut.

Her lips press into a line. "Did you punch the wall?"

"Oh, it's better than that." I chuckle. "You haven't seen the video?"

"There's a video?"

"I punched Jerry."

Her hand flies to cover her mouth, but I see her smile. I see her eyes mist. "Sorry, but that's awesome."

"That's pretty much the general response."

Her hand drops to her side, and she turns away from me. "I got a call from that reporter. I told her the story was entirely false."

"Thanks."

Her eyes are on her shoes, and she hesitates. "You helped my sister get that loan?"

Clearing my throat, I nod. "I didn't know she had a breakdown. I'm sorry she did."

"She says she didn't. She says she's never been happier in her life." The tone of her voice matches the surprise I feel. "You really helped her. I didn't believe how well she's doing until I saw it in person."

"I'm glad." As I say the words, I realize how very much I mean them. "I'd like to see her. I'd like to tell her I'm sorry for what I said."

"You would?" Her nose wrinkles as she looks up at me.

"Yes."

"That can be arranged."

Watching her, I remember holding her in that waterfall, her body naked and warm against mine. I remember feeling like I'd found what I'd been missing.

I've got to try one last time to get her back.

"Before you left, you said you didn't think I was cruel." Looking down, I rub the back of my neck with my good hand. "A long time ago, I did want to help others. It blew up in my face. It ruined three lives, and I guess I shut down."

I've never told anyone this—not even our assigned therapist.

"Because of what happened in the jungle?" Her voice is soft.

"Because of that… because of what happened after… I became so consumed with proving myself, proving I was as good or better than my dad. Proving I wasn't damaged."

"You're not the man I thought you were." Our eyes meet, and hers are misty.

"You're right." I want to hold her. "I was pretty wretched until you came along. You saved me, Raquel. You make me a better man."

I take a small step closer. "I'm in love with you."

Her eyes are blue pools of water. She blinks, and two tears hit her cheeks. Another step, and I'm right in front of her. I reach up and gently cup her cheeks in my hands. She doesn't pull away.

"I never thought I'd love anyone. I never cared about it until you walked into my life." Her hands are on my chest, and she's blinking quickly. "I'm no good without you. Will you give me a second chance to prove myself? I'll never let you down again."

It's quiet, but the chemistry between us is so strong. Her lips are so soft, so appealing.

"Say something." My voice is rough.

Her voice is soft and high. "I'll ramble."

That answer makes me smile. "At least I'll know where I stand."

She lowers her chin, and I let her step back. Clearing her throat, she adopts a professional tone. "I'm going to stay here. I decided to keep Taron's old job if the offer is still on the table."

"It is."

She steps carefully around my office as she speaks, and I drink in her beautiful form, from the beige heels she's wearing to the white jeans with rips in the knees to the cream sweater loose on her body. She's gorgeous.

"I expect all those things Jerry was talking about—the raise, the ownership share, more of a voice in meetings..."

"Of course."

"And I want a corner office."

"Done." I guess she knows I'm ready to give her anything. My cards are on the table.

She turns to face me, and her brow furrows. "You are different."

"In some ways." I take a step closer to her. "The majority is exactly the same."

I'm right in front of her. The only thing separating us is her crossed arms. "What's the same?"

"I'm still the boss."

Her lips tighten, and I think she might smile. "You're not the boss of me."

Now I'm fighting a smile. "You were always too independent."

"Can you live with that?"

"Can I touch you?" My insides are buzzing, and I want her in my arms.

Her arms uncross slowly. "I think we've reached an agreement."

"Is that a yes?"

Reaching out, she traces her fingers along the sleeve of my coat. "It's a yes, please."

My arms sweep around her.

I've got her.

Her soft body feels like heaven in my arms, and I close my eyes, pressing my lips to her brow, inhaling deeply of her hair. It's like standing on the top of a mountain. It's like facing the ocean and breathing in eternity.

Her hand touches the back of my neck, and I dip down, finding her lips with mine. Our mouths seal together, and when our tongues touch, surges of warmth flood through my stomach. She makes a soft noise, and I need to take her home.

"God, I've missed you." It's a low whisper in her ear as she presses her cheek to mine.

"I love you, Patton Fletcher."

Jesus. I didn't think I could feel any better, but those words almost bring me to my knees.

Lifting my head, I find her eyes. "You do?"

The most beautiful smile splits her cheeks, and she nods, laughing. She blinks and two more crystal tears fall onto her cheeks.

I cup her face in my hands and wipe them away with my thumbs. "You're going to marry me."

"Oh, am I?" That feisty twinkle is in her eye.

"You are." My arms tighten around her, pulling her closer. "None of this matters if you're not here."

"Then it will be Fletcher-Morgan International."

A laugh breaks from my throat, and I lift my chin, holding her tighter. "God, I love you."

"I love you." I feel her lips press against my neck. "I'm going to love being your wife."

"My little fighter."

My eyes close, and I think about those words. She's my wife. She's a fighter. She's exactly what I need on my side.

Maybe the fighting never stops, but with her in my corner, we can make it through the battles... no one left behind. She's my family.

I'll never forget.

The End.

Epilogue
Raquel

One year later

"You're fluent in Arabic, French, and... Turkish? Impressive." I flip through the résumé of the bright young man in the horn-rimmed glasses sitting across from me.

He looks like he weighs one hundred pounds soaking wet, and I briefly consider offering him my order of Extra Matzah soup with half a Turkey Rachel sandwich. But I'm a hungry pregnant lady.

Patton's having coffee, and Amir, our interviewee is drinking tea.

"I've picked up a little Spanish, but not much." He seems apologetic, but Patton's quick to reassure him.

"The ones you've listed are most important. We've been heavily recruiting in the UAE."

Narrowing my eyes, I smirk at him. My husband is finally getting his wish. I'm about to take off for six months of maternity leave, and Amir Al-Tamimi from Michigan applied to be my temporary replacement.

Patton's like a kid finally getting the new toy he's wanted for years.

"I'm so sorry." Amir looks at his watch. "I've got a class starting in twenty minutes."

"It's perfectly fine." I reach across the table to shake his hand. "We plan to go over our top applicants and make a decision this weekend. If that's you, are you available to start Monday?"

"Yes, ma'am." He does a little nod, shaking my hand.

"Great. I'm hoping I can run our new hire through the basics before I leave."

"Thank you." He turns to my husband, who has risen from his seat. They shake and he offers another thank you before heading to the door.

As soon as he's gone, I take a big bite of soup. It's so good on a cool day with the chicken broth and the spicy matzo balls, I lean back and groan.

"He's the one." Patton signals the waitress as soon as Amir's out the door. "Imagine. We'll actually have someone in the office who can tell me what they're saying when they stop speaking French."

"Or English." I take another bite of soup while he orders a tuna salad sandwich on rye. "Which they all speak."

"He doesn't have a beard."

"He's American, Patton. He was born in Dearborn." Lifting his résumé, I frown. "His math scores aren't as high as Kate's."

"We're hiring Amir. Kate doesn't speak Arabic." Turning to me in the booth, he puts a hand on my distended belly and leans forward to speak to it. "I'm sorry, Peaches. Your pretty mamma doesn't have to be so gender biased."

"Patton Fletcher!" My voice goes higher. "You have got to be kidding me."

He glances up and his brown eyes sparkle with mischief. It makes my stomach tingle, and I reach out to grab his chin, pulling him closer for a quick kiss on the mouth. "You're going to send me into premature labor."

"I forbid it." He kisses me back, turning as the waitress puts his food in front of him. "We've got our last trip to Savannah all planned out, and Peaches has to wait."

"You're not calling her Peaches. That's a dog's name."

"She's my little Georgia peach, just like her mamma."

"And if she comes out frowning with dark hair and dark eyes like her sexy daddy?"

"We'll shove her back in and let her cook a little longer." I cough a laugh, and he pats me on the back. "Smaller bites, Rocky."

"If you don't stop saying crazy things…"

"Let's get this straight." He inhales a big bite of tuna salad. "You hired Angel to head up our West Coast division…"

"It just made sense. She's in LA, and she's wonderful." I take a bite of my delicious corned turkey with cole slaw on rye.

"Dean left, and you hired Suzy to be our receptionist…"

"She's Dean's roommate. He recommended her."

"Then you hired Debra to be our social media manager…" He takes another big bite.

"She has her own website and an Instagram account with more than twenty-thousand followers. Now *we* have an Instagram account with more than twenty-thousand followers. *And* she found the security breach that let Jerry access everyone's private accounts."

"It wasn't a security breach. He stole the system access key."

"Still, she found his digital fingerprints everywhere."

"Everywhere on my files. That jackass."

I trace a finger down the side of his collar. "And now he's selling timeshares in Tempe."

"We should watch that YouTube video again."

My lips press together, but a short laugh escapes. "Is it wrong that I love it when you punch him in the face?"

He slants an eye, and I grin, shaking my head. I've learned to pick my battles with this stubborn man. He did finally stop smoking, which was my biggest worry.

Taking another spoonful of soup, I decide to gently bring up something new. "Hank would like to do a feature on us for *Nashville Notes*." I cringe, anticipating his response.

"No." He sits back abruptly, wiping his mouth with the paper napkin.

"Patton." I put my hand on his rock-hard thigh under the table.

"Rocky…" The warning tone in his voice fans the tingles in my stomach. To think it used to terrify me. Now it just makes me want to rip his clothes off… Or maybe it's the pregnancy hormones.

"He ran a retraction of that story the very next week. He's apologized profusely and has printed nothing but glowing reports on Fletcher-Morgan ever since."

"He almost destroyed us."

"That's an overstatement. In the time it took me to drive from Savannah to Nashville, you'd all but resolved the crisis."

"After twenty-four hours of hell." He polishes off the other half of his sandwich and leans back. Looking to the side he shakes his head as if remembering something distasteful. "My dad called us tacky."

My lip goes between my teeth. I know that pissed him off more than anything. Still… "NABI wants us to be their inaugural Nashville Power Couple for next year. It's a fun new feature with a photo spread…"

"Sounds like bullshit."

Sliding my plate away, I trace my finger over the sexy bump where the muscle moves in his square jaw. "Stop grinding. I think it would be great publicity."

He takes out his wallet, placing three twenties on the table. "Let's get on the road. I'm ready to be in Savannah."

I get another kiss on the lips before he slides out of the blue vinyl booth, holding a hand to help me up. I'm about the size of a whale, and while I straighten my clothes, his hand automatically rubs my baby bump. He does it all the time. Sometimes he'll lean down and kiss it, and I confess, it's incredibly endearing.

"You feel okay?" So much concern is in his pretty brown eyes. He's changed so much since that first day in the office.

"Yep. Just thinking how happy I am." He kisses me again and leads me out to the car.

We didn't plan to get pregnant so fast. After a relatively small wedding on Tybee Island, we took our honeymoon trip to Sardinia, Italy.

He kept the whole trip a total secret from me—even his new best friend Renée didn't know where we were going. I asked repeatedly... The first day we were there, he took me to *Sella del Diavolo*, or the Devil's Saddle in the Gulf of Cagliari, which he thought was hilarious. *Sexy Devil...*

It was absolutely beautiful, and we spent several dreamy days in the hills overlooking the pebble beaches before returning to Nashville and settling into married life. Now we're partners in life and in the renamed Fletcher-Morgan International.

We were as busy in the bedroom as we were outside it. Patton was happy to finally be off the condoms, and I was happy to lose the interruptions. I faithfully took my pill... Until the weekend I picked up an eye infection and had to take a short round of antibiotics. It's the only thing we can think happened.

You know how you just know certain things? I've never been pregnant, but I could tell something had changed inside me... Six weeks later, I stopped off at the drugstore on the way home and grabbed an early pregnancy test.

That night, when he got back from his jog, I had a small cake and two glasses of sparkling cider waiting. I'll never forget the way his eyes changed when I told him. They burned with a mixture of love and pride and protective fire.

He had me off my feet and out of my clothes before I finished my announcement. It's one of my fondest memories—his hands spreading across my bare stomach, his warm lips pressing just below my navel. He looked up at me and smiled, and I knew… we were complete.

For now.

He's already saying what we'll do with our next baby, which I pretend I don't hear.

Tracing my fingers in the dark hair touching his collar, I wonder how I could possibly love anyone more than I love this man. He's not a devil, but he is fierce…

Patton

"Daddy…" Marley shakes his head, taking a sip of his beer. "That's some heavy shit right there. Shaping another life…"

We're hanging out at Doc's Bar drinking Landsharks while Rocky and Renée—or Ray as my wife likes to call her—catch up on all things baby and birthing.

"You should try it sometime."

He chuckles, looking better than he has in years. "I'm still getting used to the concept of husband."

Marley and Renée were married a month ago in the same place Rocky and I tied the knot. Under a canopy on the beach while Monarch butterflies migrated all around us. Renée timed their wedding to coincide with the eastern migration of the insects from Canada to Mexico.

Of course she did.

Truthfully, I've gotten to where I appreciate my sister-in-law's eccentricities. I usually don't have patience for such things, but a lot has changed.

The day Rocky brought me here to see her for the first time since The Incident, I'd planned my whole apology speech. What I didn't know is my then-future wife had told her I'd secured her loan. I never wanted anyone to know about that…

I got out of the car and saw her on the porch of her beautifully restored home with tears in her eyes. My stomach sank. Rocky told me I'd hurt her, and while I don't usually care if people can't handle my directness, I felt like an ass. She's the sister of the love of my life.

But before I could speak, Renée walked straight across the front lawn and put her arms around my waist, hugging herself tightly to me. I hugged her back, and she whispered so only I could hear, "Thank you."

Shit, it almost broke me. I replied with my sincerest "I'm sorry," and she only looked up at me, light glowing in her hazel eyes. "You helped me more than you know."

From that day, we've been pretty close. Marley was only with me in Nashville two more weeks, long enough to give us notice, before he came here to find her.

Now he works in outside sales for a media company based in Atlanta and the two of them are like two eccentric peas in a pod.

"Ray wants to have a Blessing Ceremony for Rocky while you're here."

We've paid our tab and now we're heading out to the car. I don't like being away from my wife too long now that she's so close to having the baby.

This experience is a first for both of us, and unlike our in-laws, the Fletcher-Morgans like to have shit planned out and in a hospital with professionals all around.

"Do I want to know what that is?"

"It's an ancient Navajo tradition that focuses on the spiritual rite of passing. Rocky's becoming a mother. It's a magical time."

My eyebrows rise. "What happens in a Blessing Ceremony?"

He grins, gripping the top of my shoulder. "Woman stuff."

We're back at the house pretty quickly, to find the sisters sitting on the front porch swing. Rocky pushes herself up when I appear, and I hustle over to help her. She's so adorably huge. Around her neck is a necklace made of assorted stones and crystals and what looks like a little hand-made loop.

"What's this?" I lift it smiling into her eyes.

She grins back, giving me a wink. "It's my birth necklace. Ray made it. Each stone represents an energy she wants for the baby."

"It will remind you of the love and strength that surrounds you as you labor." Renée joins us, putting her hands on our backs. "So much good energy here. This baby will be blessed."

I put my arm around her and kiss the top of her witchy head. "Thanks, Sugar Ray."

She waves her hand at my nickname for her and starts for the door. "I'm going to make you some red raspberry leaf tea. It promotes healthy labor."

Rocky looks up at me and grins, and I pull her close to me, pinning her against my chest. It's a little harder to do now that Peaches is between us, but I still do it.

This one's mine.

After a dinner where Renée brushes her sister's hair, gives her tea, and then massages her hands and feet, we hit the feathers. I crash out almost immediately, but Rocky sits up reading. At some point she turns out the light, but it seems like only a second blinks past when I wake up confused.

Reaching to the side, I find I'm alone in the bed. I feel all around, but only a large puddle of wetness is where Rocky should be. It's too dark to see if the liquid is blood or something else... then I hear a scream that curdles my blood.

My feet don't even touch the floor. I'm out the room and flying in the direction of my wife's voice when I'm caught around the waist by a band of iron.

"Slow down! It's a contraction." Marley's at my ear, and we're both breathing hard.

His face is coated in sweat, and his eyes look as frightened as I feel. "What the fuck?" I try to push past him, but he holds me.

"Renée said not to let you burst in there like this. She said it's negative energy. You've got to be calm." He's talking fast, and I'm struggling harder.

"You're not calm!"

"That's why she sent me out here."

Another scream from Rocky, and I physically lift my friend off the ground, moving him out of my way. My hand is on the door when it opens inward, and Renée steps out, closing it behind her.

"Let me in there." I'm breathing hard, and my voice sounds like sandpaper.

"Stop this." Her eyes are wide and stern. "You can't go in there in a panic. You'll scare her to death."

"She can't have the baby here… Something could go wrong." I'm not above picking my sister-in-law up and physically moving her as well.

She puts her hands on my arms. "It's too late. She's dilated to ten centimeters. The baby is coming. If you try to take her now, she'll have the baby in a car, and I guarantee you it will be far less safe and sanitary than my little birthing pool."

The noise of all our breath fills the silence. My hands grip the doorframe so hard, I'm surprised I don't snap it like a twig. "We have to bring a doctor here."

I step back, but Renée catches my wrist. "You're not going anywhere. Martin, see if Dr. Plimpton can come."

He's running to the door almost before I can stop him. "Tell him to come. Tell him who I am. Tell him I'll pay him one hundred thousand dollars." Marley nods at the end of every sentence. "Take my car. If that doesn't work, offer him two hundred thousand."

With wild eyes, my friend heads off into the night.

Renée catches my face and looks straight into my eyes. "This baby is coming fast. She's in the right position, and Rocky is healthy and strong. There's no reason anything should go wrong. I need you to be calm. She needs you to be calm."

Swallowing my fear, I take her wrists. "I'm calm."

Calm is not as easy to maintain as it sounds.

Visible relief washes over my wife's face when I enter the room, and she starts to cry. "What's happening?"

"I heard we're having a baby." I kiss her cheek, positioning myself behind her at once, holding her back against my chest, doing everything Renée says.

"Oh, God…" She starts to cry more, and I feel her fear.

"It's okay… You've got this. You're my fighter."

Renée has her in an inflatable pool of water, and she's only wearing my old tee. "Time to push, sis."

Rocky periodically squats like she's going to the bathroom then cries out. She does it again and again until finally, Renée tells her to lean back against me. Her head is wet, and her teary eyes press against my neck. Her hands shake, hell, my hands shake. I'm shaking from head to toe, but I'm holding onto calm.

"You got this, beautiful. Your body knows what to do." I'm making it up as I go.

I'm good until she sobs into my neck. "Patton, don't let me die."

Then I just about lose my shit. "Renée…" My voice is a warning, and her hazel eyes meet mine.

"Nobody's going to die here." Her voice goes high, like a song. "We're going to welcome a new life to this magical circle of love."

Rocky shudders, and I wrap my arms around her, just above her stomach. "Come on, baby, you can do this."

"I'm so tired." She's crying, but Renée doesn't stop urging her.

"Last one. You can do it, Rocky!"

Finding a strength more powerful than any man I've ever seen, my beautiful wife rises up and focuses on her sister. She grits her teeth and we all yell as Rocky pushes one last time and like a slippery bar of soap, our beautiful little Rosalyn Rose is with us. We decided to stick with R-names for our girls. She's waving her fists and screaming her little head off.

"Oh... oh!" Rocky is sobbing.

I help lift her shirt, and Renée puts the baby on her mother's bare chest. I'm sitting in the tub now, holding my wife in my lap and cradling them both in my arms.

Renée quickly clips the umbilical cord and then wipes Rosie's little face with a sponge and cotton balls of antibiotic ointment.

"How did you learn how to do this?" I ask, watching in amazement.

She glances up at me sheepishly, and Rocky shakes her head. "Oh, no."

They both start to laugh when Renée says, "YouTube."

I don't want to know any more, and we're all saved when Martin bursts through the door, a bedraggled looking old man behind him.

"Is this the wonder woman?" The old doctor smiles when he sees Renée with her hair tied up around her head and her skirt looped between her legs like a field worker.

"She's perfect, doctor. Ten fingers, ten toes... Two powerful lungs."

Rosie is latched onto her mother's breast and her round dark eyes study us all with a serious expression I can only recognize as mine.

Pressing my lips together, I shake my head before kissing Rocky on the temple. "I think we'll have to try again for Peaches. This one's going to be a ball buster."

Her mamma only laughs and kisses her little head. "She's a fighter all right. She's going to be just like you—a heart of pure gold."

This woman. I hold her in my arms as she traces her fingers along the ink on my wrist.

Renée and my best friend join us, wrapping us in what my zany sister-in-law calls a circle of love. With Rosie here, I don't mind.

I might have started out in charge, but Rocky flipped that script. Only she would see through my brokenness and love me in spite of it all. I'm a pretty tough boss, but she's tougher than the rest. And with this little girl to seal it, she can gladly be the boss of me.

Until Rosie starts walking and talking, of course…

Thanks for reading BOSS OF ME! I hope you fell for Patton and Rocky as much as I did.

If you loved Stephen Hastings, be sure to pick up his sexy enemies-to-lovers stand-alone. Keep turning for a short sneak peek...

Coming Dec. 17, 2019: WAIT FOR ME is a sexy brother's best friend, small-town, second-chance military romance about a wounded Marine (Taron Rhodes) who returns to the farm to find the sassy girl he left behind prettier than ever and holding a baby...

Love is never simple, is it?
More details coming soon!

NEVER MISS A SALE OR NEW RELEASE!
Sign up for my newsletter and get three free stories Today:
smarturl.it/LMnews

Or sign up to get a text alert by messaging TIALOUISE to 64600 Now*
(*Text service U.S. Only.)

STAY
Special Sneak Peek

Stephen Hastings is a control freak.
He's arrogant. He's smart as a whip and sexy AF.
He has too much money. He's bossy, and he's usually right.
All I saw were his clear blue eyes, tight ass, and ripped torso.
I gladly handed him my V-card that night, ten years ago.
I was so stupid. I swore I'd never be that stupid again…

Emmy Barton works for a dry cleaner?
Yes, that Emmy Barton—long, blonde hair, bright blue eyes, pretty smile…
Sexy little ass. Smart mouth.
She was the only girl who interested me, but I was leaving to be an officer in the Navy.

Now I'm home, running my business. My life is perfectly ordered until I bump into her, divorced and struggling to make ends meet.
I hate seeing her like this. I hate that she married Burt "The Dick" Dickerson. What an asshole.

She says she hates me, but when we fight, it's all heat and lust.
I won't leave her this way.
She will let me help her and her son. She will stay…
It's a thin line between love and hate, and this line is on fire.

(STAY is a STAND-ALONE enemies-to-lovers, second-chance, marriage of convenience romance. No cheating. No cliffhangers.)

Never miss a new release!

Sign up for my New Release newsletter and get a FREE Tia Louise Story Bundle!

Sign up now!
smarturl.it/LMnews

Prologue

Stephen
Ten years ago...

Stop crying, kid. Life isn't fair.

Humans invented fair as a pacifier, because they needed justice. Animals don't know fair. In nature only the strong survive. You're kind, loving, honest? Nice try.

If you're weak, you die.

Or poor.

"What are you thinking, *Esteban*?" Ximena lowers herself carefully into a dingy-brown, worn-out armchair, and I blink these thoughts away. "You were always the smartest boy in the room."

The gray strands outnumber the black in my old housekeeper's hair. It's thinner than it was when I was a boy, and she keeps it twisted in a low bun.

"Now I'm a man." I kiss the top of her head. "And I'd wager the whole city."

Her muscles tremble from exertion, but her eyes are bright. She still greets me with a smile, just like always when I visit. "Smartest man in the city. What is that like?"

"It sucks." I look around her crumbling one-bedroom apartment.

It's a second-floor walkup, outdated but clean. She works hard to keep it clean, even with the cancer eating her insides. Even with the years passing, drawing her closer to death.

The thought of her dying fans the darkness inside me. "Where's Ramon?"

"He moved downtown. He got a good job, working at the shipyards." Her accent is thick despite all the years she's lived in Manhattan, her English sprinkled with Spanish.

"That's a long way from here."

He won't visit. He might want to, but he won't have the time or the energy to check on his dying mother.

Her neighborhood is shady as fuck, and she's too weak to climb stairs. And I'm leaving for a long time. I'll have to count on her neighbors to do what I can't.

Slipping a fat business envelope from the breast pocket of my coat, I place it under a mug on her coffee table. "This should last a while. I'll send more, but I won't be able to check on you. I'll be gone eighteen months, probably longer."

"I'm so proud of you. So proud." Her cheeks rise, and she slowly shakes her head. "A Navy officer."

Every line in her face wrinkles with her grin. Her faded purple housedress is as thin and old as she is. I remember her fat and jolly, shining cheeks and hair, every word out of my mouth would make her laugh, even if it wasn't funny. I didn't understand her, how she gave love so generously to a boy who wasn't hers. To the son of a man who didn't even consider her worth his time, who thought he was doing her a favor hiring her to keep his oversized brownstone.

She takes my hand from where she sits, and I take a knee beside her. Every time I visit she's smaller, slipping away. Her grip tightens, and the scent of her drugstore perfume drifts faintly around us, dried flowers and talcum powder. It draws a memory of me as a little boy sitting on her lap, crying against her neck after the death of my mother. She would hug me against her soft body, rocking and humming a sad song I didn't recognize.

"Your father will cut you off if he finds out you're giving me money, *Esteban*."

I exhale a disgusted laugh. "Thomas is too proud to cut me off. It would make him look bad at the club. Unruly boys are to be tolerated, bragged about even."

Her eyes close, and her head leans back as she exhales a weak chuckle. "Men are the same everywhere. *Machismo*."

Pissing wars. I rise to standing in one fluid movement. "I'll never forgive him for doing this to you."

I blame him for her illness. I blame him for her deteriorating health. I blame him for her inability to find work after he ruined her reputation. No one would hire her after he branded her a thief in his home. All the Upper East Siders shut their doors in her face, and she was left to scrounge a living wherever she could.

I've brought her money from my allowance for five years, and I'd love him to come at me for it. Pompous bastard. So worried about his appearance. So offended by a missing watch.

"He did what he had to do." Ximena still defends my father's actions. "My son stole from him. Your father could not keep me in the house after he stole."

"Ramon stole to buy you medicine. He didn't steal to party or do drugs."

He might've gotten away with it, too. If only he hadn't stolen my father's favorite Rolex—not one of the other seven he never wears.

"He did not put my son in jail." She nods her head, as if my father, Thomas Hastings has the ability to throw anyone in jail.

He's just a grown-up trust-fund brat who knows how to invest the massive wealth he inherited from our bootlegger ancestors. At least he's good for something.

Pride beams in her eyes when she looks up at me. "Now you will go and be a hero. So handsome, serving your country."

I smooth my hand down the front of my jacket, contemplating hypocrisy. "It's what my mother always wanted. Her father was in the military."

"Yes, and she can see you from above. She is so proud of you. Just like I am proud."

I study the woman who filled my mother's role for a little while. I can't heal her. I can't change her situation, and I want to leave her with happiness, not bitterness.

"Thank you, *mamá*. I love you."

"I love you, *Esteban*." She takes a slow inhale and forces a chuckle. "Now why are you here with an old woman? Why are you not out celebrating with friends? You have too much spirit. You should be with a girl tonight, release some energy."

Energy. She's encouraging me to go out and get laid. "I'm not looking for a girl."

"A boy then!" My eyes snap to hers, and I see a joking sparkle.

After all the medicine, the chemotherapy, the drugs, she refuses to be beaten. She still manages to tease me. She's the only person who can get away with it.

"I'm not gay. I'm leaving in the morning."

"Which means you have all night." She carefully rises out of her chair and takes my arm, pulling me to the door. "No more hanging around here. Go out and live your life."

I wrap my arms around her in a long hug. The feel of her bones beneath thin cotton is physically painful to me. "I'll find someone to check on you while I'm gone."

"I have my friends. I have my neighbors. Stop worrying about me." She shoos me away. "When it's my time, I'll be ready." Touching my cheek, she says her final words to me. "Be brave, *Esteban*. Laugh often. Take care of yourself."

"Take care of you." I kiss the top of her head and hesitate one last time before I go.

It's the last time I'll ever see her...

* * *

Emmy

"Harley Quinn is way sexier than Black Widow any day of the week." Burt Dickerson's voice is too loud.

He's on one of his DC versus Marvel fan-boy rants, and I'm staring into the bottom of my empty red solo cup. I need refill number four.

"Fuck that. Black Widow. Hands down." My older brother Ethan yells at him, but he's only yanking Burt's chain. Ethan doesn't give a shit about comic universes. "Give me a redhead any day. Fire crotch."

My nose wrinkles, and I want to punch my brother in the junk. "She was a blonde in the last movie. You just like Scarlett Johansson." *Why am I still standing here listening to them?*

"What's wrong with that?" He pokes me in the ribs, and I'm ready to call it a night.

It's almost midnight, and I've been watching the door so hard, my eyeballs hurt. Ethan threw this big college-graduation-slash-summer kick-off party for all his old school friends, and I made sure Stephen Hastings got an invitation.

Stephen Hastings... the love of my life.

Ethan said he wouldn't come. He laughed at me and said Stephen hates most of these guys. It looks like he was right.

God, I'm such a fucking moron. How long can I save myself for a guy who doesn't even know I exist? I'm a college woman now. Time to ditch the crush and start living my life.

I just...

I hoped.

With a sad exhale, my mind flies through all my cherished spank-bank memories of Stephen growing up… Tall, lean, dark, wavy hair that looks like he never touches it, but it's always just perfect. He was on the rowing team with Ethan, and when he'd take off his shirt… holy shit, my core clenches at the memory of his broad shoulders, his perfectly sculpted arms… So muscular and tanned. The lines in his stomach would flex, and my mouth would water like Pavlov's dog.

I'm ready to trade this beer for a pint of Ben & Jerry's, curl up in my bed, and cry.

He's not coming.

Walking down the steps, away from the landing at the door, I've reached the edge of the crowd when my brother's voice freezes my insides.

"Stephen! Hell, I don't believe it." Ethan laughs, and a few of the guys join in greeting him. "Didn't think you'd come."

"I didn't either." Stephen's low baritone tickles my lady bits, and I turn slowly to look up at him.

He's wearing a brown tweed jacket over a white button-down shirt and dark jeans. He hardly ever wears jeans, but shit, his ass is so fine in them. He always seems just a bit impatient, and when he scans the crowd, his blue eyes seem to glow from under his dark brow.

He's so fucking hot.

My heart beats faster as I contemplate my next move. He *will* see me tonight, dammit. I'm giving myself one last chance.

He turns again to Ethan, and the muscle in his square jaw moves. "I'm pulling out in the morning."

"Last day as a free man. Sucks to be you." Ethan shoves a whiskey in his hand.

He inspects the glass. "I thought it demonstrated my good character."

"Good character." Burt's loud voice interrupts them, and Stephen visibly cringes. "Still think you're better than us, Hastings?"

"Only you, Dick." Stephen takes a long drink. "Only you."

Girls actually swoon over Burt all the time, but he's nothing compared to Stephen.

"Let's join the party." Ethan puts his hand on Stephen's shoulder, and they start down the stairs in my direction. "Find a chick and get your dick wet."

"Right. That sounds like me." Stephen shrugs off my brother, and Ethan staggers away.

He pauses at the bottom, scanning the crowd with a frown. I follow his gaze over the mob of former classmates. Most are buzzed. Most are familiar. We passed each other daily at Pike Academy four years ago—until he left for Yale. Tonight we're reunited.

Girls sway in colorful silk dresses with thin, spaghetti straps, practically lingerie. Their hair hangs in waves over their shoulders and their eyes sparkle as they listen to guys tell exaggerated stories of their prowess, either in the stock market or on the playing field. The guys evaluate their breasts, their hips, their lips. I'm sure they'll be fucking like good little rabbits before the night ends. Our classmates can be so predictable.

All I know is Stephen is wide open. It's now or never.

"That's a fierce scowl." I'm amazed at how confident my voice sounds, loud and commanding. *Thanks, beer.* "Don't like what you see?"

I hop up on the bottom step beside him. It puts my head at the top of his shoulder, and I lift my chin, looking over the crowd with a scowl, imitating him. "You're right." My nose wrinkles, and I meet his gaze. "They're a bunch of horny assholes."

I manage to come off casual, teasing, and his frown morphs

into a narrow-eyed grin. "Emmy Barton. Ethan didn't say kids would be here."

His voice is like warm butter, and I'm thrilled he remembers me. "I'm not a kid anymore, Stephen Hastings. I started at Sarah Lawrence last year."

"Bully for you." He takes a drink of whiskey, but I'm stronger than his sarcasm.

"I wanted to stay close to home."

"Why the hell would you want that?"

Blinking up at him, I smile, going for honesty. "I miss my dad. I miss Ethan. I guess family feels more important when you lose someone."

"Oh, right. Sorry." He looks down at his tumbler, and his expression darkens.

My mom lost her long battle against lung cancer a few years ago. It was devastating watching her suffer, and her death was a mixture of heartbreak and relief she was out of pain. It still hurts if I think about it too much...

Stephen's mother died of cancer when we were kids, but I remember how it changed him. How he smiled less, played less.

"We have that in common, don't we?" My voice is gentle.

"It's not so fresh for me." His softens, and I'm encouraged. I'm not inside the wall, but I'm closer.

"Here you are." Burt appears at my side, putting his hand on my lower back. *What the hell?*

Stephen's eyes go to where he's touching me, and all I can think is *fuck no*.

"You're drunk." I shove Burt's hands off my short denim skirt.

He immediately puts both hands on my waist and turns me to him, leaning closer. "You're not blowing me off for this asshole are you?" His breath smells like vodka, and his flat brown eyes are intoxicated.

He makes a move like he's going to kiss me, but I duck and twirl away, moving to stand beside Stephen, holding his arm. "Stephen and I are having a nice chat. You need to call it a night."

Burt's attention turns to Stephen, and his brow lowers. Stephen is ready when Burt lunges at him. His strong arm shoots out, gripping Burt by the shoulder and holding him back.

"Walk it off, Dickerson." It's a low growl, and I know Stephen could wipe the floor with Burt's drunk ass.

"Don't tell me what to do, Hastings." Burt grips his wrist.

Stephen's fist rises, and I hold my breath. I've never seen Stephen fight, and my heart is flying. I'm sure it's about to go down when Ethan and a big guy appear. They corral Burt, dragging him to the right, and I take my chance, catching Stephen's arm and pulling him into the crowd.

He stops and straightens his jacket, jaw clenched. "That asshole. I'm taking off."

"Wait!" I gently pull his arm again. "I know where we can get a refill… away from all this."

He hesitates a beat, then our eyes meet and his shoulders relax. I quickly lead him past everybody, waving at old friends as we weave through the crowd.

Ethan put a keg out on the terrace near the wet bar, and Stephen goes to refresh his whiskey while I step over to the corner balcony overlooking Central Park. It's a beautiful night, and I can see the moon and a few stars. I make a quick wish.

Warmth at my side causes me to turn. He's standing beside me in the moonlight, dark hair, blue eyes, that dimple in the side of his cheek. "So, what's your major?"

The way he says it makes me laugh. I push a strand of long, wavy blond hair behind my ear. "Art history."

The scene flips. He actually groans, rolling his eyes and turning his back to the railing. "Not planning to work after college?"

His disgust offends me. "I most certainly am. I want to get a job at Sotheby's or at one of the museums downtown. Maybe something in SoHo. Or maybe I'll move to London!"

A moment's pause, and he slants an eye at me. "Is that so?"

"It is." My feathers are still ruffled, and I straighten my button-up cropped top. "What will you do now that you're out? Take a job with your dad? Have a wife in New Haven and a mistress in the city?"

Two can play the stereotypes game.

He drifts a little closer, and my pulse ticks faster. "Is that what we do?" His voice is low, and his eyes drop to my lips.

My voice is softer, higher compared to his. "Isn't it?"

A slight grin from him, and that humming is back in my veins. "You're smarter than I gave you credit for."

"Is that a compliment?"

"It's actually an apology. I underestimated you."

Now it's my turn to hesitate. Still, it's not like I didn't know Stephen was arrogant. It's one of the things I love about him.

"Apology accepted." Reaching out, I trace my finger down the front of his blazer. "Now. Wasn't that easy? You don't have to fight with everybody."

Taking a chance, I put my hand on his chest. It's firm and warm, and he covers my hand with his. It's a gentle touch, but it radiates heat to my chest, fanning out into my belly, warming the space between my thighs. I want this so much... I've dreamed of it. I know if he'll let me in, everything will change. He'll change.

My voice is just above a whisper. "When you look at me like that, I wonder what you're thinking."

Our eyes hold, and I know he feels it, this pull between us. My breath stills, and I'm humming with desire.

But he throws on the brakes. "I'm thinking I've had enough whiskey." His tone is level, and he releases my hand, moving away.

I have to stop him.

I can't lose this moment.

"What do you want?" I'm sassy, flirting. "Do you even know?"

He stops, giving me the full force of his scowl. "I don't want a wife in Connecticut, and I definitely don't need a mistress in the city."

Closing the distance, I put my hand on his waist this time, sliding it back and forth, working my way lower. "Maybe you need me."

He stops my downward progress with a strong grip. "You're playing with fire, Emmy Barton."

"I'd rather be hot than cold."

His grip on me tightens, and he pulls me against his chest. I can barely breathe, but I blink up to his lips, slipping my tongue out to touch mine. His erection is against my stomach, and I'm so wet.

"Are you drunk?" His voice is a rough whisper.

"No. Are you?" Stretching higher, I touch my lips to the scratchy stubble of his jaw.

Leaning down, he kisses me fast. His lips shove mine apart, and his tongue invades, finding mine. My knees start to give out, but his arm is around my waist, scooping me up against his chest.

It's a rough kiss, not kind or gentle, and my fingernails scratch up to his shoulders. A little noise escapes my throat, and he rumbles in response. Heat floods my panties.

Our mouths break apart with a gasp, and his blue eyes are blazing. "Do you want this?"

Nodding, I step back, holding out my hand. "Come with me."

He hesitates as I go to the glass doors leading to Ethan's dark bedroom. When I pause and look back, he's watching me like a predator. His hair is messy from my fingers, and his lips are parted with his breath. He looks like pure sex.

"This way." I'm holding still, hoping, until...

He follows me inside.

My shirt is ripped open. Stephen doesn't bother removing my bra. He shoves the cups down under my small breasts, and devours me, pulling a taut nipple into his mouth and giving it a bite, sending electricity straight to my core.

"Stephen..." I whimper as his large hands cup and kiss me.

I'm on fire, threading my fingers into his hair. His mouth feels so good against my skin, and he lifts me like I weigh nothing, perching my ass on the edge of the sink.

We're locked in my brother's small half bathroom, and he's making my dreams come true.

"You still want this?" His voice is hot at my ear as he shoves my skirt up to my waist.

"Yes." I gasp, gripping his neck. *God, yes...*

His belt clinks, and I wait as he rolls on the condom. Our eyes meet once more, and his burn with desire. Everything's going to change after this. He's going to fall in love with me. I just know it.

Large palms go under my thighs, lifting them, and I feel the tip of his cock touching me, probing... It's about to happen... Then all at once...

Oh, holy shit! My eyes squeeze shut, and I bite my lower lip hard, letting out a little moan of pain.

"Fuck, Emmy," he groans in my ear. "You're so fucking tight."

I make a little noise of assent, gripping his shoulders. His massive cock rips through my virginity, and it hurts so much more than I expected. He has no idea, of course, and I have no intention of telling him. I know for certain Stephen Hastings would not deflower me so roughly.

Rotating my hips, I do my best to accommodate this distinct

sense of fullness. My eyes are squeezed shut, and I focus on his scent, spicy sweat and fresh soap. It's warm and good. He groans again, thrusting faster at my movements.

"Yes…" His lips find mine, kissing me quickly, a touch of his tongue leaves me wanting more. "Like that."

His face is in my hair, and as he moves faster, somehow the pain begins to subside. It transforms into numbness, until gradually, gradually, the smallest flicker of warmth blooms in my lower belly.

"Come for me." Hot breath is at my ear, and my forehead tightens. *Can I?*

Warm hands cup my ass, lifting me off the sink and turning us to the wall. The pain is gone, and my body slides up and down against his hard pelvis. His cock glides in and out, the ridge of its head working my insides. My clit is against his shaft, and something begins to happen. Prickling warmth starts to grow. It gets stronger, and I forget everything but chasing it down.

My thighs tighten around him, and I'm pumping my body up and down, riding him, wanting that tingling heat to keep getting hotter. I'm desperate, gripping his skin and moaning as the orgasm creeps higher up my thighs.

"Fuck, Emmy." He groans, fucking me harder.

"Yes…" It's almost there. "Yes!" It's right there… the tightness in my lower stomach.

It bursts through me, and I moan so loud. It's like a million fireworks shooting through my veins. My vision goes white. I'm flying, and I feel it when his orgasm breaks, pulsing deep inside me as he comes with a loud noise.

I'm shaking. My thighs shudder and grip him, and he holds me. He holds still as we both fly through space together, soaring past galaxies, touching the stars. It's amazing.

Gradually, I blink open my eyes, and through the haze, I see us in the mirror, our bodies molded perfectly together. It's just like I dreamed it would be. My arms are around his neck, our bodies flush. It only lasts a moment.

The noise of the party outside creeps into our little cocoon. He reaches between us, lowering me to my feet as he grips the condom and quickly disposes of it. I feel like a newborn colt, my legs are so shaky.

His back is to me, and his shoulders broaden as he takes a deep breath. Then he moves to the sink to wash his hands. "It's been a while since I've done that." He sounds apologetic.

Shoving my skirt down, I straighten my bra, struggling to get a grip. "What? Bathroom fucked at a party?" I'm shook.

He cuts off the water and dries his hands on the towel as I button my shirt. I've managed to get myself together when he steps to me, putting one hand above my head on the wall and leaning close. "Had sex, period." Leaning down he kisses my cheek. "You were great."

He steps back, and just like that, he's ready to go.

"That's it?" I'm confused. The devastation hasn't hit me yet.

"I think I'll head on home." He reaches out and pats my upper arm. "Good luck at school."

I recoil from his touch. *Are you kidding me? Good luck at school?*

Loud banging startles me. A female voice shouts through the door, "Hurry up in there!"

The banging grows louder, and I go toward it, looking over my shoulder but not meeting his eyes. "Seems I overestimated you."

Pushing through the door, I run into the crowd. The party surrounds me like a wave, and I let it pull me under, drowning my tears in noise and sweeping us apart.

Get STAY today!
It's free in Kindle Unlimited.

Audiobook coming Oct. 4, 2019.

Books by
TIA LOUISE

BOOKS IN KINDLE UNLIMITED
STAND-ALONE ROMANCES
Wait for Me, coming Dec. 17, 2019!
Boss of Me, 2019
Stay, 2019
Make Me Yours, 2019
Make You Mine, 2018
When We Kiss, 2018
Save Me, 2018
The Right Stud, 2018★
When We Touch, 2017
The Last Guy, 2017★
(★co-written with Ilsa Madden-Mills)

THE BRIGHT LIGHTS SERIES
Under the Lights (#1), 2018
Under the Stars (#2), 2018
Hit Girl (#3), 2018

PARANORMAL ROMANCES
One Immortal (Derek & Melissa, vampires)
One Insatiable (Stitch & Mercy, shifters)

eBOOKS ON ALL RETAILERS

THE DIRTY PLAYERS SERIES

The Prince & The Player (#1), 2016

A Player for a Princess (#2), 2016

Dirty Dealers (#3), 2017

Dirty Thief (#4), 2017

THE ONE TO HOLD SERIES

One to Hold (#1 - Derek & Melissa)

One to Keep (#2 - Patrick & Elaine)

One to Protect (#3 - Derek & Melissa)

One to Love (#4 - Kenny & Slayde)

One to Leave (#5 - Stuart & Mariska)

One to Save (#6 - Derek & Melissa)

One to Chase (#7 - Marcus & Amy)

One to Take (#8 - Stuart & Mariska)

Descriptions, teasers, excerpts and more are on my website!

Never miss a new release!

Sign up for my New Release newsletter and get a FREE Tia Louise Story Bundle!

Sign up now!

smarturl.it/LMnews

Acknowledgments

I always find myself in this place, thinking about all the incredible people who helped me get to having a beautiful, finished novel, and just wanting to cry…

First, because of all the love and support of my amazing readers and friends. Second, because I never want to forget anybody as I thank you all.

For starters, thanks to my precious family, Mr. TL and my two daughters, for the love, for believing in me, and for PATIENCE. I love you guys!

HUGE THANKS to Dani Sanchez and Lulu Dumonceaux for all the incredible marketing and logistical support. You keep my brain straight when it's going in a million different directions, and you help me so much.

Even MORE Huge Thanks to Ilona Townsel for always being there, for dropping everything to help, and just for being the absolute best. You're my rock.

HUGE THANKS to my incredible beta squad… Lulu, Ilona, Melissa Sagastume, and Tammy McGowan, and to my awesome editor Kathy Bosman—you ladies give amazing notes.

To my Mermaid VEEPs, Becca Zsurkán, Ana Perez, Clare Fuentes, Sheryl Parent, Cindy Camp, Carla Van Zandt, Jaime Long, Tammi Hart, Tina Morgan, Jacquie Martin, and Ellie King. You ladies have no idea how much I love you all!

Kate Farlow, Parker Huntington, Harloe Rae, and every author who helped share and promote with me… What would I do without you? I love you.

Special thanks to Lori Jackson for the gorgeous cover design and all my emergencies—lol! You are The Woman. Thanks to

Champagne Book Design for making my paperbacks so beautiful, and last but never least, to Wander for that photo… ahhh!

To my MERMAIDS and my INCREDIBLE Promo Team, *Thank You* for giving me a place to relax and be silly.

THANKS to ALL the bloggers who have made an art and a science of book loving. Sharing this book with the reading world would be impossible without you. I appreciate your help so much.

To everyone who picks up this book, reads it, loves it, and tells one person about it, you've made my day. I'm so grateful to you all. Without readers, there would be no writers.

So much love,

Stay sexy,

<3 Tia

About the Author

USA Today bestselling, award-winning author Tia Louise has been a teacher, a book editor, a journalist, a magazine editor, and finally a novelist of super hot and sexy romance.

All her heroes are alphas with hearts of gold, all her heroines are smart, sassy ladies who love them, and all her endings are happily ever after.

A lover of the beach, dark chocolate, strong coffee, and sparkling wine, Louise lives in the Midwest with her trophy husband and two teenage geniuses.

Signed Copies of all books online at:
http://smarturl.it/SignedPBs

Connect with Tia:

Website: www.authortialouise.com

Pinterest: pinterest.com/AuthorTiaLouise

Instagram (@AuthorTLouise)

Bookbub Author Page: www.bookbub.com/authors/tia-louise

Amazon Author Page: amzn.to/1jm2F2b

Goodreads: www.goodreads.com/author/show/7213961.Tia_Louise

Snapchat: bit.ly/24kDboV

** On Facebook? **

Be a Mermaid! Join Tia's **Reader Group** at *"Tia's Books, Babes & Mermaids"!*
www.facebook.com/groups/TiasBooksandBabes

www.AuthorTiaLouise.com

allnightreads@gmail.com

Be a Mermaid! Join Tia's **Reader Group** at *"Tia's Books, Babes & Mermaids"*

www.AuthorTiaLouise.com

allnightreads@gmail.com

Made in the USA
Monee, IL
09 June 2022